IN *LOVING MEMORY*

WINONA
KENT

DIVERSIONBOOKS

Also by Winona Kent

Persistence of Memory
Cold Play
Skywatcher
The Cilla Rose Affair

Diversion Books
A Division of Diversion Publishing Corp.
443 Park Avenue South, Suite 1008
New York, New York 10016
www.DiversionBooks.com

For more information, email info@diversionbooks.com

First Diversion Books edition July 2016.
Print ISBN: 978-1-68230-078-7
eBook ISBN: 978-1-68230-077-0

I'd like to thank the following people, without whose assistance this novel would be much less authentic, and much the poorer for detail.

Karen Eldridge, for her diligent visits to Balham and Tottenham Court Road, camera at the ready.

The Cambridge Man, for his inspiration and suggestions.

London Underground, for their cooperation and assistance, and Simon Cook, Area Manager for Balham and Tooting Bec stations, for his notes, diagrams, photos, and clarifications.

Nick Cooper for his excellent book, *London Underground at War*.

Katy Green at the London Transport Museum, for her patient answers to my inquiries about fares, escalators, lifts, and Underground stations in 1940.

My uncle, Mike Kent, and my mum, Sheila Kent, for sharing their vivid memories of the Blitz.

My husband, Jim Goddard, for his knowledge of World War Two tactics and weaponry, and for his patience and understanding.

CHAPTER ONE

December 1849

It was a perfect winter's night. The trees sparkled with hoarfrost, and the ground crunched underfoot as Matilda and Silas Ferryman made their way towards Sewell Manor, on the eastern edge of Middlehurst, deep in the New Forest.

The manor's owner, Joseph Sewell, had accumulated his fortune in the Caribbean Islands, where he held vast tracts of land that produced sugar. Bringing his wealth back to the village, he had constructed a mansion on the grandest of scales, with pinnacles and turrets, and so many bedrooms Matilda had a difficult time imagining what they could all be used for, since Joseph Sewell himself was a widower, and only three of his eight children still lived there. The manor was known throughout the land for its fabulous gardens and ornamental ponds. And although it was frozen over now, in the summer the pond closest to the house boasted an enormous fountain, which Matilda had viewed personally on three separate occasions.

Each Christmas, Joseph Sewell was seized by the spirit of the season and opened his grand hall to the villagers, who were invited inside for hot mulled wine and freshly cooked mince pies. And there was always a performance by the mummers, who toured the public houses and manors with a play about St. George and the Dragon, and gratefully received whatever compensation was offered in return.

Matilda's father, Cornelius Quinn, was a master blacksmith in Middlehurst. Joseph Sewell was his most important customer, and this fact alone guaranteed that Matilda's family was among the first to be invited each year to the Christmas celebrations. It also meant they would be met at the door, warmly welcomed, and given a table at the front of the hall, so that they would not have to stand with the commoners.

Matilda was most appreciative of this concession, as her knees gave her unceasing trouble, especially in the chill of winter.

The grand hall on this night was lit by hundreds of candles, some contained in a massive chandelier hanging from the ceiling, others upon tables, and still more held by sconces attached to the walls. A huge fire crackled in the stone fireplace at one end of the room, and sprigs of freshly cut holly and mistletoe and branches gathered from evergreen trees were scattered all about for decoration. The whole of it lent the room a delicious Christmassy scent.

"Welcome! Welcome!" Joseph Sewell was, as always, at the door to guide Matilda and Silas to their table. "I trust you are well, Mrs. Ferryman!"

"As well as can be expected, sir," Matilda replied.

Two fiddlers at the front of the hall were providing the means for a dance. Matilda watched with a certain amount of envy as her brother, Thaddeus, took a turn on the floor with Edwina Sewell, Joseph's eldest daughter, who was of a marriageable age and, consequently, had no shortage of suitors.

Oh, to be young again, Matilda thought, and unencumbered by rheumatism and catarrh, and an unabated cramping of the stomach and the bowels.

"Will you have some mulled wine, Mrs. Ferryman?"

"Thank you, I believe I shall." Matilda accepted the cup from Mr. Sewell. "Hot drinks provide such comfort to one's digestion."

She sat down, and drank her wine, and observed with languid interest as her husband engaged her father in a conversation about anvils. Silas worked for Cornelius Quinn, the offer of employment having been extended the very same night that Silas had asked for

Matilda's hand in marriage. It was a convenience that had benefited everyone, for although Matilda's mother had given birth to three sons, none of them had shown any interest whatsoever in learning their father's trade. Thaddeus was a police constable, and Robert and Maurice had become schoolmasters, one employed in Middlehurst, the other in nearby Sway.

There they were now, with their respective wives and all of their children, including the two yet to be born. Mr. Sewell was leading them, negotiating a path through the celebrating villagers to the Quinn family tables at the front of the hall.

Matilda searched the room for Thaddeus. He had finished dancing with Edwina Sewell, and was now discussing something in earnest with her brother, Bertram, a young lad who had a fine future in store as the sole male heir to Joseph Sewell's fortune.

Matilda caught Thaddeus's eye and signalled to him.

"Would you indulge me, dearest brother, and escort me outside for a breath of fresh air?"

"Oh, but you can't!" Bertram exclaimed. "The mummers are about to come in!"

The impending mummers caused Matilda to become even more impatient. She knew who most of them were: they were the sons of New Forest commoners. Tradition required they appear in disguise, and so their clothing was garish, and their faces were variously blackened, or hidden underneath large hats decorated with rags and ribbons. Last summer, she had chased several of them out of her garden as they attempted to steal apples from her tree.

"It is the same play every year," she remarked. "I do believe I must have the entire dialogue committed to memory by now."

One of the boys, made up like Father Christmas, was clearing a space for their performance at the front of the grand hall. Matilda recognized him as the ringleader of the apple thieves.

"But that's the charm of it!" Bertram argued. "We all know the story. That's what makes it so enjoyable."

Matilda was about to take issue with his definition of enjoyable, but Maurice and Robert and their wives and children had arrived.

"Good evening, Matilda." Maurice's wife, Nancy, took the lead in greeting her, as she did every year.

"Merry Christmas," Matilda replied, bestowing formal embraces upon her, Maurice, Robert, and Robert's wife, Harriet, who was due to give birth within days. "Do have my chair, Harriet. I shall fetch another."

Another was located, and, with considerable effort, Matilda dragged it back to the table, where Eveline, Maurice's six-year-old daughter, immediately appropriated it.

"Child!" Matilda admonished. "Manners! If you please!"

"Go and fetch your own chair, Evie," Maurice replied, with good humour. "You know your aunt suffers greatly from pernicious knees."

"Is it your pernishest knees which always make you so bad-tempered, Aunt Matilda?" Eveline inquired.

"I shall help you find another chair," Maurice decided, trying very hard not to laugh.

"I hate Aunt Matilda," Eveline whispered as Maurice led her away.

Matilda sat down. "That child needs a good hiding."

"Fortunately," Nancy replied, "Maurice and I entertain somewhat more enlightened thoughts concerning child-rearing than you, Matilda. It is a pity you and Silas were not blessed with offspring."

Robert's youngest son, Lionel, tugged at the bottom of his father's coat.

"Why have Aunt Matilda and Uncle Silas not been blessed with offspring?" he asked.

"For goodness sake!" Matilda said, growing very red in the face. "Children should be forbidden to speak in the company of adults. Seen and not heard, that is my preference. And, preferably, not even seen."

"We know, Mattie," Robert replied. "Next year I shall ask Mr. Sewell to set a separate table for us on the other side of the hall, so—happily—you will be spared further distress."

Maurice returned with Eveline—but without a chair.

8

"Never mind," he said to her. "You can sit on my shoulders instead." He hoisted her up. "There you are, Evie. You're taller than the mummers now!"

"What is the play about, Papa?"

"Well," said Maurice. "There's a King…and a Turkish Knight…." He winked at Matilda. "And, of course, a very fierce and vexatious Dragon…"

"I shall remove myself," Matilda announced. "I am going outside."

"You do that every year, Mattie. The less enlightened might think you didn't enjoy Christmas at all."

"I dislike the mummers. You may remain here, Maurice, unencumbered by vexatious dragons, to partake in the enjoyment."

Father Christmas was beginning his speech, delivered in rhyming couplets. Matilda got to her feet. As she did so, her husband disengaged himself from his conversation with Cornelius and intercepted her.

"I shall accompany you, my dear," Silas said, taking her arm. "I cannot allow you to venture out on your own into the dark. There are far too many dangers lurking in the woods."

"Thank you," Matilda replied, a little surprised. During past Christmas celebrations, Silas had rarely noticed when she had taken her leave to escape the dismally amateur theatrics at the front of the hall, and her nieces and nephews, who were intolerably bothersome. "I shan't be long. It is cold tonight, and my knees will no doubt protest the chill tomorrow."

• • •

In the days that followed, there would be much attention paid to the exact time that Matilda Ferryman had departed with her husband, and the exact time that Silas Ferryman had returned, minus his wife. Matilda had been taken ill, he explained, and he had been obliged to accompany her home, where he put her to bed with a hot water bottle. Whereupon she had insisted he return to the festivities.

The discovery, later that night, of Matilda's bloodied body, her throat cut and her clay hot water bottle in pieces upon the floor, was the subject of much horrified conversation among the villagers. It was assumed that the motive of the killer must have been robbery. Matilda had been educated, with an aptitude for numbers, and, as a result, had been made responsible for the oversight and care of her father's accounts.

Indeed, after Cornelius Quinn had been admitted to the Ferryman home to witness the aftermath of the terrible crime firsthand, he had immediately discovered that his considerable savings, of which Matilda had been appointed guardian, had vanished.

Also missing was a locket, which had belonged to Matilda's mother, Jemima. Matilda had inherited it, and it was her favourite piece of jewellery. It was not an inexpensive trinket.

Christmas was bleak for the Quinns, but not—surprisingly—for Silas Ferryman, whose recovery seemed uncommonly quick, according to Thaddeus Quinn's practised eye.

Thaddeus and Silas were of a similar age, and they had attended lessons together, had grown up in close proximity, and were likened, by some, to be as close as brothers. And because he knew Silas as well as a brother, it was Thaddeus's contention—which he shared with no one except his superior at the Middlehurst constabulary— that they need not look beyond the environs of Middlehurst for the man who had taken his sister's life.

"What is your proof?" Chief Constable Mathers inquired, as he sat with Thaddeus in the quiet brick building that served as their headquarters, as well as the village lockup.

"Their marriage was not a happy one," Thaddeus replied. "My sister confided this to me upon several occasions."

"A possible motive," Chief Constable Mathers agreed.

"And Silas is unable to provide proof of his whereabouts for more than an hour. It is only a ten-minute walk to my sister's cottage, and a ten-minute walk back. Which leaves forty minutes unaccounted for, and I'm almost certain it does not take that long to see an unwell woman safely to bed. Where was he, sir, and what was he doing?"

The Chief Constable contemplated his cup of tea, which he had made before they had begun their conversation. "What do you make of the theft of the money and the locket?"

"The locket held some monetary value, but I do not think that is why he removed it. I think he took it as a token, if you will. A remembrance. And as for the money…. I'm of the firm belief that Silas Ferryman has planned this for some time, and that he will shortly quit this village, and relocate elsewhere. Perhaps Southampton. Or even London."

"You have given considerable thought to this."

"I have feared for some months that Silas was about to abandon Mattie. I could not, sadly, predict that his decision would take a deadly turn."

"How do you suggest we proceed?"

"With your agreement," Thaddeus replied, "I shall invite him to attend an interview, so we may put some pertinent questions to him, and consider what he has to say for himself."

• • •

And so Thaddeus set out to visit his father's blacksmith shop.

What he found upon his arrival did not entirely surprise him. Silas Ferryman was preparing to depart the premises, and was dressed not in the leather apron and shirtsleeves of his trade, but in a cloak. He had with him a case, which appeared to be fully packed.

"Are you leaving us, sir?" Thaddeus inquired.

"What of it?" Silas replied.

"An unexpected development, that is all."

"My wife is dead," Silas said. "There is no purpose in my remaining here."

"Will you agree to a small diversion? Chief Constable Mathers has some questions he would like to put to you about the night of Matilda's murder."

Silas seemed hesitant. He contemplated his case, which was

resting upon the floor. Then he picked it up quickly. "Very well. If he must."

It was not until they were nearly upon the constabulary that he decided to flee.

Silas Ferryman was in excellent form, and his years as a blacksmith had conditioned his body well. He was easily able to outrun Thaddeus, even with the additional burden of his case, and so the pursuit became a matter of who would become winded first.

Unfortunately, the route Silas chose led precisely nowhere, except into a field occupied by some cattle. The cattle had deposited upon the ground what nature had designed, and Silas was not fleet-footed enough to avoid it. His boot thus mired, he tumbled forward. He quickly scrambled up and was off again. However, Thaddeus had, in the meantime, caught up, and in a matter of moments was upon him, seizing his arm and throwing him once more to the ground.

"I am arresting you, sir!" Thaddeus shouted, catching his breath, but even as he uttered the words, he was aware something was not quite right.

Indeed, everything was not quite right. The grass beneath his feet was no longer in evidence. In its place was a hard substance, which he had not before encountered. And the quiet of the December afternoon had been replaced by rumbling sounds he was also unfamiliar with, and disagreeable smells, and sights.

To his right, contraptions seemed to travel without the aid of a horse. There were no trees and no fields, and there were definitely no cattle. There were, however, people—both men and women—and they were dressed in highly peculiar clothing.

Thaddeus's surveillance was short-lived, as he was summarily struck over the head by Silas Ferryman, and rendered unconscious.

And that was all Thaddeus Oliver Quinn could recall, until he opened his eyes some minutes later, in response to an urgent voice inquiring about the state of his health.

The voice belonged to a gentleman wearing a uniform not unlike his own, though of a decidedly unfamiliar design.

"What is this place?" Thaddeus said.

"You are in London, sir. And you appear to have had a nasty knock on your head."

"Yes," said Thaddeus, as the fog in his mind cleared, and he became aware, once again, of the strangeness of his surroundings.

"Can you tell me your name, sir?"

"Quinn. Constable Thaddeus Quinn. From Middlehurst."

"Indeed, sir. And the date? Can you recall what day it is?"

"I cannot," Thaddeus replied, after a moment.

"It is the 28th of December, sir. 1939. And where, might I inquire, is your gas mask?"

CHAPTER TWO

Now

Mr. Deeley was attempting to make tea.

Lying in bed upstairs, Charlie could hear him pottering about in the kitchen. He'd located the Brown Betty teapot, and the tea itself, which was kept in three boxes on a little shelf underneath the window.

Earl Grey. English Breakfast. Yorkshire.

She hoped it was Earl Grey, which was her favourite on a lazy Sunday morning.

Tap on, water in the kettle.

The next bit was the tricky part.

"Plug the kettle into the wall," Charlie said to herself, repeating what she'd told Mr. Deeley the last time he'd decided to surprise her with breakfast in bed.

Fortunately, she'd got downstairs before the entire cottage had gone up in flames. Her kettle, however, had been reduced to a toxic lump of melted plastic in the sitting room fireplace.

The sitting room fireplace was now off-limits to Mr. Deeley. For food preparation purposes, anyway.

She could not smell anything burning. Excellent.

"Mrs. Collins!" Mr. Deeley called from the bottom of the stairs.

"Yes, Mr. Deeley?" she inquired.

He had a first name. Shaun. But it was impossible to call him that, as impossible as it was for him to call her Charlie. And anyway, it suited them. John Steed had never addressed Mrs. Peel by her Christian name. And Emma Peel had only ever referred to the most important man in her life as Steed.

"Do you wish your eggs hard boiled, or soft?"

In fact, Charlie wished them scrambled, but she dared not suggest this to Mr. Deeley, as it would mean butter, and a frying pan. Boiled eggs were simple, and involved only water in a pot. He could be trusted with that.

"Are you all right with the cooker?" she checked.

"Yes," Mr. Deeley said, with a little less certainty than Charlie would have preferred. "I have turned the handle, and the surface is hot. I have placed the eggs in the water. And the pot is now upon the fire."

"The fire...?" Charlie faltered, sitting up in bed.

"Forgive me," said Mr. Deeley. "It is a turn of phrase I cannot easily abandon. The pot is upon the hob. And you have not yet replied to my question, Mrs. Collins."

"Soft boiled," Charlie replied. "Please."

She heard him go back into the kitchen. In the years before Mr. Deeley, she had more or less abandoned cooking. Proper cooking, anyway. The microwave oven had been enough, because there was only herself to look after.

But since Mr. Deeley's arrival three months earlier, preparation of food had become an altogether worthwhile—and surprisingly pleasant—pastime.

The old AGA that her mum had bought decades earlier still sat abandoned in its alcove, a useful place for putting newspapers and odds and ends that hadn't yet found a more permanent home. But taking its place, at the end of the counter underneath the window, was a newly installed electric cooker, with a double oven and grill, and a four-element ceramic hob. It was upon this hob that Mr. Deeley was now attempting to boil eggs.

"Mrs. Collins," he called, again, from the bottom of the stairs.

"Yes, Mr. Deeley?"

"You have not yet replied to my other question."

Charlie smiled. "That is because," she said, "I have not yet had ample time to consider it."

He was coming up the stairs.

He paused at her open bedroom door, and knocked.

"You may come in, Mr. Deeley. I'm perfectly decent."

Mr. Deeley entered and stood at a modest distance from Charlie's bed, his eyes averted.

"Mr. Deeley," Charlie reminded him. "You've seen me in a far less respectable state than this. And I have seen you in an altogether less respectable state than the clothes you're wearing now."

What he was wearing now was new jeans, and the white cotton shirt he had worn when he escaped from prison in 1825. The loose sleeves were rolled halfway up his forearms, and he was without shoes or socks. He looked, Charlie thought, quite dishy. For someone who was more than two hundred years old.

"The circumstances of our mutual disrespectability," Mr. Deeley said, trying very hard to maintain his composure, "were… were…."

He stopped, struggling to find the right word.

"Dire?" Charlie suggested.

"Indeed. Dire. Yes."

"If we'd been given more than one hour together," Charlie said, "I suspect our circumstances might even have progressed to direness in the extreme."

"Ah," said Mr. Deeley. "And therein lies my dilemma. For I feel, Mrs. Collins, that our mutual consummation of nature's urges must lead us to an inevitable, yet not unpleasant, conclusion."

"We did not consummate nature's urges," Charlie reminded him. "Much as we both had wished it so. That circumstance has yet to be… concluded."

Mr. Deeley approached the side of her bed. He knelt on one knee, and took Charlie's hand in his.

"Then marry me, Mrs. Collins," he said, looking into her eyes. "For I will not accept a refusal."

"Mr. Deeley…" Charlie paused. "It's not necessary to be

married in order to conclude the circumstances you and I began in your prison cell in 1825. Truly."

"But I wish to spare you a terrible dishonour, Mrs. Collins."

"What dishonour, Mr. Deeley? I don't understand."

"If we should so conclude said circumstances, Mrs. Collins, and not once but upon regular and, with hope, frequent re-examination... you would soon be with child. And I could not bear to see you scorned by the villagers."

Charlie clasped both of Mr. Deeley's hands in hers.

"Mr. Deeley," she said. "There are ways to prevent such occurrences. Extremely reliable ways. I'm in no rush to become a mother. We may conclude to our hearts' content."

Mr. Deeley's face brightened.

"And these methods are well-known to you? And without attendant danger?"

"Extremely well-known," Charlie assured him, adding a kiss. "And completely without danger. Now then, what about those eggs?"

• • •

The eggs had been boiled to perfection. Charlie added toast and butter, and ginger marmalade, and poured the tea—it was, in fact, Earl Grey—with milk and sugar. Mr. Deeley sat on one side of the old wooden table in the kitchen while Charlie faced him on the other, with some sprigs of freshly picked autumn-flowering Clematis from the garden completing the setting.

"Mrs. Collins," Mr. Deeley said. "Forgive my curiosity, but the knowledge you imparted to me earlier has intrigued me greatly. Have you the means at hand to prevent an unintended outcome to a possible...happy conclusion...?"

Charlie laughed. "I do indeed, Mr. Deeley. In fact, I took the necessary steps three months ago. It was rather pre-emptive of me, I know. But under the circumstances, I felt it a wise precaution."

"Does it involve a concoction? A disagreeable unguent composed of foul-smelling ingredients?"

"It does not, Mr. Deeley. It involves a tablet."

"Things have much improved," Mr. Deeley remarked, "from two hundred years ago. My knowledge is intermittent. However, one cannot share a kitchen table with servants, particularly the housemaids, without gaining some understanding of this… delicate subject matter." He paused. "Do you then place this tablet in the specified location… so as to interfere with what… issues forth?"

Charlie laughed.

"No, Mr. Deeley. I swallow it with my morning tea, and that's all that's required. Chemistry and biology take care of the rest. Look."

She pulled the packet of tablets from her bag and showed it to him. Then she took one out of its slot and popped it into her mouth.

Mr. Deeley shook his head in amazement.

"I am much cheered by this news," he said. "And as such, I believe we should consider concluding our circumstances at the earliest possible opportunity."

Charlie laughed again. "I do love you, Mr. Deeley," she said. "It's a wonder I discovered you single and not spoken for in 1825. Were there no attractive and marriageable young ladies at all who had caught your eye?"

Mr. Deeley knew all about Charlie's husband, Jeff, and the car accident that had killed him five years earlier. She'd told him everything. They'd visited his grave, delivering a fresh pot of flowering geraniums. But Mr. Deeley himself had been very circumspect about his own romantic past.

"There was a young lady," he began carefully. "Miss Jemima Beckford. The eldest daughter of Mr. William Beckford."

"From Beckford Farm?" Charlie guessed. The farmhouse, near Stoneford, was long gone, and the outbuildings reduced to dereliction. And the land upon which the buildings had once sat was tumbling into the sea, a few feet every year.

"Yes, the same. It was rumoured that Mr. Beckford provided a safe house for smugglers, although it was never proven. In any case, it was his daughter that I loved. And I would have married her, had tragedy not intervened."

"Oh, Mr. Deeley," Charlie said. "I'm so sorry…."

"There is nothing to be sorry about," Mr. Deeley replied. "The tragedy was another gentleman. Miss Beckford was, unhappily, not constant in her affections. She accepted a proposal of marriage from Mr. Cornelius Quinn, the son of the village blacksmith. And six months following, gave birth herself to a son, whom she named Thaddeus."

"Six months following," Charlie mused.

"A not uncommon occurrence," Mr. Deeley provided. "When human nature is allowed to pursue its most inquisitive course."

"Mr. Deeley," Charlie said. "If this is not too indelicate a question…did you allow your human nature to pursue its most inquisitive course with Miss Beckford at any point prior to her wedding to Mr. Quinn…?"

"It is not too an indelicate question, Mrs. Collins. We had, in fact, given free rein to our inquisitiveness upon four separate occasions prior to the wedding. I had every reason to believe Miss Beckford would soon become my wife. And as she had not provided any indication to the contrary, we happily indulged."

"Mr. Deeley," Charlie said carefully. "Might it be possible that Thaddeus Quinn was not actually the son of Cornelius Quinn?"

"That complication had occurred to me," Mr. Deeley replied. "Alas, Mr. and Mrs. Quinn took up residence some distance away, in Middlehurst, when young Thaddeus was no more than a few months old. It was therefore impossible for me to observe his features and his character, to determine whether there might be some likeness to myself. And so, Mrs. Collins, that is where it was left. He would have been nine years of age when you made my acquaintance. And, in truth, I had not loved another since Jemima. Not as I love you now."

"Oh Mr. Deeley…."

Charlie was lost for words. She had wondered why a man in his midthirties, in 1825 Stoneford, should not be spoken for, but until now, it had not seemed overly important to know the answer.

But the idea that he might have had a son did fill her with a sense of intrigue. She made up her mind to investigate further.

"Finish your breakfast, Mr. Deeley. It's time we put in an appearance at the museum."

19

CHAPTER THREE

The Stoneford Village Museum building had once been the vicarage attached to St. Eligius Church. It was there that Charlie spent her days, immersed in her role as Historical Guide and Interpreter. It wasn't actually necessary for her to work. She'd acquired quite a nice sum of money from the sale of a rare deck of Tarot cards that had come into her possession earlier in the year. But she enjoyed the history, and she enjoyed sharing that history with the museum's visitors. And so she'd stayed on as a part-time, unpaid consultant.

Charlie walked with Mr. Deeley to the Old Vicarage, their journey taking them past the Village Green and the ancient Village Oak. It was October, and the sun was shining wanly through a high marine haze. Children on the green kicked a football around.

There weren't many tourists; in the summer, Stoneford, on the south coast of England, was awash with visitors. All of the little shops and coffee places around the Village Green did a roaring trade, as did the concessions closer to the beach, which were just down the road, at the bottom of a low, sandy cliff. The Village Museum was always on their list of Things to See. Because of this, Charlie had installed a shop in the vicarage's entrance hall, selling posters and mugs and T-shirts, as well as smugglers' loot, gypsy tambourines, and other souvenirs inspired by the displays.

She unlocked the vicarage's front door and switched on the lights. The shop stayed dark, its inventory locked away, an apologetic sign on its empty display shelves stating it would open again in June.

She wasn't expecting many visitors. Once the summer rush was over, Stoneford reverted back to what the locals had always known it as, a former fishing village that had once been notorious as a haven for smugglers and pirates. An out-of-the-way stop on the coastal road, midway between Southampton and Bournemouth. The museum was open only on weekends now, and even then just for half days.

If anyone did pop in, Charlie's office was in the vicarage's kitchen, at the back. She kept the door open and could appear at a moment's notice for an impromptu tour of the museum's latest display, a yearlong tribute to Stoneford during the Blitz. And Mr. Deeley was employed outside, using his nineteenth-century handyman skills to restore the derelict coach house to its former glory.

Charlie sat down at her desk and switched on her computer, while Mr. Deeley went through to the back garden. In the summer, he provided historical tours of the village in a horse-drawn wagon borrowed from a local farmer. Now that the tourists had stopped coming, he was a bit at loose ends. In 1825, he'd been the head groom at Stoneford Manor, on top of the hill overlooking the village. It wasn't really the kind of skill that transferred easily into the twenty-first century. Like Charlie, he didn't need to work. Indeed, he couldn't work, since he had no identification and didn't officially exist. But, like Charlie, he needed to do something to occupy his time. Today, he was painting the doors of the old coach house, located at the bottom of the garden.

Charlie went online to her favourite family tree site, thinking she might look up Thaddeus Quinn.

She loved digging into the past. She was just old enough to remember a time before the Internet, when her essays at school were researched, not by googling, but by enlisting the helpful assistance of Mrs. Bamber at the village library. Endless fingerings through the cards in little wooden catalogue drawers. Pencilled reference numbers on slips of paper, a wander through the stacks of bookshelves. Sitting in front of a dodgy microfilm reader, whirring weeks of newspapers through the winder, battling queasiness not unlike seasickness, trying to follow the text.

The Internet had come along just in time for her university degree in history, igniting and facilitating a passion for research into her family's past. In the old days, she'd have spent months ploughing through dusty birth, death, and marriage records in local council offices, and christening entries in church ledgers. But with everything now online, what previously would have taken years could now be accomplished in a matter of mouse clicks.

Charlie signed into the website and was about to type "Thaddeus Quinn" into the search box when the front door to the vicarage opened.

Charlie stood up. And when she saw who it was, she sat down again. Reg Ferryman, the proprietor of The Dog's Watch, a historical coaching inn that, centuries earlier, had serviced carriages, horses, drivers, and passengers. These days it was, like many of the buildings in Stoneford, Grade II listed. That hadn't stopped Reg from coming up with dozens of plans to renovate the place, all of them roundly disallowed at council meetings.

Reg hadn't given up. He'd turned his sights to other properties and other endeavours, and was currently eyeing the Old Vicarage as a venue for his latest idea, a Hampshire rip-off of the London Dungeon.

"Afternoon," he said, walking through to the kitchen and stopping in front of Charlie's desk.

"No," Charlie replied. He was repulsive. And greasy. And he smelled like last week's mopped-up beer.

"I haven't said anything yet."

"I know what you want, and the answer's still no."

He'd offered her a job managing his new attraction. Because the Old Vicarage was not, for some unfathomable reason, listed with English Heritage. It was an oversight Charlie had taken steps to remedy, but the process was slow. At this rate, the Old Vicarage would be gutted and turned into the Hampshire House of Horrors before English Heritage even had the time to consider Charlie's application.

"You'll change your mind once you see this wreck of a place transformed into an unmissable seaside attraction.

Midnight slaughters. Cut-throat smugglers." His eyes lit up. "The Plague Pirates."

"I don't need a job," she reminded him.

"So you say."

Reg Ferryman was a very poor loser. He had briefly been in possession of one of the Tarot cards that had made Charlie's fortune. The one missing card that had been necessary to complete the deck. But it was, by law, hers. And the law had prevailed. It was Charlie's considered opinion that Reg Ferryman's plans for the Old Vicarage were personal payback for being cheated out of his share of the loot.

"What about your friend? That Deeley bloke. He'd be a good bloodthirsty murderer. He looks the part."

"No," Charlie said. "Go away."

"The Middlehurst Slasher."

Charlie knew all about the three women who'd been found with their throats cut, near Middlehurst in the New Forest, in 1849. Stoneford was only a short drive away from the area where their bodies had been located. The killings were all fairly grisly, and had never been solved.

"Since one of the victims was married to one of my distant ancestors. A personal connection. Just saying…"

"Go away," Charlie said, again.

"I will," Reg replied. "But I just wanted you to know, I've got a meeting with the Village Council on Wednesday. We're discussing the sale of this building. To me. There are some who would like to see Stoneford put back on the tourist map. There are some who could do with the employment and the knock-on benefits."

"Please leave, Reg."

"I'm going."

And he went.

Charlie sent herself an e-mail. *Call English Heritage tomorrow. Urgent.*

Then she sent herself another one. *Arrange to have Reg Ferryman disembowelled. First display for the Hampshire House of Horrors.*

There was no way that man was going to be allowed to dismantle the Stoneford Village Museum, with or without his distant connection to the Middlehurst Slasher.

• • •

"We're in luck, Mr. Deeley," Charlie said. "Josephine Quinn has put the entire family tree online."

Mr. Deeley had paused his afternoon's labours in the coach house and was now sitting in the comfy armchair beside the vicarage's huge kitchen fireplace, drinking a cup of tea and reading the Sunday papers on Charlie's iPad. After an initial reticence, followed by absolute wonder, and then, finally and very rapidly, rampant curiosity, he'd taught himself the basics of internetting.

Not bad, Charlie thought, for someone who'd arrived only a few months earlier from a time when the steam engine was just being explored as a method of transportation. And when useful electricity wouldn't be invented for another sixty years.

"Who is Josephine Quinn?" Mr. Deeley inquired.

"She's the wife of Samuel Quinn. Quinn Motor Services. On the High Street."

She clicked through the pages of familial links.

"Here we are. Jemima Beckford and Cornelius Quinn. Married in January 1816 in Stoneford. And there's Thaddeus Oliver Quinn, born on June 11th of that year. Oh."

Mr. Deeley got up to look over Charlie's shoulder. "What is, 'oh'?" he inquired.

"After they moved to Middlehurst, they had three more children. Matilda, Robert, and Maurice. But Jemima died. June, 1825. Giving birth to Maurice. Look."

Mr. Deeley looked, and the expression on his face became genuinely sad. "Oh," he said, softly. "Indeed. Then she had been gone for only a little time, when you and I met. And I had not known."

"How could you know?" Charlie asked, gently. "They lived in another village, eight miles away."

"Her father might have said. William Beckford. He and I often had cause to converse. He would have attended her burial. And yet he said nothing to me."

"Who knows why people act the way they do?" Charlie said. "Perhaps he felt it was a kindness not to. Sometimes it's better to say nothing, to spare another's feelings, than to say something and cause further hurt."

Mr. Deeley didn't reply. He walked back to the armchair, and sat for a little while, silent.

Charlie continued hunting through Josephine Quinn's family tree. It was Maurice Quinn from whom her husband, Samuel Quinn, had descended, down through the generations.

What then of Thaddeus?

Josephine Quinn seemed to have lost interest in him, preferring instead to focus on Maurice's family line.

Charlie went back to the website's genealogy area and consulted the census records. A census was taken every ten years in England, starting in 1841, and the information those lists provided was invaluable for tracking elusive family members. Yes, there he was. Thaddeus, Robert, and Maurice, all still living with Cornelius in Middlehurst in 1841, although Matilda had disappeared. Married and moved away, most probably. She'd look into that later. She could see that by the time of the next census, ten years later, Robert and Maurice had also left the family home…and so had Thaddeus. Cornelius was living alone.

Charlie searched all of 1851 for a mention of Thaddeus Oliver Quinn.

Nothing.

And in 1861?

Nothing there either.

Charlie checked every census up to 1911, the last that had been released for public perusal.

There were no records of him at all.

Perhaps he'd simply wanted to avoid being counted. People could be peculiar that way. One of her own cousins had successfully avoided every census in his lifetime, yet he'd lived, quietly and happily, in splendid bachelorhood, with only his birth and death noted in official records.

Perhaps Thaddeus had died. Or left the country.

Or run away to sea.

Charlie did a worldwide search for Thaddeus Oliver Quinn, and discovered... nothing.

No marriage or death records, no passenger lists or seamanship papers. No portraits or old photographs. Nothing at all.

Charlie let her breath out.

It wasn't as if he'd had an ordinary name. There seemed to be only one Thaddeus Oliver Quinn in existence. And, sometime between 1841 and 1851, he had disappeared from the face of the earth.

She looked up as the front door to the vicarage opened again and a woman came into the entry hall. She was dressed in a hat and coat that looked as though they'd come straight out of wartime England. She had a round, full-moon sort of face, and very red cheeks, and a haircut that made Charlie think that a hairdresser had upended a bowl on her head, and snipped all around its rim. Her expression was one of diligent inquiry.

"Hello," Charlie said, warmly, going out to greet her. "Welcome to our little museum."

The woman's face burst into a smile. "Oh! Jolly good! Glad I've found you open. I heard all about your World War Two Blitz display and I thought to myself, 'I must have a go.' Any possibility of a look round?"

Charlie had to stop herself from laughing. The only adjective she could think of to describe this woman was exuberant. Her words were positively bursting from her. And, in spite of looking no more than forty, she seemed delightfully old-fashioned.

"Yes, of course," she said. "Please come this way."

Charlie led the woman into the Blitz Room. There were displays showing the damage done by Luftwaffe bombers who'd sometimes included Stoneford in their demolition runs to nearby Southampton.

Before and after photos, and what the bomb sites looked like today. Pictures and stories from the evacuees that Stoneford had taken in at the start of the war, in 1939 and 1940. Fragmented bricks, blackened by fire, and a small mound of 1940s coins, fused together by the heat of an explosion.

Next to the melted coins, by way of comparison, was a saucer filled with the real things: several little silver sixpences, a chunky thrup'nny bit, a handful of giant copper pennies and a couple of one-shilling pieces.

In one corner of the room, she'd mocked up a kitchen and furnished it with some of the things one might find in a 1940s home: a vintage gas cooker, pantry shelves, a washing-up sink, a broom and dustpan. The pantry was filled with boxes and jars and tins of food: National Dried Milk, Bird's Custard, OXO. Cocoa and dried eggs. All of them looked quite new, largely because Charlie had created them from scratch. She'd collected empty tins and boxes and replaced their labels with ones she'd found online and run off on the museum's colour printer.

The woman seemed very taken with Charlie's kitchen.

"My word," she exclaimed, examining the National Dried Milk box, "this does look familiar."

"Really?" Charlie said.

"Oh yes. I've seen photos. From my grandmother's kitchen."

She leaned over, as if to share a very big secret.

"My grandfather was a very keen photographer, you see. Insisted on documenting everything. Including their house. And their garden. And the road they lived on. He took masses of pictures, every year of the war. I ought to donate them to something. I'm sure they'd be useful."

"He must have been a very lucky man," Charlie said. "I understand it was extremely difficult to get film for cameras during the war."

The woman tapped the side of her nose.

"Black market," she said. "Easy when you know how."

She walked across to the other corner of the display, where

Charlie had installed a bedroom. She'd created it using her own grandmother's recollections and, indeed, some of her grandmother's things. Charlie's Nana Betty was notorious for never throwing anything away.

There was a double bed covered with a deep red satin eiderdown, and a dressing table with three mirrors, and on top of the dressing table were bottles of violet scent, a silver brush and comb set, face powder and lipstick, and a pearl necklace.

Beside the bed was a big old oak wardrobe that she'd scrounged from Edwin Watts, who owned the antiques shop near the Village Green. Nana Betty had allowed Charlie to take away some skirts and blouses and a dress that she'd worn during the war. But she'd been extremely reluctant to lend her any of Charlie's grandfather's clothing. Pete Lewis had died in 1970 and Charlie understood Nana Betty's feelings completely. She'd held onto all of Jeff's things, too… his shirts and trousers, his favourite suits and ties. His two guitars—a Gretsch and a battered old Fender Strat—both stowed in their hard travelling cases and kept safe, in the spare bedroom, with his collection of CDs and his playlists… as if he might wander back one day, and want to go out gigging again.

But Nana Betty had surprised Charlie in the end and had relented, giving her a beautiful hand-knitted V-neck pullover with a Fair Isle pattern of rust, brown, yellow, green and blue: "Keep it safe, my darling. It's one-of-a-kind. And it belonged to a man who was one-of-a-kind."

Charlie had hung it with care in the wardrobe, supplementing it with some vintage men's shirts and trousers and a suit jacket she'd found online.

The exuberant little woman who had come to visit the museum seemed particularly drawn to the pullover.

"My Nana donated that," Charlie said. "She knitted it herself, during the war. Amazing to think it was all those years ago."

"How extraordinary!" the woman exclaimed. "It is absolutely marvellous. Is she still alive?"

"Oh yes, very much so. Quite ancient, in her nineties. But my

28

Auntie Wendy pops in to see her every day, and takes her out for a walk. Would you like to see the Anderson shelter we've got in the back garden? Sandbags and everything."

"Yes, please!"

They went outside. At the bottom of the garden, Mr. Deeley, having finished his cup of tea and his perusal of the Sunday papers, had taken up his paintbrush once again and was busily coating the coach house's nondescript grey doors with quite a lovely shade of Drawing Room Blue.

The shelter was just to the left of the coach house, dug into the earth with its back up against the garden's brick wall. The woman observed the careful arrangement of sandbags around its entrance and admired the vegetable garden growing on its roof. And then she clambered inside to have a look at the wooden slat bunk beds.

"I must say, this is all terribly realistic-looking," she said, climbing back out. "Kudos to whoever's the genius responsible."

"That would be me," Mr. Deeley volunteered modestly.

"Well done you, then!"

"He researched it all online," Charlie said, "and found an old abandoned shelter in someone's back garden in Totton. We drove over in my cousin's van and took it apart and brought it back here. Mr. Deeley dug a hole and put it all back together again using the original wartime instructions."

"Well, it's absolutely authentic," the woman said.

Mr. Deeley gave a little bow. "Your kind words are most appreciated."

"My Nana's got one just like this in her back garden in London," Charlie added. "She wouldn't dig it up after the war. I think she's quite attached to it, really. Reminds her of my grandfather. He was a pilot in the RAF."

"Ah yes, the brave fighters up in the sky. What did he fly? A Spitfire?"

"A Spitfire," Charlie confirmed.

"Bravo him. I'm much more fond of the Spitfires than the Hurricanes. Though they were both the absolute heroes of the war."

29

She took out an old-fashioned pocket watch, the sort that Charlie had seen in photographs, and opened it.

"Gosh, look at the time. I must, with utmost apologies, take my leave. Thank you so much for the tour."

"My pleasure," Charlie replied.

"And mine," Mr. Deeley added. "Please do come again."

"I shall make every effort," the woman promised, letting herself out through the garden gate.

• • •

After the museum had closed for the day, and while Mr. Deeley was scrubbing away the remnants of Drawing Room Blue in the shower, Charlie continued her research into Thaddeus Oliver Quinn. She'd had an idea that perhaps he'd committed some heinous crime and had, as a result, been transported.

She scanned the trial records at the Old Bailey, the prison registers, the lists of convicts packed onto ships bound for Australia.

Nothing. Absolutely nothing.

A tapping on her kitchen door interrupted her research. She got up to see who it was.

"Nick!"

Nick Weller was her first cousin, Auntie Wendy's son, a physicist who lectured at Wandsworth University in London, but who spent his summers—and his term-time weekends the rest of the year—in Stoneford, where he'd grown up.

"Come in," she said. "What brings you round at this hour?"

Nick limped into the kitchen. His right leg had been mangled in the same car accident that had killed Jeff and, as a result, he relied on a cane to help him walk.

"I've just had a call from Mum," he said. "Sorry, Charlie… it's Nana. Mum found her in bed this afternoon when she went to check on her. She'd passed away in the night."

Charlie felt dizzy. She was prevented from falling by Mr. Deeley, who, coming downstairs after his shower, saw her legs buckle and rushed to catch her.

"It's Nana Betty," she said, hanging onto him. "She's died."

"I'm so sorry," Mr. Deeley whispered, into her hair, as he helped her into the sitting room, and sat her down in the comfy armchair by the fire.

Nick followed, leaning on his cane.

"Was it her heart?" Charlie asked, trying not to cry.

"Very likely. Mum said she looked peaceful. As if she'd just fallen asleep and not woken up."

"That's all right then," Charlie said.

Nana Betty had been physically frail, but in full possession of all her faculties, her mind still brilliant. She'd lived alone in Balham, in the little terraced house where she'd grown up.

And now, she was no more.

Her passing was not entirely unexpected. But still, it was like a punch to the stomach. You expected your Nana to live forever. You didn't dare think about a time when she might not be there.

Charlie's mind was racing with last memories. The last time she'd visited. The last present Nana Betty had sent her, for her birthday, a month earlier—a card-stock kit that you assembled, a perfect replica of Balham Underground Station. It was still sitting on top of the AGA, waiting to be cut out and glued together. Along with the kit, Nana had included something that had made Charlie smile. It was a fragment of white glazed pottery tile, the sort that lined the station tunnels on the Northern Line, where Balham was located. Where she'd got it from, Charlie had no idea. But it was a perfect gift, something that her Nana had known she would treasure.

The last time she'd spoken to her had been the day before yesterday, on the phone. She'd rung out of the blue, and at the end of their chat, had signed off with, "Bye-bye, my darling. God bless."

As if she'd had a feeling. As if she'd known.

"Let me know what her doctor says?"

"I will," Nick said. "And I'd think her funeral would be in about a week's time. You OK?"

"Just sad," Charlie said with a sniff. She couldn't hold the tears off for much longer, and she was beginning to go numb. She'd felt this way before, but much, much worse, after the police had told her about Jeff.

"Perhaps I ought to put the kettle on," Mr. Deeley offered. Charlie was still clinging to his hand.

"Yes, please," Nick said. "I could do with a strong cup of tea myself."

CHAPTER FOUR

Mr. Deeley had never been on a train.

The world was just becoming aware of steam locomotion when Charlie had made his acquaintance in 1825. Railways had yet to be built. And Stoneford was never destined to be included on a main line to London, or on a branch line to anywhere else.

The nearest station to Stoneford was Middlehurst, the same Middlehurst where Jemima had gone to live with Cornelius Quinn and Thaddeus. It was a ten-minute drive north along a country road that meandered past woods and copses, golf courses and farmers' fields, and ended just inside the southern boundary of the New Forest.

Once, encampments of gypsies had inhabited the New Forest. To both Charlie and Mr. Deeley, it had always been a mystical, magical sort of place. There were woodlands and heathlands, grassy meadows and scrubby bogs. And there were witches and fairies and ghosts, the tales of which had peppered each of their childhoods.

The railway station at Middlehurst seemed to have been painted from a picture book. Built in 1886, it featured a red brick station house with white and dark blue trim. The Victorian decorations were repeated on Platform 1, which accommodated the through services to Southampton and beyond. A scalloped wooden canopy, supported by blue and white cast iron pillars, sheltered passengers from the weather.

"Don't go too near the edge," Charlie warned as Mr. Deeley studied the tracks, and then the view from the platform along the tracks, first east and then west.

"Why?" he asked.

"Because you might topple over," she said.

"And what if I should topple over, what then?" Mr. Deeley replied, teasing her. "It is a short journey down. I would not suffer an injury."

"You would if the train was coming," Charlie said. "You'd be run over. Or electrocuted. And then you'd be dead."

She kept an eye on him as he wandered along the platform, fascinated by what it had to offer: a machine for dispensing tickets; another containing sweets and cold drinks; a round white passenger Help Point; bench seats and storage sheds for bicycles.

He was on his way back to where Charlie was standing when she recognized the round-faced woman who had come to the museum to look at the Blitz display. She was carrying something wrapped in what looked like a piece of old sacking, tied up with string, and she was hurrying towards Charlie.

"Hello," Charlie said.

"Ah!" the woman replied. "Jolly good! Just the person I wanted to see. I went to the museum but it was all locked up. I rang the telephone number for inquiries posted on the door and spoke to a frightfully helpful young woman."

"Natalie King," Charlie said. "My office manager."

"The very same. Miss King told me you were on your way to London. I'm so glad I've caught you because I've got something you might find interesting."

She unknotted the string and unfolded the burlap. Inside was a charred and pockmarked piece of metal the size of Charlie's fist, a rusty fragment of something that had obviously survived a great blast.

Charlie took the piece of metal into her hands and examined it.

Mr. Deeley, meanwhile, had returned from his exploration of the platform. "This is a most interesting artefact," he observed.

"It's a piece of shell casing," the woman replied. "From an anti-aircraft gun during the war, I should think. I discovered it in a field while I was walking one day, and was wondering where it might best be housed. Do you think it would suit your museum?"

"Brilliant," Charlie said. "Yes. Thank you. It would. I know exactly where I can put it."

"There's something else which makes this terribly interesting," the woman said. "It seems to possess a rather unusual quality."

She produced her pocket watch, opened it, and held it close to the lump of metal.

"Do look."

Charlie and Mr. Deeley both looked. And then looked again. The hands of the pocket watch were winding backwards, very slowly.

The woman drew the clock away, and the hands ceased their movement.

She held it close again, and the hands, once more, began to tick backwards.

"What's causing that?" Charlie asked, intrigued.

"Haven't a clue," the woman replied. "Possibly an instance of unusual energy... possibly some sort of magnetic effect. It is, without a doubt, a very special piece of shrapnel."

"Then I promise I'll keep it safe."

Charlie wrapped it back up in its burlap covering, and placed it in her bag.

"I well remember my first train journey," the woman mused, turning to Mr. Deeley. "I was very small, and living in a village that was much like Stoneford. My parents were taking me to see London, and what an adventure that was!"

"I am very much looking forward to it," Mr. Deeley replied. "But how do you know it's the first time I am travelling aboard a train?"

"It's written all over your face, Mr. Deeley," the woman replied, amused. "I'm an excellent judge of character. I can tell you're excited."

"I am," he admitted. "Although the circumstance of our travel is less than happy."

"Ah," the woman said, "yes. Yes, of course."

She turned to Charlie. "Miss King did tell me about the funeral arrangements. So terribly sorry about your grandmother. It's never an easy thing, is it?"

"Thank you," Charlie said. "She was lovely."

"I know," said the woman, turning back to Mr. Deeley. "You'll not be disappointed with London, I promise. And here I must here bid you a hasty farewell, as I seem to be required elsewhere."

"Wait," said Charlie. "Can I have your name and contact information? So that I can properly note the donation in our records?"

"You can put me down as Mrs. Ruby Firth," the woman replied. "And you'll always be able to find me—I'm never far away. Good morning!"

And she rushed off.

"Is my delight at climbing aboard a train for the first time really so evident upon my face, Mrs. Collins?"

"Everything is evident on your face, Mr. Deeley. Sometimes you remind me very much of a child, filled with wonder at every new discovery."

"I believe it would be a disservice to you, Mrs. Collins, to mention that you sometimes remind me of my mother."

"I hope I don't, Mr. Deeley."

Wisely, Mr. Deeley said nothing further, as the 09.33 from Weybridge to London Waterloo came into view on the tracks to the west.

• • •

Mr. Deeley was studying Charlie's clever phone. The train was provisioned with Wi-Fi, and he was making full use of it, exploring a website that featured English serial killers.

"Here we are," he said. "The Middlehurst Slasher. The unsolved murders of three unrelated women who all lived in the same geographical area, in or near the village of Middlehurst. The first was Annie Black, aged seventeen, the unmarried daughter of a farmer, who, with her mother and three sisters, was employed as a maker of straw bonnets and hats. She was last seen by her father, walking towards the village, where she had arranged to meet a gentleman wishing to buy a special bonnet for his wife's birthday.

Her mutilated body was found in a stand of trees very near to where the current South West train line runs, between Middlehurst and Brockenhurst."

Mr. Deeley glanced up at the trees, and at the rolling land streaking past the window of the train.

"Very near to here, I should think."

"Yes," Charlie agreed. "And when her body was located, it was noted in the police files, but not widely reported, that a cherished bracelet she had been wearing was missing."

Mr. Deeley returned to the details on Charlie's mobile.

"The next victim was discovered some three months later, in August 1849. Mary Potter, aged thirty-four, the unmarried daughter of a brick-maker. Her father reported he had last seen her on the morning she set off to visit her cousin in nearby Huddleswood. She never arrived, and her body was found some three weeks later, under a bridge, close to Middlehurst. Her throat had been cut, and a silver ring which she had inherited from her grandmother had been stolen."

Mr. Deeley consulted the window once again. The train was travelling over just such a bridge.

"And the last. Matilda Ferryman. Who was married to Silas Ferryman."

"The distant ancestor of Reg Ferryman," Charlie mused. "The Stoneford Ripper-Offer."

Mr. Deeley laughed, and then grew suddenly serious. "This is of interest, Mrs. Collins. Did you know that Silas Ferryman was employed as a blacksmith in the village of Middlehurst, and that he worked with his father-in-law, Cornelius Quinn?"

Charlie looked at Mr. Deeley.

"I didn't," she said. She paused. "Matilda... Matilda Ferryman? Could this be the same Matilda we looked up earlier? Jemima's daughter? Matilda Quinn?"

"It would appear so," Mr. Deeley replied, reading further. "Matilda Ferryman was discovered dead in her bedroom after attending the annual Christmas celebration at Joseph Sewell's Middlehurst manor with her husband."

"Hang on, " Charlie said. "Joseph Sewell. Father of Edwina Sewell. Who married my great-great-something ancestor Augustus. You met him!"

"Indeed," Mr. Deeley replied. "I could hardly forget that particular encounter, Mrs. Collins."

"Etched forever in my mind, Mr. Deeley, for your bravery and your sense of honour. So, a personal connection on both sides. How fascinating! Do carry on!"

"Matilda Ferryman was discovered dead in her bedroom after attending the annual Christmas celebration at Joseph Sewell's Middlehurst manor with her husband. It was further discovered that her father's fortune, which was considerable, had been stolen. As was a locket, Matilda's favourite piece of jewellery. It was assumed that poor Matilda had awoken and confronted the thief, who had attacked her in the bedroom and cut her throat. Although she was married, and her body was discovered in her home, and not outside, Matilda Ferryman has always been considered the third victim of the Middlehurst Slasher, because of the identical method in which she was killed." Mr. Deeley gave the clever phone back to Charlie. "I should like one of these of my own."

"I'll get you one when we come back," Charlie promised, "as long as I can be certain you won't be spending all your time on dating sites."

"What is a dating site?"

Charlie smiled. "Never mind," she said. "If you have to ask, you don't need to know."

But Mr. Deeley's mind was already occupying itself with other matters.

"I had often thought of visiting London when I was employed at Monsieur Duran's manor," he said. "It was a wish I entertained, for a time when I might have been able to afford the days away, and the fare aboard the coach."

He paused.

"If the war was more than seventy years ago, how is it the lady at the train station came by that piece of shrapnel lying in a field? I think it unlikely to have been there all of this time, undiscovered."

"Who knows?" Charlie mused. "Another New Forest oddity. The mysterious collaboration of geology and time. It's not altogether unheard-of. Bits and pieces of the past are always popping up to the surface, where you least expect to find them."

. . .

Waterloo Station was, at half past eleven on the morning of Friday, the 11th of October, nothing short of chaotic. Mr. Deeley stayed close to Charlie as she led him through the platform turnstile and onto the brightly lit main concourse.

Since arriving in the twenty-first century he had not ventured much beyond Stoneford. The journey to Totton to dig up and disassemble the air raid shelter had been a notable exception.

And now, here he was, transplanted into the middle of a bustling railway terminus, which swarmed with an excess of people that, at this hour, might well have rivalled the entire population of Stoneford in terms of numbers.

He suddenly stopped walking and grasped Charlie's arm, tightly. "Mrs. Collins."

"Don't panic," Charlie said. "I don't like crowds, either."

"It is not so much the abundance of individuals," Mr. Deeley replied, "as the realization, Mrs. Collins, that I have absolutely no idea where I am. I am... lost. Is this London?"

"This is London. Well, one of its train stations, anyway. Waterloo. London's outside."

"Waterloo," Mr. Deeley said. "Is it named as such, in order to commemorate the battle?"

"I think it's named after the bridge that's nearby. But yes, Battle of Waterloo. 1815."

"I remember it well," Mr. Deeley replied. "And, in fact, I counted among my friends several former soldiers who had fought there, and lived to tell the tale. One of them even recalled catching a glimpse of Napoleon, astride his horse, although it was from a very great distance, and only for a few seconds. If only they could know that a bridge, and, indeed, an entire railway station, would be named after the place where they had forfeited their arms and legs. And lost their compatriots."

"You're a walking history book, Mr. Deeley. Your life, before you met me, must have been absolutely fascinating."

"I'm glad you think so, Mrs. Collins. For I considered my previous life perfectly ordinary, and certainly without anything outstanding to recommend it. It is my new life, here, which I find full of fascination."

He raised his head, and took stock of his surroundings.

"Have you some sort of diagram as to where we are to proceed next? A navigational chart?"

"On my phone, yes. But we won't need it. We're going by tube."

"A tube?" Mr. Deeley hung on to Mrs. Collins's arm for dear life. "Why must we be enclosed in a tube?"

"It's another train. But it runs underground. Down there." She pointed to the station's floor.

Mr. Deeley seemed frozen in place, unable to move.

"Are you all right, Mr. Deeley?"

Mr. Deeley took a moment to compose himself. "I am, Mrs. Collins. Although, I must confess, I am not without some small degree of trepidation. We have arrived here aboard a vehicle which does not require horses and owes its rapid forward motion to the same force which empowers the lights at night inside your cottage. Now, you inform me there is a similar vehicle which tunnels through the earth like a worm possessed."

"A worm possessed," Charlie mused. "I've never heard it called that before. Very apt. Come with me."

Mr. Deeley reluctantly followed Charlie to the Underground entrance.

"Wait," he said. "These steps are in motion."

"Yes, it's an escalator."

"We do not have such things in Stoneford."

"We're lucky to have buildings with more than two storeys in Stoneford, Mr. Deeley. Don't look down. Just put one foot in front of the other, step on, and hold onto the handrail. I'll be right behind you."

Mr. Deeley hesitated, and after several false starts, managed to coordinate his feet with the moving stairs.

"Stand on the right," Charlie added.

"Where does this wind come from? It is impossible!"

"It's caused by the trains in the tunnels," Charlie replied. "They fit very tightly, and as they move forward they push the air in front of them."

Riding down the escalator, just behind Mr. Deeley, Charlie recalled her earliest memories of the Underground, visiting Nana Betty with her parents. There was a remembrance, tucked away in her mind, of her three-year-old self's wonder at the escalator, and that very same wind blowing up from below, and the sound the train made when it was still in its tunnel but approaching the station, a throaty kind of muffled roar.

"All right?" she checked.

"Yes. It is quite wondrous, Mrs. Collins."

He was staring at the line of people riding the up escalator, opposite. Suddenly, Charlie caught a shadow of sadness on his face.

"What is it, Mr. Deeley?"

"I was in mind of a journey I once undertook, Mrs. Collins, from Stoneford to Southampton. It was twenty miles there, and twenty miles back again, and when I returned, the housemaids and the cook, the butler, and my friend Mr. Rankin, the gardener, were all so eager to hear of my adventures. They savoured every last detail, at supper, and at breakfast the following morning. They spoke to me of nothing else for days."

He looked back at Charlie.

"It is indeed strange," he said, "to realize that all of the people I grew to know, and to love, have been dead for nearly two hundred years. I thought of them just now. I thought of what tales I would share with them, of all of my travels…."

"You have no one left to tell," Charlie said, softly. "I'm so sorry, Mr. Deeley. I didn't even think of that."

"You must accept none of the blame. It was my decision to undertake the journey from my time to yours. And this has been, without a doubt, the most exciting adventure of my life. But I confess, Mrs. Collins, I do, upon occasion, feel a trifle misplaced, and caught very much out of my time."

They had reached the bottom of the moving steps.

"Step off quickly, and don't look down," Charlie advised. "There you are. Your first escalator. And next, the fabulous Northern Line. The worm possessed."

CHAPTER FIVE

"This station," Mr. Deeley said, as their train arrived at Balham, "was opened on December 6th, 1926, as part of the Morden extension of the City and South London Railway, which later became known as the Northern Line."

In the half hour that had elapsed since they'd ridden the down escalator at Waterloo, Mr. Deeley had managed to make himself something of an expert on the Underground. He'd accomplished this by once again referring to Charlie's mobile, and making use of the excellent free Wi-Fi that was provided at each station.

"Wikipedia is your friend," Charlie mused.

"We are indeed fortunate to be occupying the third carriage of this train. We should disembark by way of Door Three, which will align us almost perfectly with the Way Out."

"I'm going to put you in charge of our travels next time we're in London," Charlie said, following Mr. Deeley as he led her off the train, and onto the platform and through the short passageway to the escalator landing.

"There are forty-eight steps up to the booking hall," Mr. Deeley continued, "in a configuration of sixteen, then sixteen, and then another sixteen."

He looked up at the steps.

"We shall take the escalator," he decided.

He stepped onto the moving stairs, barely looking at his feet.

At the top, in the ticket hall, Mr. Deeley paused in front of a small plaque fixed to the wall, above a row of seats, and read aloud what was written there.

"'In remembrance of the civilians and London Transport staff who were killed at this station during the Blitz on the night of 14 October 1940."'

"I can tell you what that is before you look it up," Charlie said, taking her phone back and switching it off before stowing it safely in her bag. "It's a memorial to something that happened during the war. London was heavily bombed and a lot of people only felt safe if they slept in the Underground. So this station was used as a shelter. On that night, October the 14th, a bomb fell on the High Road outside, and it broke through to one of the platform tunnels downstairs. It shattered the mains and the sewers and the tunnel filled up with earth and water and it killed nearly seventy people. They've never been completely sure about the exact total."

"You know much about this occurrence."

"Nana Betty used to tell me stories about it. She was a young woman in 1940. But she wouldn't go down in the tube. She always hated it, and even refused to use it when it was safe, after the war ended."

"It is strange," said Mr. Deeley, "that she should have felt that way. I find this Underground a compelling fascination. And I would have thought that the shelter in her back garden was far less accommodating. At the very least, the Underground station would have been warm and dry."

Charlie smiled, a little impishly.

"On the other hand, that Anderson shelter's where my mum was conceived. Or so Nana Betty always claimed."

"I would not ever have thought of such a place as being conducive to romance," Mr. Deeley replied, also with humour, and a tiny hint of naughtiness. "Perhaps you might show it to me...?"

• • •

It was a short walk from the tube station to Nana Betty's little house at the end of the terrace on Harris Road, and, from there, a slightly longer ride in Nick's van to the cemetery.

Charlie sat at the back of the chapel with Mr. Deeley, listening to a clergyman talk about Nana Betty as though he had known her well, when in fact he had only learned her name and her circumstances the day before.

Charlie's mum and Nick's mum had arranged the funeral. And although they meant well, Charlie was of the opinion that Nana Betty would have much preferred a simple remembrance, followed by an even simpler cremation, with none of the ceremonial trappings that were now taking place.

"It is for the comfort of those left behind," Mr. Deeley whispered, sensing Charlie's unhappiness.

"I know, Mr. Deeley. I'm just sad. I'm afraid you're not seeing the best side of me just now."

She looked at him, and saw that there was sadness in his eyes as well.

"What is it, Mr. Deeley?"

"Would you forgive me if I used these moments to grieve for Jemima? I was not given the opportunity to say goodbye to her in my previous life. And although she chose another over me, there is still a small corner of my heart which cannot dislike her."

Charlie took his hand. She loved his fingers, which were long and a bit rough—he'd been a groom, after all, lugging feed and hay to Monsieur Duran's horses, caring for them on a daily basis, and mucking out their stalls.

"I don't mind at all, Mr. Deeley. And I'm absolutely certain Nana Betty wouldn't mind either."

She glanced behind her. They were sitting next to the aisle, and it would be a simple thing for her to quietly slip away.

"I think I need to go outside," she whispered, excusing herself, avoiding Nick's questioning look.

It was a glorious afternoon, a crisp October day, misty and overcast, and the cemetery was very quiet. Charlie wandered among the graves, reading the inscriptions absently, not really taking in what had been carved into the stones.

She felt closer to her grandmother out here. It was as if Nana Betty had come out for a breath of fresh air as well, having grown impatient with the goings on inside the chapel. And she was walking beside her, *tsking* over flowers that had been left untended and wilting on burial plots, admiring a clever sentiment captured in stone, remarking on the simple beauty of some moss.

Charlie stopped in front of a tiny marker under a tree.

She had to read the inscription twice. And then a third time.

In Loving Memory
Thaddeus Oliver Quinn
Aged 34
Killed by enemy action
Balham Underground Station
14th October 1940

Kneeling down, she cleared away some dead leaves and a few random weeds that had sprouted up around the weathered little headstone. And then she glanced up to see Mr. Deeley, standing near the door to the chapel, looking for her. She waved to him, and he joined her in front of the little grave.

"Look," she said.

Mr. Deeley stared at the tiny marker.

"How can this be?"

"I don't know. There was only one Thaddeus Oliver Quinn. I searched all the way up to the present. Born in 1816, in Stoneford. And no date of death. This couldn't be the same man."

She took out her phone to access her favourite family tree website.

"There is absolutely no record of a Thaddeus Oliver Quinn dying in the UK in October 1940. Or in 1939. Or 1941. Or in any year at all. It has to be a mistake."

She walked across to a nearby wooden bench and sat down. Mr. Deeley sat next to her.

"Still," she said, thoughtfully. "It was wartime. All sorts of mix-ups must have happened. Life was completely chaotic. I'll contact the cemetery's people when we're back in Stoneford and ask them if they have any more information."

"It is very peculiar," Mr. Deeley said thoughtfully. "But, Mrs. Collins, why must we assume that we are the only two ever to have travelled from one century to the next? Surely there could be other individuals who have done the same?"

"You're suggesting that Thaddeus might have been a time traveller?"

"If he is my son, why not? Perhaps the ability to travel in time is an inherited talent. Like music. Or writing. Or holding lengthy conversations with horses."

Charlie smiled. She contemplated the little grave marker again.

"It's still odd that there was no official record of his death, even in 1940. And especially if he died in that bombing. Don't you think?"

They sat in silence for a few moments more. And then Mr. Deeley remembered what he'd come to tell Charlie.

"Your grandmother's casket is being taken to the place where it will be interred, beside your grandfather. Will you go and say goodbye to her?"

"I think I'd rather not, Mr. Deeley. I'd rather just sit here and think about how she was when she was alive. How I remember her. I don't want my last memory of her to be a box being lowered into the ground."

"Then I will sit with you as well," Mr. Deeley decided. "If you are amenable."

"Nothing would please me more."

• • •

Nana Betty's little house in Harris Road had belonged to her parents, Bert and Marjorie Singleton. Bert was a far-sighted greengrocer who'd started out with one small shop in a parade near the tube station. He had grand plans, though, and was eventually able to grow his single business into a small chain of food shops throughout south London.

Nana Betty, being an only child, had never felt a need to live anywhere else. And there was a notorious lack of housing during the war and for years after it ended. So after she'd married Pete Lewis on Christmas Day in 1940, they'd stayed on, occupying the large back bedroom. And then, after the war was over, Bert and Marjorie had moved to Epsom, leaving the house to Betty, and the management of the food shops to Pete.

Charlie's mum had been born there, and Nick's mum too. Uncomplicated births, attended by a midwife.

There was a small front garden, separated from the pavement by a brick wall with a green-painted wooden gate, overgrown and in desperate need of some grooming. When Pete was alive, the garden had been his pride and joy. Charlie had seen photographs, mounted in old-fashioned albums with sticky-backed picture corners. But after Pete had died his domain had been allowed to grow wild, almost as an unspoken tribute to him.

Inside the house, Charlie's mum and Auntie Wendy had planned a reception for Nana Betty. They'd appropriated the tiny kitchen, and were distributing sandwiches, slices of Battenberg, and hot, strong tea to the three dozen people who'd come back from the funeral to reminisce, shed a tear, and catch up on family gossip.

Charlie escaped to the back garden with Mr. Deeley.

"This is where Nana Betty used to spend her mornings, sitting in the sun, drinking tea and reading the papers," she said.

"This" was a little area with paving stones and large fired clay flowerpots, which in the summer contained pansies and geraniums, a riot of colour and scent. And beyond the paving stones lay a tidy patch of lawn, with two rock-rimmed fishponds and a border of ivy along the two wooden fences. A path made out of more paving stones led to the famous Anderson shelter, half buried in the ground, overgrown with a jumble of ivy.

"It is as I imagined," Mr. Deeley remarked.

"Come with me," Charlie said. "I'll show you the shelter."

Nana Betty's shelter, like the one in the museum's back garden, was made of corrugated steel panels that had been bolted together in six sections and buried three feet down into the ground. A layer of earth had been shovelled on top of its roof, which, since 1939, had been home to successive tangles of ground cover. It was thus neatly camouflaged from view, and those who were not acquainted with Nana Betty's best-kept horticultural secret often overlooked it completely.

The three-foot drop to the shelter's floor from its entrance meant that you needed to climb down a very rickety ladder in order to gain access. Charlie negotiated this carefully, lowering herself backwards into the hole, acutely aware that heels and a skirt were not the best clothing to be wearing for this activity. Mr. Deeley followed, crouching down in the doorway, then bypassing the ladder altogether and jumping.

It was dark inside, and damp, and it smelled of earth and mildew and age. Charlie flicked on her phone's torch, illuminating the shelter with a bright white light. The shelter was filled with things left over from the war: an old wooden bunk bed along one wall and a single bed along the other, as well as some homemade shelves, in a very poor state of repair. Over the years, the shelter had been turned into a makeshift garden shed, so it also contained a folding chair, a spade, a rake, several buckets and a lot of clay pots, and a very large red tin watering can.

Charlie unzipped her bag and dug out the piece of shrapnel Mrs. Firth had given her. She unwrapped the piece of sacking.

"How peculiar," she said. "Feel this, Mr. Deeley. It's *hot.*"

Mr. Deeley put his hand on the shrapnel.

There was, suddenly, a very loud *WOOMF.* The old wooden boards underneath Charlie and Mr. Deeley's feet seemed to bounce, and the clay flowerpots on the shelves jumped. The light in Charlie's phone blinked out.

They were plunged into darkness.

"What was *that?*" Charlie said. "Thunder?"

"I do not think it thunder, Mrs. Collins," Mr. Deeley replied, sensibly. "In fact, if I did not know better, I would suspect it was the sound made by something exploding."

"Bloody hell, Mr. Deeley."

49

Still holding the piece of shrapnel, Charlie scrambled up the ladder and out into the garden. Mr. Deeley clambered after her.

Now there was the sound of gunfire. Charlie was fairly certain it was some sort of gunfire, anyway, a rapid *BANG, BANG-BANG-BANG, BANG*, deep and rumbling, from somewhere to the south of where they were.

A solitary plane flew overhead, soaring away to the north, its propellers chopping the air.

And now a young pregnant woman was running out of the kitchen door of Nana Betty's house.

"Bloody Germans!" she shouted. "Just as I'm having my tea. In! In! Get in with you!"

Charlie and Mr. Deeley ducked back into the shelter. The young woman followed, then switched on the torch she was carrying, illuminating the interior with a dim and eerie glow.

It was not the same interior Charlie and Mr. Deeley had just left.

The beds were now covered with blankets. The homemade shelves looked new and solid, and held half a loaf of bread, a packet of biscuits, a couple of magazines, a bottle of water, a first aid kit, and a wind-up clock.

"That's the second daylight raid this week," the young woman complained, sinking onto the bottom bed in the bunk. "Have a seat. Cramped but cosy. And guaranteed to save us from everything except a direct hit, so they say. Sorry for the rude introduction. Have you come from next door?"

Charlie glanced at Mr. Deeley.

"Yes?" she guessed.

"Thought so. Ruby said she'd sent you a letter, but I don't suppose you got it. Bloody air raids. Disrupting the post, disrupting the trains."

"We didn't get her letter," Charlie confirmed.

"If only she'd sent a text message," Mr. Deeley added.

Charlie tried not to laugh. "If we'd known, of course we wouldn't have come," she added quickly.

50

The young woman looked puzzled. "What on earth is a text message?"

"It's Mr. Deeley's joke," Charlie said. "He's been reading a science fiction novel where nobody talks to each other anymore. They just send each other written messages on their phones."

"Sounds positively dismal. Well, the text of the message I'm to give you is that Ruby's been called away by her brother in Basingstoke. Some sort of emergency. But she'll be back Sunday, and if you two did show up, I'm to look after you. I'm Betty Singleton, by the way."

"Charlotte Duran," Charlie said, looking at Mr. Deeley. "And this is Shaun Deeley."

"Very good. And Junior here..." she patted her tummy, "... rum lot, being born into the middle of this, but what can you do. We should have been more careful."

She placed her torch on the shelf and offered them the packet of biscuits.

"Cadbury's Teatime," she said. "My absolute favourite."

CHAPTER SIX

11 October 1940

"There you are. Best sound in the world."

Betty poked her head out of the shelter and glanced up at the sky as the All Clear siren began to wail.

"You can see the planes' vapour trails," she added. "It always gives me a lovely feeling, knowing they're up there, chasing down the bombers. I know a bloke who's posted at Biggin Hill. That might be his Spitfire. Anyway, come inside and have something to eat. I was just about to make supper when bloody Moaning Minnie went off."

Charlie and Mr. Deeley followed Betty back to the house, past rows of cabbages, potatoes, Brussels sprouts and beets that had taken over the once carefully manicured lawn.

"Why did you take issue with my comment about text messages?" Mr. Deeley asked Charlie curiously.

"Because they don't have text messaging where we are now," Charlie said. "No mobiles, no Internet. No television, in fact, because all the technology was diverted to the development of radar. They only had basic telephones, and even that was considered a luxury."

And it was most peculiar, she thought, entering a house that you knew from the present, and seeing how it now looked in the past. The wallpaper was decidedly different—beige, with a repeating pattern of tiny pink rosebuds on a lattice background. But the fireplace looked exactly the same, faced with deep red glazed terracotta, similar to what was on the outsides of tube stations in

Central London. An oval mirror hung over the mantle, and upon the mantle sat a wind-up clock— the same oval mirror and wind-up clock that had always been there.

In front of the garden door, she recognized the same big wooden dining table, with its ornately carved legs, that Nana Betty had inherited from her parents. And the huge walnut sideboard dating from the turn of the century that had always occupied the corner between the fireplace and the table. Charlie remembered investigating its drawers as a child and discovering all manner of curiosities: green stamps and plastic popper beads, needles and thread, tiny bottles that had once held perfume, a tin of pipe tobacco.

Heavy blackout curtains hung in the windows and across the garden door, which Betty had opened to admit the last of the late-afternoon October sun. Paper blast tape criss-crossed the exposed glass, creating an odd, diamond-shaped design.

"You sit there," Betty said, indicating a familiar pair of wooden chairs that had never quite matched the table. "I'm afraid supper's only soup and a bit of minced beef. But I think I've got enough to stretch it to four. I'll just go and put the kettle on again."

"Your rations," Charlie said. "Of course. This is terribly generous of you."

"It's perfectly all right," Betty replied, going into the little kitchen and carrying on their conversation through an open square hatch cut into the common wall. "Any friends of Ruby's are most definitely friends of mine. Besides, I get a bit extra because I'm expecting. And Mum and Dad have gone down to Epsom to look after my granny—she's got bronchitis. So there's just enough to spare."

Charlie watched through the hatch as Betty lit the gas stove, placed the kettle on the ring, and then set about making the soup. She diced tiny pieces of mushroom, potato, and onion, sautéed them in the tiniest dollop of butter, then popped them into a pot with water, a teacup of milk, a bit of cornstarch and a sprig of parsley.

"Four...?" Charlie inquired.

"Yes, we've got a lodger. Well, I say lodger, but he's also a bit special to me. He was bombed out, poor love, so we've let him come and stay in our little bedroom over the stairs. He works at my dad's greengrocers."

With the pot simmering on the stove, she came back to the dining room.

"Let's have some music, eh? Take our minds off Jerry and that dreadful murder across the way."

A walnut-veneered Marconi occupied pride of place on a table on the other side of the fireplace. Another object that was still there, Charlie thought, more than seventy years later, and it still worked, valves and all.

Betty switched the radio on. It took a moment to warm up to a clarinet-driven tune Charlie didn't recognize at all.

"*Frenesi*," Betty provided. "I adore Artie Shaw."

"Which dreadful murder?" Mr. Deeley inquired.

"Oh yes!" Betty said, with rather more enthusiasm than Charlie expected. "You wouldn't have heard about it. Mrs. Bailey, from across the road, her eldest daughter, Angela. Found dead on a bomb site just over there." She nodded in the general direction of the tube station. "Her throat was slashed from ear to ear."

Charlie looked at Mr. Deeley.

"Do you know any more details?" she asked.

"From what I've heard, she disappeared after going out to see her friend from work, last Saturday evening. When she didn't come back, poor old Mrs. Bailey thought she'd been caught out in an air raid. They assumed the worst... until yesterday, when workers clearing the site found her body. But that house had been bombed on October the 4th, and there weren't any casualties. They were all sheltering down in the tube station."

"So her body had been put there by someone else, after the fact."

"Sometime after this past Saturday, yes. And something else. Poor old Mrs. Bailey said her Angela was wearing a brooch when she went out. Very distinctive, made out of gold, with three small flowers. And whoever killed her had taken it. Such a dreadful thing to happen. Makes you wonder, doesn't it?"

"Indeed," Mr. Deeley agreed.

"And do you know, I've had ever such a funny feeling, since then, that someone's been watching me. When I go out. I've actually stopped walking and had a good look round, it was that strong a feeling. I've not seen anyone… but you just never know, do you?"

She went back into the kitchen to check on the soup, leaving Charlie and Mr. Deeley alone with Artie Shaw.

"Doesn't this remind you of the Middlehurst Slasher?" Charlie said, quietly.

"I was about to say the very same thing, Mrs. Collins."

"It's a coincidence, I'm sure. But still…"

"Is it not also a coincidence," Mr. Deeley said, "that the woman we met on the platform at Middlehurst Station has the same first name as the woman who lives next door to Betty? And even more strangely, that she was expecting us to arrive?"

"If I didn't know better, Mr. Deeley, I'd be tempted to say that really was more than a coincidence."

"And this may seem indelicate of me, Mrs. Collins, but your grandmother does not appear to be married."

Old habits died hard, and Mr. Deeley was still very much a gentleman of the nineteenth century, in spite of his valiant attempts to embrace the twenty-first.

"She isn't," Charlie said. "We always knew Nana was expecting my mum before she married Pete… but I definitely didn't know she was seeing someone else at the same time. Mum's never mentioned it. I wonder if she even knows? Or if Pete did? He's that Spitfire pilot Betty was talking about. They're due to be married in about two months' time. Betty's going to borrow a wedding dress from her aunt, and Pete's going to be in his RAF uniform."

"Your grandmother has much in common with Jemima Beckford," Mr. Deeley remarked, not unkindly. "I confess to some further trepidation. Since we appear to have landed in the same time as the war display in the museum… are we likely to have explosives drop upon our heads from the skies?"

"Hopefully not, Mr. Deeley. I know we'll be safe here, anyway. This house survived the Blitz quite intact."

A repeating double ring interrupted their conversation, and Betty rushed out of the kitchen to answer it.

"Telephone," Charlie explained to Mr. Deeley, as Betty's animated voice drifted into the dining room from the front hallway. It was a quick conversation.

"Our lodger," she said, pausing at the open dining room door. "He's bringing some figs and apples, so we'll have a proper pudding for afters."

She returned to the kitchen, the tea kettle, and the soup.

Some minutes later, there was a *rat-tat-tat* at the front door, followed by the key turning in the lock, and Betty hurried out of the kitchen again.

"Hello, my lovely!"

There was a long pause.

Charlie got up from the table and, curiously, peeked around the open dining room door.

Betty was lost in a passionate kiss and a loving embrace.

Charlie tiptoed back to the table, and Betty brought the lodger into the dining room.

"Here he is," she said, holding his hand tightly. "My favourite greengrocer. This is Charlotte and this is Shaun, all the way from Stoneford. Pals of Ruby's. They got caught out in the raid earlier, and now we're fast friends."

Betty's favourite greengrocer was of average height, with dark brown hair, and in his midthirties. He wore a suit jacket and flannel trousers, and underneath, a white shirt and a dark red tie. In his hands he held a flat tweed cap. And he smelled rather nice, Charlie thought. Imperial Leather. She recognized the scent.

He dug into the pockets of his jacket and pulled out two slightly bruised apples and a handful of figs, which he presented to Betty.

"Here you are, my love."

"I'll just pop back into the kitchen with these," Betty said, taking the apples and figs with her.

"Very pleased to meet you," Charlie ventured.

"As am I," Mr. Deeley added, politely.

"Thaddeus Quinn," the lodger replied, with a grin, shaking each of their hands in turn. "And you've come all the way from Stoneford? That's where I'm from—originally, anyway. Where I was born. Jolly pleased to make your acquaintances."

CHAPTER SEVEN

Mr. Deeley could not take his eyes off the dark-haired gentleman.

Neither could Charlie. She watched him open the sideboard and remove a set of Blue Willow china cups and saucers. It was the same Blue Willow china that Nana Betty had nurtured through the decades, and that was still in the sideboard more than seventy years later, nearly intact. One cup cracked and one saucer broken. Minimal chips. They had been lovingly preserved.

"I know of a Thaddeus Quinn," Mr. Deeley said, with care. "He was born in Stoneford but he grew up in Middlehurst."

"I was raised in Middlehurst. But I'm almost positive I've never met you."

"When were you born in Stoneford?" Mr. Deeley asked.

"Thirty-four years ago. Eleventh of June."

"And how long," Charlie asked, "have you been working for Betty's father?"

"Not long at all," Thaddeus said. "How long has it been, Betty?"

"Less than a year," Betty answered from the kitchen. "December, wasn't it? Dad was left short-handed when everyone joined up. And you've got bad feet, haven't you, darling? Not fit for duty. Lucky for Dad. And Thad. Goodness, I've rhymed." She laughed. "Here we are!"

She carried a tray from the kitchen with a Blue Willow teapot, a little silver bowl containing her precious ration of sugar, and a small glass bottle one-quarter filled with milk.

"Will you be Mother, Thad?"

"Only if you are," Thaddeus joked, pouring out the tea. He winked at Charlie and Mr. Deeley. "I had no plans for fatherhood, but there you are. One of these days you'll have to make an honest man of me, Betty."

"You only have to ask," Betty replied.

She gave Thaddeus a quick, but very fond, kiss, and then went to the sideboard, and opened a drawer, and brought out some knitting. Charlie recognized the pattern immediately. It was the front part of the Fair Isle pullover that her grandmother had loaned her for the wartime display at the museum.

"Coat off," Betty said, and Thaddeus removed his jacket, so that she could hold the unfinished pullover up to his chest to judge how well it was going to fit.

"It's coming along nicely," Thaddeus judged. "Soon be finished. Just in time for the cold weather."

"Just a few more rows," Betty replied. "I'll stitch it to the back tonight, if I'm not too tired, and you can have it tomorrow."

"Lovely," Thaddeus replied. He looked at Charlie and Mr. Deeley. "Isn't she marvellous?"

"She is, indeed," Mr. Deeley replied. "Have you a pattern, Betty?"

"I do."

She retrieved it from the drawer in the sideboard, a page torn from a women's magazine, and showed it to Mr. Deeley.

"Excellent," Mr. Deeley replied, studying it.

"Don't tell me you know how to knit," Charlie said.

"I do, in fact."

"You continue to surprise me, Mr. Deeley."

"I am not without my uses."

He returned the pattern to Betty, who put it back in the sideboard drawer, along with the unfinished pullover, and then drew the heavy blackout curtains.

Going back to the kitchen, she returned with the pot of soup, and the minced beef, which she'd fried with some chopped onion and cloves and peppercorns, and a large sliced carrot from the garden.

"Tuck into this," she said, "before the bloody sirens go off again."

"Your house won't be bombed," Charlie said.

"No?" Betty laughed. "You're quite sure of that, are you?"

"Quite sure," Charlie said.

Thaddeus finished his supper quickly, and checked the clock on the mantle over the fireplace.

"I must be off," he said. "Space at the tube station's first come, first served. They start lining up outside at half past two in the afternoon! Too early for me, though I always end up getting my little pitch at the top end of the northbound platform. Also favoured by employees of London Transport."

"Not spending the night in the Anderson shelter?" Charlie asked, surprised.

"I prefer the tube station," Thaddeus replied.

He kissed Betty goodbye, and was gone.

"He's a bit of a snob," Betty said, confidentially. "He likes to hobnob with the station master. He says it's good for Dad's business, but I know better. The air raids terrify him. He feels safer in the Underground."

· · ·

While it was still daylight, Betty made sure the rest of the blackout curtains were drawn throughout the house.

"Don't want to risk our ARP man Mr. Braden shouting at me to put out the lights," she said as she took Charlie and Mr. Deeley upstairs. "He'd put the fear of God into anyone, bellowing at you from the road. I'm sure he's single-handedly got Hitler on the run."

On the landing at the top of the stairs were four buckets—one empty, two filled with sand, and one with water, along with a small spade and a folded blanket.

"Mind how you go. Dad insists on having them up here in case of firebombs. I think they'd be better downstairs in the front hall, but the Air Raid Precautions pamphlet's his ruddy bible and he won't be swayed."

Charlie smiled. Betty sounded just like her own mother. *I know better. He won't be swayed.* It was fascinating.

"I'll just show you where the bedroom and loo are. Have you not brought any cases with you? Ruby told me you'd be staying the weekend."

"We did," Charlie said. "What's happened to our suitcase, Mr. Deeley? I thought you had it."

She looked at him askance, her expression not entirely serious.

"I thought you had taken charge of it," he replied.

"Oh dear," Betty mused.

"I think, in all of the excitement, we must have left it on the tube," Charlie concluded, feigning distress, with mixed success. "Mr. Deeley's never been to London before."

"Never mind," Betty said. "I'm sure if you check with London Transport, someone will have handed it in. One of my old uncles once left a glass eye on the seat beside him. God knows what he was thinking, taking it out at Clapham Common. But there it was, a week later, at the Lost Property Office, waiting for him to identify it and claim it. This is the loo."

Like the dining room, Nana Betty's bathroom had changed very little in seventy-odd years. The walls were covered, up to eye level, in black and white ceramic tiles. There was a long, deep, enamelled tub; an airing cupboard; a small mirror; and a sink under the window that overlooked the back garden. And there was an old-fashioned toilet, with a wooden seat, an overhead water tank, and a chain that you pulled to flush it.

"I have not seen this before," said Mr. Deeley.

"Not got one where you come from?" Betty inquired.

"Not of this design," Mr. Deeley replied.

"Ah," said Betty, with a knowing nod. "I know what you mean. We're all modern around here but some of the very old houses, other side of the Common…" She leaned over to whisper confidentially. "Outdoor privies."

"Ah yes," said Mr. Deeley, "I recall such conveniences with great clarity. And I am very grateful I must no longer rely upon them when answering the call of nature."

Betty showed them the large back bedroom. "This is mine," she said. "And where Junior will be sleeping when he—or she—decides to put in an appearance. I haven't got a cot yet, but we've still got a few months to find one. My cousin's little girl was born three weeks ago and she's spent her entire life so far in the pulled-out bottom drawer of her mum's dressing table!"

And then Betty opened the door to the largest bedroom, at the front of the house, overlooking Harris Road.

"Mum and Dad's room," she said. "You two can sleep in here."

In the present, Charlie knew, this was Nana Betty's room, the room that she'd died in.

She recognized the white tiled fireplace and the tall oak wardrobe in the corner, which in the present still contained all of Pete's clothes, and the matching dressing table with its three-part mirror, underneath the windows.

But the comfortable-looking double bed was different, as were the blankets and the pink silk eiderdown.

"Unless you want to join me in the shelter," Betty added. "I go down there as a matter of habit these days. Saves me getting up in the middle of the night if there's a raid. If I'm honest, apart from the noise of the bombs, the bloody ack-acks over on the Common frighten the life out of me. And I'd be glad of the company." She looked a little bashful. "I'm used to Mum and Dad being in the bunk bed."

"I think we'll be all right here," Charlie said.

Betty pulled open her parents' dressing table and in one drawer discovered a rather fetching nightgown, and in another, a pair of men's striped pyjamas. "Freshly washed," she said, holding them up. "I'll just go and see what we've got in the airing cupboard."

She abandoned them momentarily, and then returned with an armful of sheets and pillowcases, and two towels and two flannels.

"I'll leave these with you if you want to have a wash. Though it'll have to be cold water, I'm afraid. The boiler's coal-fired, and we only put it on for a short time on Sundays, so we can all have a bath. If you're really desperate for a basin of hot water I can boil the kettle again."

"This is very generous of you," Charlie said.

"Nonsense," Betty replied. "Ruby would do the same for me, if my friends showed up unexpectedly. But if you do change your mind about the shelter, dress warmly. It's bloody cold once the sun goes down. And damp."

She left them alone again, and went downstairs.

"Well," said Charlie, sitting down on the bed beside Mr. Deeley.

"Well indeed," Mr. Deeley replied. He tucked a feather pillow into its cotton case. "What are we to make of this Thaddeus Quinn, Mrs. Collins? Do you believe this gentleman could be my son?"

Charlie looked at him. "Do you?"

"He does bear a striking resemblance to Jemima. His nose, in particular. And his eyes. And I suspect if you had looked closely, Mrs. Collins, you might have seen my chin, and my mouth."

Charlie drew a pillowcase over the second feather pillow, and plumped it up on her lap.

"He was very vague about the year of his birth. The day and the month match... but if he is really your son, of course he wouldn't be able to tell anyone that he was born in 1816. Even if Betty knows his secret—and I doubt she does—he has no idea who you are. Or me. We're just friends with the woman next door, a couple of people who turned up unexpectedly in the middle of an air raid."

"There is something more to consider," Mr. Deeley said, with some hesitation. "If the headstone in the graveyard is correct, then he is destined to die in three days' time when a bomb drops upon the tube station. He admitted himself that he regularly takes shelter there."

He stood up, and walked out of the bedroom, and opened the door to the room over the stairs where Thaddeus Quinn slept. It was only a little bigger than a cupboard. It had a window and enough room for a single bed and a chest of drawers. And it had been, for as long as Charlie could remember, the repository for things that weren't needed anymore, but which Nana Betty could never bring herself to throw away: round cardboard hatboxes and faded cushions, outdated lampshades and discarded books, suitcases with steamer stickers on them and worn-out shoes.

Here and now, in October 1940, it contained nearly all of Thaddeus Oliver Quinn's earthly possessions.

"To know that I will lose my son—whom I have only just now met for the first time—is devastating enough. But even worse than that is the knowledge that he is the father of the child Betty is carrying. For that would make you, Mrs. Collins, my great-granddaughter. And I am not altogether certain that I am able to come to terms with that. It is a tragedy beyond all comprehension."

He sat down upon the narrow single bed.

"I shall sleep here... lest the temptation of sharing your bed, Mrs. Collins, lead me to act in a way that both of us might quickly regret."

CHAPTER EIGHT

Moaning Minnie had not woken Charlie from the deepest of sleeps. Nor had the drone and heavy throb of the German planes approaching. Not even the whistling drop of the bombs and the incendiaries, faintly and in the distance at first, and then louder and closer, shaking the very foundations of the house.

What did wake Charlie was the monumental explosion across the road as Mrs. Crofton at Number Twelve received a direct hit.

The resulting blast shattered the glass in the windows of the bedroom where Charlie was sleeping. The protective paper tape criss-crossing the panes prevented the larger shards from exploding inward, as did Marjorie Singleton's best lace net curtains and the heavy blackout material that Betty had made sure was pulled across at sunset. But the metal window frame was twisted off its hinges. And small fragments of glass had shot across the bedroom through the gaps as the blast had blown the fabric aside.

And Charlie had woken up screaming.

Glass and dust and bits of metal and brick covered the bottom half of her bed. The room was filled with smoke and the smell of high explosives. The triple mirror on top of the dressing table was bent over, its panels split. And through the vertical gap in the blackout curtain, Charlie could see the flicker of flames.

And then Mr. Deeley was by her side, holding her. She could feel his heart beating as hard as her own, and his breathing was heavy and frightened.

"I didn't know," Charlie said. "I'm sorry. I knew this house was never hit. I didn't know about the one across the road."

"Have you been injured?"

"No," Charlie said. "No. Just scared to bloody death. What about you?"

"I am unhurt."

They held each other for long moments, listening to the throb of the plane engines overhead, and the roaring thundering boom of the big anti-aircraft guns on the Common a few blocks away, and the unceasing shudder and shake as more bombs fell, some nearby, some further away.

Then they heard the jangling bells of a fire engine, and an ambulance, and people were shouting in the road. And there was something else: a woman's voice, crying desperately, muffled by fallen bricks and wood.

"We must help," said Mr. Deeley.

. . .

There was no shortage of volunteers. Mr. Braden, the ARP warden, had already begun the search for Mrs. Crofton and her two children. He knew the layout of their house and where they were sleeping. And while the firemen sprayed water on the flames, he dug in with the first rescuers, who scrambled to clear the debris and burrow down to where Mrs. Crofton was trapped, in what had once been her cupboard under the stairs.

"She had a shelter in the back," one of the neighbours, Mrs. Lane, was saying, to anyone who would listen. She'd appeared in her nightdress and slippers, with her winter coat thrown over her shoulders and her hair in curlers. "Wouldn't go in it, said it was too damp, always filling up with water. Said it was warm and dry and safe under the stairs. Just goes to show you, doesn't it."

Charlie climbed into the ruins of Mrs. Crofton's house, joining Mr. Deeley and half a dozen others as they gingerly removed bricks, one by one, to try and locate her.

Finally, after what seemed like hours, there was a breakthrough. A white hand reached out of an impossibly small space. There was a cheer, and more digging, more careful removal of debris. And at last, Mrs. Crofton was pulled free from the hole in the ground, her nightgown in tatters.

A woman ambulance driver wrapped her in a blanket and helped her onto a stretcher, and she was carried into the road.

"My babies," she moaned, as she was lifted into the ambulance.

"How many?" the driver asked.

"Two. They were with me in the cupboard."

"Tommy and Lindy," said Mrs. Lane. "Ever such lovely children."

"How old?" one of the diggers asked.

"Two and a half, and four."

"Two children!" the digger shouted to the men standing in the rubble, and the search began again, in earnest.

At some point, the bombing ceased, and the anti-aircraft guns on Tooting Bec Common stopped their barrage. The Luftwaffe flew home. The searchlights, criss-crossing their beams into the black October sky, blinked out.

The All Clear sounded.

And the road fell silent.

The diggers stopped working, and listened.

Nothing.

"Tommy!" one of them shouted. "Lindy! Can you hear me?"

Nothing.

Mr. Deeley crouched down, and peered inside the small cave beneath the bricks.

"Give me a light," he said.

A torch was produced, and he shone it into the hole.

"See anything?"

"I am not certain," Mr. Deeley said.

"I think I hear something," said the first digger, the one who had been talking to Mrs. Crofton.

They listened again.

"Child crying. There."

The crying was coming from an entirely different place, several feet away from the hole that Mrs. Crofton had been pulled from.

But it was beneath an impossible tower of fallen and broken bricks, and splintered beams of wood.

Mr. Deeley shone the torch into the hole again.

"There is room for me to crawl in," he said.

"It's unstable, mate. The whole lot'll collapse in on top of you."

"Then you will have to dig me out as well," Mr. Deeley replied.

He manoeuvred himself into the tiny opening, and dragged himself forward. Charlie watched as his legs disappeared, and then his feet.

"Bloody hell, Charlotte. Your Shaun's a bit of a daredevil, isn't he?"

It was Betty, roused from her sleep, joining the others in the road.

"It's one of the things I love about him," Charlie replied. "He's much braver than me."

"Well, you were right about my house not being bombed. This time, anyway. Is Mrs. Crofton all right?"

"Yes, she's in the ambulance. But she's very shaken."

"Poor woman. There but for the grace of God… It could have been us. But it wasn't. Do you often have thoughts like that about things? I get a little crawly spidery feeling, all up and down my arms. And that's when I know what I'm thinking definitely will happen— or definitely won't happen. And I'm nearly always right."

"I sort of have a sixth sense," Charlie said. "I sometimes know about the future. It's very difficult to explain though."

She paused. *Why not? Where was the harm?*

"For instance," she said, "I have a very strong sense that your baby's going to be a girl. And you'll call her Jackie. And you'll have another little girl, too. Wendy."

"Another!" Betty laughed. "That'll be news to Thad."

In the ruins of Mrs. Crofton's house, the men had all stopped working, lest they cause more rubble to fall in on the tiny tunnel where Mr. Deeley was.

Suddenly, there was shouting, and Charlie's heart stopped. Part of the excavation had given way. The men scrambled to keep the opening clear.

A few moments later, a small boy was pushed through the debris, into their waiting hands. And a few moments after that, a little girl scrambled to safety. Both were covered in cuts and dust, but appeared to be otherwise uninjured.

The beam of the torch shone out of the hole, followed by Mr. Deeley's hand, which one of the diggers grasped. Finally, Mr. Deeley himself was dragged into the fresh air.

"Well done, sir," said one of the diggers. "Cup of tea?"

A mobile canteen had arrived, and the two women inside were dispensing hot drinks to the firemen and the rescuers. Mr. Deeley happily accepted a large mug of milky tea and a relieved hug from Charlie. The ambulance drove away with Mrs. Crofton and her children.

"I'm going to have to have a word with you about your heroic deeds," Charlie said, observing her companion through newly admiring eyes. He looked rather amazingly rugged, she thought, with his dusty, tousled hair, a night's growth of stubble on his face, and his shirt unbuttoned and torn open by the exertions of his tunnelling. "What if the rest of the house had collapsed and you'd been killed?"

"Then you would have been left with the certain knowledge that I'd died a heroic death," Mr. Deeley replied, not entirely seriously.

Charlie checked to make sure Betty was out of hearing distance. Yes, there she was, exchanging opinions with Mrs. Lane about the merits of an Anderson shelter as opposed to a cupboard under the stairs.

"You know what you've done," she said. "You've gone and changed history. You rescued those two children. They might have died, otherwise."

"Or," Mr. Deeley said, "at dawn, those digging might have unearthed them without my help, and delivered them safely into their mother's arms. Who is to say what might have been, with or without my influence?"

"Forgive me." It was the man who had brought Mr. Deeley his mug of tea. He was fair-haired and tall, in his midthirties, and wearing clothes completely impractical for rescue work. He looked as if he'd come from a night on the town: a white shirt, black trousers, a loosened tie, a dinner jacket, and shoes that must once have been quite new and polished but which were now covered in dirt and soot and dust. "I overheard what you said just now. You're speaking of time travel, are you not? And the complications which may occur when one finds oneself having to make a decision about whether or not to act?"

"Yes," Charlie said, a little warily. "Hypothetically, of course. We were trying to imagine what might have happened if we hadn't interfered."

"I'm a time travel aficionado myself. H.G. Wells wrote about it rather well, I thought, though he allowed his socialist political leanings a little too much influence in the narrative. Have you read *The Time Machine*?"

"Yes," Charlie said, "a long time ago."

"I have not," said Mr. Deeley, "but I shall add it to my list of books to investigate. Will it download to your clever iPad, Mrs. Collins?"

Charlie gave Mr. Deeley a cautionary look, but the gentleman did not appear to be concerned.

"I would love to discuss the concept of time travelling with you further," he suggested. "I find the idea variously frightens people, or worries them, or causes them to dismiss me as an impossible eccentric. But your outlook encourages me. I'm staying at the Bedford Square Hotel in London. Do you know it?"

Charlie shook her head.

"It's on Bloomsbury Street, near the British Museum. Will you meet me there tomorrow?"

"I'm not sure…" Charlie began.

"Tube to Tottenham Court Road," the gentleman suggested. "Then a short walk to the British Museum. It's across the street. Shall we say lunch time?"

"Mr. Deeley?" Charlie checked.

"I think this might be arranged," Mr. Deeley replied.

Charlie's silence was interpreted as consent.

"Excellent. Until tomorrow then."

The gentleman took his leave.

"Wait!" Charlie shouted after him. "What's your name? Who should we ask for?"

But the gentleman was gone, swallowed up by the darkness.

"Is the British Museum far?" Mr. Deeley inquired, as they crossed the road and went back into Betty's house.

"Yes, all the way up in central London. What a strange man."

"Why is it strange for someone other than ourselves to believe in the possibility of travelling in time? He will have a long walk tonight. Unless there is a train."

"Not likely, Mr. Deeley. Perhaps a bus. Though I'm not sure if they ran all night during the Blitz."

The light was on in the dining room, where Betty was hunting for something to write on.

She settled on the back cover of a little blue booklet, *War-Time Cookery to Save Fuel and Food Value.* "There," she said, turning around to acknowledge Charlie and Mr. Deeley, who had paused in the doorway. "October the 11th, 1940, Charlotte Duran says I am going to have a little girl. And I will name her Jackie. And a sister for Jackie, and I'm going to call her Wendy."

She smiled, then finished her thought.

"And, she says, my house will not be bombed."

She put the pencil and the booklet in a drawer in the walnut sideboard.

"Crawly spidery feelings," she said, to Charlie and Mr. Deeley, rubbing her arms. "Let's see if we can salvage a bit more sleep before dawn."

Charlie followed Mr. Deeley up the stairs. At the top, on the landing, he paused, turned, and without words, wrapped his arms around her, enfolding her. He smelled of soot and dirt and brick-dust and the insides of houses when you've knocked them down

71

and exposed their old pipes and underpinnings. The protective cave of his armpit smelled like sweat, and the scent of the soap he'd used that morning in the shower, in Stoneford. Something lemony lime and very male-ish that he'd bought after using up all of her Florentyna Shower Crème from Marks and Spencer.

"I think you really are a hero," Charlie said. "In case you had any doubts."

"I did nothing special, Mrs. Collins. Any other man of honour would have done the same."

"Perhaps not so readily, Mr. Deeley. Or so fearlessly."

He silenced her with a kiss. A strong kiss, and a passionate one.

"Good night, Mrs. Collins," he said.

"Good night, Mr. Deeley."

CHAPTER NINE

The bomb in the night had damaged the gas mains, so there was nothing to cook breakfast with. And there hadn't been enough time to heat the coal-fired boiler for a wash.

"I'm so sorry," Betty said, offering Mr. Deeley and Charlie some bread and butter, a little cheese, and an even littler portion of rhubarb and ginger jam. "This jam's all I can get these days, and they're threatening to ration that after Christmas! I can't even make you tea. But at least we've still got lights. And the taps are working. Keep calm and carry on, eh?"

"We shall wash with the cold water from the tap," Mr. Deeley replied.

"Speak for yourself, Mr. Deeley," Charlie said. "I'm not quite as stoic as you are."

"As you may recall, Mrs. Collins, I still consider the constant hot water in your cottage a curious luxury."

"He used to work in a very old-fashioned country house," Charlie said, to Betty. "Dodgy plumbing. And the man who owned it was a French count. Completely mad. Kept horses and a carriage. Mr. Deeley was his groom."

"How absolutely fascinating!" Betty replied. "You'd be quite at home here, then. We've no shortage of horses and carts. Our rag and bone man's got one. And our milkman. They'll have a job coming down Harris Road today, though. Have you looked outside?"

Charlie took the opportunity to do just that while Mr. Deeley was in the loo, braving five inches of October-chilled tap water in the deep, old-fashioned tub.

There had, in fact, been two bombs. The first had fallen farther down the street, which had severed the gas mains. The second had landed squarely in Number Twelve's back garden, scoring a direct hit on the empty Anderson shelter and causing most of the house in front of it to collapse. If Mrs. Crofton had, indeed, been huddling inside the shelter with her two children, they would have been killed instantly.

The irony was not lost on Charlie as she walked across the road. The house was collapsed, nothing left but broken bricks and splintered timbers and roof tiles. The homes on either side were severely damaged and completely uninhabitable. As were two of the houses on Betty's side of the road, in the direct line of the blast.

She heard a small noise behind her and turned around, thinking that Mr. Deeley had finished his bath and come outside to have a look at the devastation with her. But no one was there.

Odd.

She could have sworn she'd heard Betty's front gate clicking shut.

She started back across the road. Betty had been fortunate. Once the windows were replaced, there would be little to betray the fact that there had been any damage at all.

And there was Thaddeus, walking towards her from the end of the road, in his tweedy cap, with his hands in his pockets, whistling.

"Hallo," he said jovially. "Jerry's made a bit of a mess, eh? Glad everyone's all right. I've managed an hour away from the shop so I can organize someone to come round and mend Betty's windows. And I imagine it'll be a bit of a shock for Ruby when she gets back tomorrow. Her windows have all gone as well."

• • •

Both Charlie and Mr. Deeley's clothes were filthy, a consequence of their overnight activities in the wreckage of Mrs. Crofton's house.

"Look at the state of you," Betty said. "We can't have you wandering into the Bedford Square Hotel looking like a pair of tramps, even if it is wartime. It's respectable. I've had tea there."

She rummaged around in her bedroom wardrobe, deciding on

an olive green and cream dress made of crepe de chine, with a fitted waist and a flared skirt.

"There you are," she said, holding it up for Charlie to see. "It's just about your size. And I'm sure Dad won't mind me lending your friend something presentable."

"Am I not presentable now...?" Mr. Deeley inquired, joining them in the bedroom. He did look very well-scrubbed, Charlie thought. His hair was clean, and he'd also managed to shave.

"You'll certainly have everyone's attention if you show up for lunch wearing that," Charlie laughed, eyeing the three large towels he'd wrapped around himself to preserve his modesty.

"I have just what you need," Betty promised. "Come with me."

In the tall oak wardrobe in the front bedroom, Betty found one of her father's white shirts and a grey knitted pullover, and the trousers belonging to one of his lesser-used suits, which were rather baggy and held up with braces.

"And, of course, a tie," she decided, selecting one of dark blue silk. "He only ever wears it for special occasions, and church."

"Now we look like a proper wartime couple," Charlie mused, after Betty had gone and Mr. Deeley had exchanged his towels for Bert Singleton's best Sunday clothes.

In one of the trouser pockets, he discovered three tiny slips of paper with printing on both sides, and a tiny hole punched into one corner of each.

"Bus tickets!" Charlie said. "Used."

In the other pocket was a peculiar little box, which upon further investigation was revealed to contain a collection of tiny wooden sticks.

"And what are these?"

"Swan Vestas," Charlie said. "Haven't you seen them before?"

"Not at all."

"Of course," Charlie said, remembering how, in 1825, embers had been carefully preserved in the kitchen fireplace, then used to light candles, rushlights, other fires for cooking.

"What is it they do?"

"They're matches, Mr. Deeley. They create fire. Like this!"

She removed one of the matches, struck it against the rough surface on the side of the box, and was rewarded with an instant flame.

"If only these had been invented when I lived at Monsieur Duran's manor," Mr. Deeley marvelled. "What a lot of drudgery might have been dispensed with.... And what foresight displayed by Betty's father, to carry the means for a fire with him in his trousers!"

Charlie looked at him. "Are you being naughty again, Mr. Deeley...?"

"Me?" he inquired, assuming an expression of utter innocence. "What makes you say that?"

"Nothing," Charlie replied, matching his tone of innocence with one of her own. "Anyway, Bert smoked a pipe. I remember Mum telling me. She used to love the smell of the tobacco before it was lit."

"I shall keep these safe," Mr. Deeley decided, "in the event of some emergency requiring a fire." He smiled at her. "Or the sudden appearance of a pipe." He turned his attention to the necktie. "How is this arranged?" he asked, holding the two ends in his hands.

"I'll show you," Charlie said. "Half Windsor, I think...Watch in the mirror."

She created the knot, sliding it up under his shirt collar.

"There you are.... I haven't done that since Jeff died. He was hopeless at knotting his tie."

Mr. Deeley's own winter overcoat, black and long and what Charlie liked to term "dramatic," completed his new wardrobe.

"You're as respectable as me now," Charlie mused, as they went downstairs. "And you look smashing in a proper shirt and tie. I could easily get used to that."

• • •

Balham Underground Station looked almost exactly the same as it had the day before, when Charlie and Mr. Deeley had arrived for

Nana Betty's funeral. Except that concrete blast walls had been put up in front of the two entrance buildings—one on either side of Balham High Road—and the station's white Portland stone facings were stained black by smoke and grime.

Mr. Deeley paused at the top of the stairs leading down to the booking hall in the larger Station Road entrance.

"We are required to purchase some sort of ticket, are we not?" He checked the pockets of his overcoat. "I have some coins."

He produced them, and Charlie counted them up.

"Five pounds and fifty-five pence," she said. "I think I've got a little bit of money in my bag. Oh. Damn."

"Is five pounds and fifty-five pence not enough?"

"I think it likely would be quite enough, Mr. Deeley, if our coins were from 1940. But everything changed in 1971 with decimalization. This money won't mean anything to them."

Mr. Deeley thought for a moment, then disappeared down the stairs to the booking hall. He reappeared a few moments later.

"There are no ticket checkers in evidence," he said. "I suggest we avail ourselves of an excellent opportunity to commit a minor dishonesty, Mrs. Collins, and, in haste, descend to the trains."

As Mr. Deeley had correctly observed, the two wooden passimeters in the booking hall were unoccupied, as was the ticket inspector's booth.

There were, however, several uniformed station staff lurking in the general area, and so, spotting a solitary ticket machine against the wall, Charlie made a brief show out of pretending to insert some coins and receiving two printed tickets in return.

Then they proceeded to the escalators which, Charlie noted, were made of wood, not metal.

"And this wind," said Mr. Deeley, "smells like the chimney in your cottage."

Charlie smiled. It was true. The heady scent of creosote and wood had not been in evidence on Friday.

She had seen black and white photographs of tube stations during the war, crowded with shelterers, a narrow strip of platform beside the tracks kept free for the movement of passengers. Balham's northbound tunnel looked exactly the same as it had in the photos, except it was midmorning, so there was no one sheltering, only a handful of men and women waiting for the next train to arrive.

Compared to the brightly lit and recently renovated Balham of yesterday, it was dingy and dark, with low-wattage lamps in yellowed shades, and small posters stuck to the walls, all of them seeming to have something to do with food: Ovaltine. Bovril. OXO cubes. Rules about sheltering and reminders about rationing. Dire warnings about eavesdroppers and spies.

Is Your Journey Really Necessary?

"When the bomb drops on Monday night," Mr. Deeley said quietly, "which platform will be affected?"

"This one," Charlie replied.

"And will it be the entire length?"

"Almost. Although I think the people sheltering in the middle and at the southern end were able to get out in time. The sludge and debris and water spilled over through a passageway onto the southbound platform, too. But it wasn't as bad on that side."

She studied the northern end of the platform, past the big old-fashioned clock jutting out from the top of the curving wall.

"There's a very famous picture of all the rubble that poured through the breach in the tunnel roof. It's almost up to the height of that clock, and then it tapers down as it travels towards the southern end of the station. The hands of the clock are stopped at two minutes past eight."

Mr. Deeley walked slowly past the clock, which at that moment was indicating nearly half past ten. He continued all the way to the end of the platform, pausing at the northern-most cross-passage to study the yawning black mouth of the running tunnel. Then he turned and walked all the way back to the southern end, in deep contemplation.

"It is very unsettling, owning the knowledge of what is yet to come," he said, returning to where Charlie was standing. "Nearly

seventy people will die. Men and women. And very small children…
and my son."

He paused, looking sad.

"Is there nothing we can do to save them?"

Charlie looked at him. "I don't know what we can do, Mr.
Deeley. If we tell the stationmaster that no one should come down
here to shelter on Monday night, he'd want to know why, and if we
told him, he'd want to know how we knew. And then, he'd probably
have us arrested as German spies."

"Perhaps a note, written anonymously…?"

"We'd be interfering with history, Mr. Deeley. And there's
no guarantee anyone would take an anonymous note seriously.
Would you?"

"We might still be able to save Thaddeus. If we were to
delay him…."

"But if we interfere… if we stop him from sheltering down
here on Monday night… what then? Perhaps Betty will end up
marrying him, instead of Pete. And then what will happen to Auntie
Wendy? And Nick, and his two sisters? Pete was Auntie Wendy's
father. She might end up not being born at all, and then neither
would Nick. And then where would you and I be, Mr. Deeley? It
was Nick who brought us back to the present when you and I first
met, in 1825. If we'd stayed in that time, you'd have been a fugitive
on the run in France… and I'd have died a horrible death from a
burst appendix."

"But your mother will be born, regardless. That will not
change. And neither will the identity of her father. That has already
been decided."

Mr. Deeley took her hand, and held it in his own.

"I cannot bear to contemplate that you are my great-
granddaughter, Mrs. Collins. It is impossible. And it causes me such
great unhappiness. In truth I would rather take my leave of you now,
and not ever see you again, than have to live with the knowledge that
I cannot ever hope to marry you."

"Oh, Mr. Deeley, please don't say that. Perhaps I was wrong.

Perhaps Cornelius is Thaddeus's father after all, and not you. It was just a guess on my part."

A sound like the emptying of a large drain echoed at the far end of the platform. The wind began to pick up. Moments later, a red 1938-vintage train rattled into the station.

"I'm so sorry, Mr. Deeley... I just don't know what we can do. And I don't know why we're here. Perhaps the gentleman we're meeting for lunch will give us some answers."

CHAPTER TEN

The interior of their carriage was completely unlike the flashy red, white, and blue Northern Line train they'd taken from Waterloo to Balham the day before, with its bright blue seats and yellow poles. Everything was painted green. The window-frames were made of varnished wood, and the windows themselves were covered with anti-blast mesh, with a small diamond-shape cut out, presumably to allow passengers to see the station names. The seats were upholstered with a scratchy red and green moquette, the floor appeared to be made out of the same slatted wood as the escalators, and there were peculiar round knobs dangling from the ceiling on stiff stems.

"What are those?" Mr. Deeley asked, watching, fascinated, as they swayed in a coordinated dance while their train clattered through its tunnel.

"They're for the passengers who have to stand in rush hour. Something to hang onto."

Because it was Saturday, the usual office workers were at home, and their carriage was sparsely populated. Two gentlemen reading newspapers. A solitary woman nodding off. Farther down, a tired-looking mum with two children, and two more men, both sitting facing forward, with their heads leaning against the windows, dozing.

"They all seem so exhausted," Charlie said. "I suppose I would be too, if I was woken up by air raids every night."

Mr. Deeley picked up a frayed pocket Underground map that a passenger had left on his seat when he'd got off at Kennington. He studied it as the train drew into Charing Cross, clattering along its long curved platform. The woman with her two children got off.

Two men got on, sitting across from one another at the far end of the carriage.

"I am disappointed we will not be passing through Trafalgar Square," he said. "Is it named after the battle?"

"It is. And it's got a huge column, with a statue of Horatio Nelson at the top. I'll show it to you later, if we've got time. It's a very popular meeting place."

"Strange to think that a monument of such historical significance exists now, commemorating an event which occurred when I was fourteen years old. And that there is an Underground station directly beneath it. What would my friends from Monsieur Duran's manor make of it all, Mrs. Collins? Ned Rankin, and Mrs. Dobbs?"

"I'm sure they'd be as astounded as you, Mr. Deeley. The London of now is nothing like the London of their time. In fact, the London of now has barely anything in common with the London of *my* time."

Their train was on the move again, back into its running tunnel, on its way to Strand.

"What is this place called Piccadilly Circus?" Mr. Deeley inquired, again consulting the map. "Are there dancing bears and other exotic beasts?"

Charlie laughed. "It's very famous intersection. The traffic used to go in a circle, which is how it got its name. From the Latin. And there's a fountain. It was erected in 1892 and on top of it is a winged statue that most people call Eros. Although officially it's supposed to be his brother, Anteros. The Angel of Christian Charity."

"Not the Greek god of love...?" Mr. Deeley mused. "He who smites maids' breasts with an unknown heat...?"

Charlie gave him a look, and Mr. Deeley smiled. It was a smile that lasted all the way through Strand and Leicester Square, to Tottenham Court Road, where they got off the train and rode another noisy wooden escalator to the surface.

At the top, there was a passimeter. And a uniformed inspector, checking tickets.

"Um," Charlie said.

Mr. Deeley thought for a moment.

"Allow me," he said.

He approached the barricade.

"Hello," he said.

"Morning," the inspector replied. "Ticket please."

"We, how you say? *Viatores*. Visitings."

Charlie put her hand up to her mouth and bit her finger. Mr. Deeley's foreign accent was atrocious.

"Oh yes?"

"Yes. Here is *denarius*."

He held out the coins from the pocket of his overcoat.

The inspector peered at Mr. Deeley's 5p, 10p and 20p pieces.

"Have you got a ticket?" he said, very slowly, clearly and loudly, as if Mr. Deeley was deaf.

"*Tikkit...*" Mr. Deeley said, turning, befuddled, to Charlie. "*Tikkit. Quid est* tikkit?"

Charlie stared at Mr. Deeley, and then offered the man in the uniform her own collection of coins.

"*Tikkit?*" she suggested.

"No, not a ticket." The inspector was clearly losing his patience. "Look, I don't know where you two are from but you need to have our money, or a ticket, to travel on the tube. Where did you begin your journey?"

"Ah," said Mr. Deeley. "*Sic.* Buenos Aires."

"No, mate. Which station on the Underground?"

Mr. Deeley looked at Charlie again. "*Quod est* station?"

"Tottenham Court Road," Charlie replied, with a perfectly straight face.

"That's *this* station," said the inspector. "Where did you get on?"

A queue of weary travellers was forming behind them.

"Where did you get on?" he repeated.

"I'm really sorry," Charlie said. "We got on at Balham. My friend was having a little joke. We haven't got tickets."

"I'm not in a mood for jokes. Or for time-wasters. Does your friend speak English?"

"Unaccountably well," Mr. Deeley confessed. "My most sincere apologies."

"Pay up then, and be on your way."

"Ah," said Mr. Deeley, "and therein lies our dilemma… as we are without appropriate funds."

The ticket inspector gave Mr. Deeley a suspicious look.

"You've got a very dodgy way of speaking for an Englishman," he said. "Come on, then, let's see your identification cards."

Mr. Deeley glanced at Charlie.

"We haven't got our identification cards," Charlie said. "We lost everything in an air raid. Ration books, gas masks, the lot. I'm so sorry. Please let us go. I promise we'll pay next time."

The inspector was clearly of two minds. "You've given me very good reason to suspect that you may, in fact, not be telling me the truth and that you may, in fact, be in this country illegally…."

"We've come from a little village in Hampshire," Charlie said. "It's called Stoneford… and it's our first time in London. We're really very sorry for causing you such trouble…."

"Go on, mate," said a tired-looking man, in line behind them. "Let 'em through and then we can all get on with our day. If they was German spies Hitler would have made sure they had enough money for their fares. None of this mucking about."

The inspector looked at Charlie and Mr. Deeley, and then relented.

"Out you go, then. Next time I won't be so lenient."

He stepped aside, and Charlie and Mr. Deeley were free to leave.

"My utmost apologies," Mr. Deeley said, as they climbed the steps to the street.

"Never mind. We weren't arrested. They're all a bit on edge… you saw the posters. Everyone's a potential spy." They reached the surface. "And where did that come from? Buenos Aires…?"

"Are you not in awe of my knowledge of world geography,

Mrs. Collins? I have used your clever device for many more things than perusing newspapers and watching the YouTube."

"That wasn't Spanish, though, was it?"

"It was Latin. At last, I have found a use for the classical education inflicted upon me by the very aged and imaginatively diminished Reverend Hopwood Smailes."

Charlie laughed.

"*Hic est a pretium in via,*" said Mr. Deeley. "Here is a busy road."

"Stop showing off."

"Were you not required to study Latin at your school?"

"I was not," Charlie replied. "Thankfully."

She looked around, trying to get her bearings in the damp, misty morning. It was not the London that she knew. In their present, in the time they had come from, this intersection was the site of a massive and ongoing construction project to accommodate the new Crossrail station. It was all demolition and hoardings and detours.

Here and now, there was very little that Charlie actually recognized. Just up Tottenham Court Road, she could see the Dominion Theatre, which appeared now to be a cinema—but it was closed, perhaps because of the air raids.

Across Oxford Street she could see a posh-looking Lyon's Corner House restaurant. In front of her stood tall, ornate lampposts, topped with filigreed metalwork. The bollards and traffic lights, and the posts the traffic lights were mounted on, were all painted with broad black and white stripes, presumably to aid navigation in the dark when the blackout was in effect.

Oxford Street itself was crowded with boxy-looking motorcars and red and white double decker buses. And over the way, the pavement entrances to the tube station were swathed in anti-blast concrete blocks and black and white painted corrugated steel, the familiar Underground roundel propped reassuringly on top.

"Which way, Mrs. Collins?"

"To our right, I think."

They crossed over Charing Cross Road and began to walk east, in the direction of the British Museum.

"I do not like the smell of London," Mr. Deeley decided. "It is nothing like what I had imagined."

"Nothing like what I'd imagined either, Mr. Deeley."

"This is the smell of coal. And things which have been burned. It reminds me of last night. Buildings which have been demolished. Broken bricks and gunpowder."

They walked together along New Oxford Street, past walls pockmarked by shrapnel, and defiant, hastily printed signs: *Business as Usual, Mr. Hitler... Bombed But Not Beaten*. And everywhere underfoot was the crunch of crumbled bits of brick and glittering tiny fragments of glass. They passed roads they could look down and see gaps in, like teeth that had been knocked out of the neighbourhood's mouth. And bits of buildings with their ends lopped off raggedly, exposing rooms with furniture but no outside walls. The remnants of peoples' lives, lost in the smouldering grey smoke.

"What are these things in the sky?" Mr. Deeley asked, pausing to look back towards central London.

Charlie looked too. Over the city hung hundreds of floating, silvery objects, suspended in midair like a flock of giant birds.

"Barrage balloons," she said. "They're meant to prevent the enemy planes from flying in low."

"I should think they are there also to provide reassurance to the people living underneath them," Mr. Deeley said, thoughtfully. "I did not know that there existed a power so great as to cause this much destruction."

"And there's worse to come," Charlie said, sadly. "One day I'll tell you how World War Two ended. The Battle of Trafalgar pales by comparison."

"In the time we came from," said Mr. Deeley, "is there still much of this to be seen?"

"Not much," Charlie said. "Everything was rebuilt. Or torn down and new buildings put up in their place. I was born too late, but my mum remembers bomb craters and walls propped up with timbers and big empty plots of land where offices and houses used to stand, well into the 1960s."

They had reached Bloomsbury Street. They turned the corner and walked north.

And there it was. Not quite at Bedford Square, but close enough that the establishment could get away with expropriating its name.

"*Hic est* the hotel," Mr. Deeley said.

It had, Charlie thought, seen better days. An imposing Portland stone archway curved over its big front doors, flanked by a pair of matching stone columns. The grey stone facade carried on along the building's ground floor, which was lined with ornate windows that she imagined had once been dressed with deep blue velvet curtains, but which now just looked shabby and faded. Higher up, soot blackened the white window sashes, and the windows were streaked and dirty.

Inside, the same shabbiness prevailed. The marble floor looked in need of a good cleaning. There was a reception desk with dull brass fittings, and, across from it, two lifts, one of which wasn't working, as evidenced by a handwritten apologetic sign on a stand. A curving marble staircase led to the upper floors, foot-worn, its banisters in need of a thorough polish. And of course, placed at strategic points throughout the lobby, were the requisite buckets of water and sand, along with several very used-looking stirrup pumps.

It was respectable, Charlie thought, remembering Betty's words. Or had been, before the war. Now it just seemed weary. Exhausted—like the Londoners she'd observed on the tube.

"Hello! So pleased you've come!"

It was their fair-haired gentleman, looking far more presentable in daylight than he had the night before. He'd exchanged his dusty bomb site clothes for a comfortable grey wool suit, with a clean white shirt and a deep red tie.

"Are you hungry? I'm starving. There's a pleasant restaurant here. And it's nearly lunchtime. Will you join me?"

CHAPTER ELEVEN

The restaurant was adjacent to the hotel's reception area, and was, to Charlie's surprise, nearly full. She had thought that wartime austerity would have affected eating establishments—if only because of the shortage of food—but this was evidently not the case.

An efficient gentleman in formal attire seated them at a table beside one of the windows with the faded blue velvet curtains.

The lunchtime diners were mix of men and women, the men mostly in suits, the women in rather functional-looking skirts and blouses. Charlie guessed they were people who had business in London. Shoppers, perhaps, or those who worked or lived nearby, or who had made the hotel their home, on a temporary or full-time basis. On nearby racks hung their overcoats and hats, and on the floor beside their chairs their gas masks, in cardboard boxes, awaited the attack that was never going to materialize.

Luncheon menus were offered, and a waitress in a black dress, white pinafore, and black-and-white cap arrived almost immediately to take their orders.

"As you can see," the gentleman said, helpfully, as if he'd been reading Charlie's mind, "the food in restaurants is not rationed. It is what makes living in this establishment such an attractive proposition. But you are only allowed a fish course, or a meat course, one or the other, not both. Also, icing has been banished from the cakes, which I consider particularly appalling."

"Highly inconvenient," Mr. Deeley agreed. "I shall therefore go without."

"Fried fillet of cod, I think," the gentleman said, to the waitress, whom he seemed to know quite well. "With mixed carrots and turnips. And a cup of tea, if you wouldn't mind, Violet."

Charlie glanced over the single-page menu. There were really only a handful of choices. Nothing appealed to her at all, and she found herself, rather shamefully, longing for something familiar and comfortable. A Big Mac. Or something from Burger King.

"I shall have meat pie and chipped potatoes," Mr. Deeley decided.

"I suppose I'll have the same," Charlie said.

"Tea for both of you?"

"Yes please," Mr. Deeley replied. "Since I'm to be denied a satisfactory confection for afterwards."

Violet collected their menus, and left.

"Let us begin," the gentleman said, "and thereby, I hope, allay any concerns we may harbour about one another. May I know your names?"

"I'm Charlotte and this is Shaun."

"Thaddeus Quinn," the gentleman replied, extending his hand across the table, and shaking each of theirs in turn.

"Sorry…?" Charlie said.

"I thought that might be your reaction. Thaddeus Quinn."

"My curiosity," said Mr. Deeley, "is aroused by my knowledge of the existence of a second individual with exactly the same name as the one you have just given us. Are you familiar with this gentleman?"

The fair-haired man laughed.

"I understand your scepticism, sir. And yes, I am familiar with him. But he is not Thaddeus Quinn. He is called Silas Ferryman. He has stolen my identity, and used it as his own. No doubt if you were to ask him for some form of official document to prove who he is, he would be unable to supply it."

"Silas Ferryman," Charlie repeated.

"The name is known to you?"

"It is," Charlie said. "Where we live, in Stoneford, Reg Ferryman is the proprietor of The Dog's Watch Inn. And one of his ancestors, in the 1800s, was called Silas. He was married to a woman named

Matilda, who was a victim of a serial killer they nicknamed the Middlehurst Slasher."

"Indeed. I hope you are now able to understand my very keen interest in the idea of travelling in time."

Their tea arrived in cups with saucers, accompanied by a little china jug of milk, and a matching bowl containing precisely six lumps of sugar. The fair-haired gentleman poured the milk into his tea, and stirred in two of the six lumps.

"Do continue," Mr. Deeley suggested, when Violet had gone.

"I shall. In December 1849, I was a police officer employed at the constabulary in Middlehurst, when my sister, Matilda, was brutally murdered. As you have described, she was the last of three women who had been discovered over a period of two years with their throats cut. It was my contention that they needed not look far beyond the four walls of my sister's cottage for the killer."

"Silas Ferryman was the Middlehurst Slasher?" Charlie said.

"That is my belief. He was unable to provide proof of his whereabouts for more than an hour on that night. And as for a possible motive, my sister's marriage was not a happy one. They had no children. This was not by accident, but by deliberate design, and the design was of my sister's making. She disliked, shall we say, the act that would lead to issue. Almost as much as she disliked her husband."

Charlie nudged Mr. Deeley. "Wait until Reg Ferryman hears about this."

"I determined that I would interview Mr. Ferryman, but I arrived at his place of employment only to discover he was about to quit the village. I pursued him on foot, and had hold of his arm, when, unaccountably, I discovered the two of us were no longer in Middlehurst, in 1849, but in here, in London. And that, unaccountably, we had undertaken a passage of nearly a hundred years into the future. Unfortunately I was then struck over the head, which rendered me insensible. Ferryman fled. I have only very recently been able to locate him once again. Which is why I was to be found loitering in Harris Road last night."

"If you were a police constable in 1849," Charlie said, "where's your uniform?"

"I assure you I do have in my possession a proper police uniform—it was what I was wearing at the time—however it is not with me at this moment. It is hanging in the cupboard, upstairs, in my room."

"And do you have any papers which might prove you are who you say?" Mr. Deeley inquired.

"None which specifically state my occupation," the gentleman replied. "For which I apologize, but in 1849, it was not required, especially in a village the size of Middlehurst."

Their lunches arrived.

"Thank you, Violet. Have you given any thought to my invitation to dinner this evening?"

The waitress looked slightly embarrassed. "Not yet, Mr. Quinn."

"Never mind. Plenty of time."

Violet hurried away, and Charlie investigated her meat pie. The crust was rather nice, but she wasn't altogether certain what was underneath it. She had a terrible feeling it might be rabbit. She had never eaten rabbit, and wasn't sure what it would actually taste like. A cursory investigation resulted in the conclusion that it was not rabbit at all, but beef and kidney, and that the pie also contained carrots, peas and potatoes.

"You still doubt me," the gentleman suggested. "And my intentions."

Charlie didn't say anything.

"What are your intentions?" Mr. Deeley inquired.

"Having at last located Silas Ferryman, my only desire now is to return him to 1849, to face justice. You are staying at Number Twelve, are you not? The home of the Singleton family?"

"We are," Mr. Deeley replied.

"I have had the house under observation for some days. I did not see you arrive. Are you related to the family?"

"We're friends with Ruby, Betty's next door neighbour," Charlie said, not untruthfully. "We came to see her, but she was away."

"She has gone to Basingstoke," Mr. Deeley added.

"Betty simply offered to let us stay with her until Ruby comes back."

"Tomorrow," Mr. Deeley said helpfully.

"Yes, I am acquainted with Mrs. Firth," said the fair-haired gentleman. "So you know nothing about this fellow who is calling himself Thaddeus Quinn? And you have nothing to do with him?"

"Nothing whatsoever," Charlie lied. "We've only just met him."

"Then I must advise you, he is a thief as well as a killer. After dispatching my poor dear sister, he made off with a considerable sum of money. He is also capable of deception upon a grand scale, maintaining a pleasant demeanour which masks an evil, duplicitous personality."

He paused as Violet returned to remove the remnants of Charlie's meat pie, and the empty plates belonging to himself and Mr. Deeley.

"What have you for afters?" the fair-haired gentleman inquired.

"Today's sweet is steamed fruit roll with custard, Mr. Quinn. And there's also a very nice raisin roll, with custard. An apple tart, with custard. Stewed figs, and custard. And gooseberry tart."

"With custard?"

"Of course."

"Then I shall have the gooseberry tart," the fair-haired gentleman decided. "Anything for you two?"

Charlie shook her head.

"I shall sample the stewed figs," said Mr. Deeley.

"And another cup of tea, if you wouldn't mind, Violet. Still thinking about dinner…?"

"I'd have to let my mum know…. She always has supper waiting…."

"Do, then. It would make such a nice change for you. And afterwards we could go dancing."

"And then you'll see me home safely? There's ever such funny people about. That poor girl down in Balham…"

"I promise I shall see you home, safe and sound."

Violet left again, and was back a few moments later with his gooseberry tart, and a bowl of stewed figs for Mr. Deeley.

"Yes, then?" the fair-haired gentleman prodded.

"Yes," Violet decided.

"Shall we meet outside? Seven o'clock? Give you time to change into your civvies and put on some fresh lipstick?"

"Yes," Violet said again, more certain of herself this time.

"Lovely. See you at seven."

"How is it," Charlie said, when Violet had again gone, "that you were able to finally locate this Silas Ferryman person?"

"Indeed," Mr. Deeley concurred. "It seems to me that London is a very large city. The fortuitousness of your luck astounds me."

But before the fair-haired gentleman could respond, a siren very close to the hotel began to moan, which precipitated a decisive and unanimous groan from the restaurant's customers, and an immediate rush for hats, coats, and gas masks.

The maître d' of the restaurant cleared his throat importantly, and shouted out instructions so that he could be heard above the air raid warning.

"Ladies and gentlemen, if you'll follow me please, I'll escort you down to our cellar!"

• • •

The hotel's air raid shelter had, in a previous life, been its nightclub. But the nightclub been closed down for the duration of the war, and its dance floor and seating area turned into emergency accommodations for the hotel's guests.

There was a sleeping space at the back, with beds and folding cots, for patrons disturbed by night raids. And at the front, adjacent to what had once been a well-stocked bar, a waiting area had been created with surplus chairs and a few tables, to accommodate those displaced by the Luftwaffe's daylight bombing runs.

It was into this front waiting area that Charlie, Mr. Deeley and the fair-haired gentleman were ushered, along with the other customers from the restaurant, all of the hotel's daytime staff, and a number of guests who had been evacuated from its upstairs rooms.

It was, Charlie observed, a rather interesting cross-section of London life. Not nearly as intriguing as the collection of secret agents, displaced aristocrats, and near-cousins of royalty whom she'd read about moving into London's top-flight hotels at the start of the war. The Bedford Square Hotel was not luxurious, and it was not as handily located as its West End counterparts, the Ritz and the Savoy. Nevertheless, their fellow shelterers were an instant source of fascination to her. Men wearing military uniforms from several different countries. WAAFs and women from the Voluntary Services. Chambermaids and front desk clerks. One or two gentlemen who looked like newspaper reporters but could just as easily have been German spies.

"Well," the fair-haired gentleman said, tucking into the remains of his dessert, which he'd had the presence of mind to bring with him as the restaurant had been abandoned. "At least the gooseberry tart will be safe from Hitler."

"Why did you invite us to lunch?" Charlie said. "Other than our mutual interest in time travelling."

"But it was that very thing," the fair-haired gentleman replied. "My curiosity was aroused when I overheard your conversation about altering the future. I knew that Silas Ferryman had moved into a room at Number Twelve, and because I observed that you, too, had come from there, I wondered whether you and he had been previously acquainted."

"You must therefore now be satisfied," Mr. Deeley said, "that we have never before encountered this fellow who calls himself Thaddeus Quinn."

"He is not Thaddeus Quinn," the fair-haired gentleman repeated, a little impatiently. "He is a poor impostor."

"Whoever and whatever he is," Charlie repeated, "we've never met him before."

"But you *are* time travellers."

"Yes, but only by accident. We didn't come here deliberately. We went into an air raid shelter and all of a sudden it was 1940."

In the far distance, Charlie could hear *thuds*. Rumbling explosions, at intervals, growing louder as they travelled closer. And with each *thud* came a small corresponding shake in the earth surrounding the hotel's cellar. Nervously, she reached for Mr. Deeley's hand. Last night's bombing had been one thing, but this was quite another. She had no idea if the Bedford Square Hotel had survived the war without being damaged.

"I understand your dilemma only too well," the fair-haired gentleman said. "As I explained, I shall make it my principal task to return Ferryman to the time we originally came from. Of course, he would prefer to see me dead before he would ever allow that to happen, as I appear to possess the one thing he does not: the ability to travel backwards and forwards in time, at will."

There was another loud *THUD*, and Mr. Deeley observed the ceiling, which housed a number of electric lights that swayed perceptibly with each increasing explosion.

"Might we not be better accommodated underneath one of these tables?" he suggested.

"Nonsense," said a well-heeled fellow who was sitting nearby. "Built like bunkers, these old hotels. I reckon we could survive anything down here except a direct hit. They say the Prime Minister's got an underground bolt-hole just like this where he eats, sleeps, and runs England."

"Yes," Charlie said, "Churchill's War Rooms."

She stopped. Loose lips *could* sink ships. She would say nothing further about the British government's top-secret headquarters underneath the Treasury building in Whitehall. Even though she'd toured its restored site twice (it was, in the present, one of the branches of the Imperial War Museum), had seen the Map Room and Churchill's Bedroom, and had bought a *Dig for Victory* poster and a *Keep Calm and Carry On* mug in the gift shop. It all seemed rather far away and superficial now. Something jolly and entertaining, like the Blackout Ration Chocolate Bar that went for £4.50, or the tin of Ration Tea for £5.00.

The real thing was going on outside, and all around her. She hung onto Mr. Deeley's hand just a little bit tighter.

The fair-haired gentleman finished his gooseberry tart, and placed the plate on the floor beside his chair.

"You now know a good deal about me," he said, "however I know precious little about you. If you don't mind my asking, what time have you come from? And what are your last names?"

"We have come from seventy-three years in the future," Mr. Deeley replied.

"And we are Charlotte Duran and Shaun Deeley," Charlie said.

"Deeley?" the fair-haired gentleman repeated, just as an enormous BANG jarred the room, as if it had been struck by a giant battering ram. Everything shook. The lights dimmed and flickered, but did not go out.

Charlie dived under the table, and was quickly joined by Mr. Deeley and the fair-haired gentleman.

Another immense BANG and a THUD shook the shelter's walls, floor, and ceiling. And then something—a beam or a supporting pillar—gave way with a horrible creak and a deafening crash. And Charlie was thrown across the floor, as the lights arced and went out, and the room was plunged into utter darkness.

• • •

Someone—perhaps it was the well-heeled gentleman—was singing. Something by Vera Lynn, brave and full of optimistic fortitude.

Others in the darkness joined in, their voices tinged with weary humour.

Quickly, torches were located and switched on, and the room was illuminated once more, if only in small round patches. People were lifting pieces of ceiling off themselves and organizing improvised first aid stations. The air was filled with dust. The man who had been singing checked on Charlie.

"You all right? Everything intact? Nothing broken?"

Charlie sat up. She tested her arms and legs, wrists and ankles.

"Nothing's broken," she said. She looked around. "Where's Mr. Deeley?"

"There's nobody else here."

"But he was underneath the table, beside me. There."

The table they'd been sitting at was in pieces on the floor, demolished by a large slab of concrete which had crashed down from the ceiling. The slab of concrete was also in pieces.

The man shone his torch on the wreckage. And then all around the debris that had scattered nearby.

Mr. Deeley was not there.

"Anyone here called Deeley?" he shouted into the darkness.

His question was met with silence.

"Let's have a little walk around the room," he suggested. "Perhaps he's been injured and they've got him bandaged up somewhere."

But the search proved fruitless.

Mr. Deeley was not there.

And neither, it seemed, was the fair-haired gentleman.

CHAPTER TWELVE

The All Clear had sounded. The air raid was over.

There were more torches now, and more rescuers—men from the ARP, in arm-bands and tin hats—helping the hotel guests, the chambermaids, the front desk clerks, and the customers from the restaurant climb out of the devastated cellar.

Charlie blinked as her eyes adjusted to the sudden daylight at the top of the stairs.

There was an immense hole in the front of the hotel. Its outer wall had been blasted away, and part of the floor had collapsed into the cellar. People were being herded around a gigantic crater in the middle of Bloomsbury Street, to the safety of the pavement beyond.

"All right, my love? Can I just have a look to make sure you're not hurt?"

It was another volunteer with an armband and a tin hat, a woman. Charlie allowed herself to be superficially examined. She wasn't badly injured, aside from some scrapes and a bruised knee. But her clothes were covered in the dust from fallen bricks and masonry, and the shoulder strap of her leather handbag had been torn away at one end.

Something was digging into the back of her neck. Her hand went instinctively to the little silver chain belonging to the necklace she never took off. At the bottom the chain hung a name, also fashioned in silver: MRS. COLLINS. It had been a surprise birthday present from Mr. Deeley. She felt for the clasp. It was bent, nearly broken.

She pressed the fragile ends of the clasp back together as she searched around her. Where was Mr. Deeley?

"What's your name, my love?"

"Charlie. Charlotte. Collins. Lowe. Duran."

She realized she sounded confused. She *was* confused.

"And can you tell me what the date is?"

"1940. It's October the 12th, 1940."

"And when's your birthday?"

"Thirteenth of September."

"What year were you born?"

"1979," Charlie said.

The woman in the tin hat turned to have a word with one of the rescuers. "Possible concussion," Charlie heard her say.

And then, she saw the stretcher party.

They were carrying casualties to an awaiting ambulance.

And there was Mr. Deeley. On one of the stretchers.

The two men carrying Mr. Deeley placed his stretcher on the pavement, out of the way, and then abandoned him to go back inside the hotel.

Charlie pushed past the woman in the tin hat and ran to where Mr. Deeley lay, covered in dust.

"Mr. Deeley," she said, kneeling on the ground beside him. "Shaun."

He wasn't moving.

He wasn't breathing.

Charlie touched his hand. It was cold, limp, unresponsive.

She'd taken a lifesaving course. She knew how to look for vital signs, how to do rescue breathing and CPR. She'd once saved someone's life after they'd been overcome by smoke in a fire.

She couldn't feel Mr. Deeley's pulse.

She touched his face, lightly, lovingly.

Cold.

It was almost as if he was asleep.

He wasn't breathing.

This couldn't be.

The steps for CPR raced through her mind. *If the victim is not breathing begin chest compressions. Push down*...how many times? She couldn't remember. *Push hard and fast.*

She started to pump, trying to recall what came next. This was ridiculous. She knew this. *She knew this.* Why couldn't she remember?

She stopped the chest compressions, then tilted Mr. Deeley's head back and lifted his chin. She pinched his nose. She covered his mouth with her own until she saw his chest rise. *Two breaths, one second each. Then back to the chest compressions.*

"There, my lovely. Nothing more you can do for him now."

It was another ARP volunteer, another man, another armband, another tin hat. And he was pulling her off Mr. Deeley.

"No!" she shouted. "No! Let me do this! I know what I'm doing!"

But they didn't know about CPR in wartime London. They didn't know about rescue breathing. Charlie struggled to free herself from the man, but he was holding onto her, and then another man appeared, to make sure she couldn't go back to Mr. Deeley.

"He's not dead!" she cried. "I can save him! Please let me try!"

But the men wouldn't listen. And they refused to let go of her. They forced her sit down on another part of the pavement, where she couldn't see him.

"Can you tell me his name, lovely? He doesn't have any identification."

The second man had a little notebook and a pencil.

"Shaun Deeley," Charlie said miserably. "Shaun Patrick Deeley. Please let me go back to him!" She stood up again, but was caught by the first volunteer as she fell back down to the pavement, dizzy and disoriented.

"Date of birth?"

"November. The twelfth."

"Do you know the year?"

"1791," Charlie said vacantly.

The woman volunteer had come back, this time with a cup of tea.

"She's a little bit confused," the man with the notebook said. "She's had a bad knock to her head. Have a cuppa till you're feeling better, love."

Charlie drank the tea. This couldn't be. *This could not be.* Mr. Deeley couldn't die. They were meant to be together in time. Not separated. Not like this.

The first man knelt down in front of Charlie. "How are you related, my love? Is he your husband?"

"No," Charlie said, fighting back the tears. "No… we are… we were going to be married… he kept on asking me to…and I kept on saying no…."

"Never mind, my love. It's wartime. We don't any of us know whether we'll be here tomorrow. Remember the good times you spent together, eh? You loved him and he loved you and that's all that matters. If he's watching from afar, he's smiling. He knows. I'll have to arrange to have him taken away, my love, but if you leave me your details, I'll make sure someone's in touch about certificates and burial. Are you on the 'phone?"

Charlie nodded.

"Can you just give us your address and number, then?"

The second man was waiting, his pencil poised over his little notebook.

"Number Twelve, Harris Road," Charlie said. "Balham. I'm staying with Betty Singleton."

"And the telephone?"

"I'm sorry," she said. "I can't remember. Look it up in the directory. Bert Singleton. On Harris Road. In Balham."

"I'll do that," the man with the notebook said, writing Betty's father's name next to the notation. "Here we are then, love. They've come to take him away now."

They helped her to her feet, and allowed her to watch as the stretcher party lifted Mr. Deeley up from the pavement and carried him to the back of a waiting ambulance.

"Wait!" Charlie shouted, running over to them.

They waited.

Both looked away as Charlie kissed Mr. Deeley, tenderly, touching his fingers and his lips, his forehead, his cheek. Was it her imagination? Was there warmth there?

"Goodbye, Mr. Deeley," she whispered. "I'm so sorry. This wasn't meant to happen. It's a horrible trick of history."

She watched, in tears, as they closed the door at the back of the ambulance, and drove away.

It was Mr. Deeley's body, but it was not him. The part of him that had inhabited his body had already left. She had kissed an empty shell, the physical thing that had housed his soul. And his soul had gone somewhere else.

She turned away from the ambulance and began to walk.

• • •

It seemed she had been walking for a very long time. But then, she had no idea how long she'd been unconscious in the cellar, nor how long it was before she'd been rescued. And it seemed like only minutes that she'd spent sitting on the pavement…but, in fact, it must have been more like hours.

And now it was getting dark.

In spite of broken windows and shattered bricks, the other buildings she passed were largely intact. But there was a fire burning somewhere; its smoke billowed into a grey and hazy sky. And there was a fresh and acrid smell of detonated explosives.

It seemed as if she was walking west. Yes, it was west. She'd passed Tottenham Court Road and found her way to Oxford Street. She was surrounded by broken brick and stone, and pockmarked cornices and chipped columns and boarded-up windows. She crossed the road and walked down the long grand avenue that she recognized as Regent Street.

But then it was necessary to stop walking, because the road in front of her was blocked. The Portland stone columns and facades of the buildings on either side of the street were freshly scarred by flying shrapnel. All of the glass in all of the windows had been blown out, their frames twisted and torn. Regent Street itself was fractured. Water cascaded from a broken water pipe into a river that flowed down towards Piccadilly Circus, swamping an abandoned taxi and several cars. Broken bits of wood and stone were strewn everywhere, and men in tin hats wielded large brooms, sweeping glittering crystals of glass off the pavement and into the gutter. Charlie could see evidence of yet another fire, now out, with every window and doorway blackened.

She negotiated her way down to Piccadilly Circus, as darkness fell at last, and the blackout took effect.

In the present that she'd come from, Piccadilly Circus was a riot of electric lights, huge LED advertisements flashing on the sides of buildings, traffic humming, the famous fountain a gathering spot for sightseers and Londoners alike.

Here, in 1940, the giant ads had been switched off. She could still see them in the moonlight: a huge clock proclaiming *Guinness is Good for You*; giant letters spelling out Bovril and Schweppes. On another corner, Wrigley gum was the prescription for Vim and Vigour, while Brylcreem was The Perfect Hair Dressing. Charlie could also see where the famous fountain was. But it had disappeared beneath protective hoardings advertising National War Bonds.

The shiny black taxis were still there, too, and private motorcars, their running boards and bumpers painted white and their headlamps dimmed. And she could see any number of red and white double-decker buses. And instead of sightseers, there were soldiers in uniform, and men and women dressed up for a night on the town.

Charlie ached, watching their determination to get on with life in spite of the war. After Jeff had died, she'd purposely isolated herself, shutting herself off from anything that even hinted at being a couple. Because she was no longer one half of a whole. She was the lopped-off bit, the fragile part that was left standing, propped up with timbers, after the other part was destroyed. And she had lived that way for five years, in mourning, the grief never very far away, the calendar on her kitchen wall permanently marking the day that Jeff had ceased to be.

And then, that July, Mr. Deeley had come into her life. Impetuously, madly, completely unexpectedly. He had banished her grief and put an end to her mourning. She was part of a whole again, one half of two, and filled up with an emotion that had been too long absent from those long, dark days.

She had been happy.

Had it only been since July?

Had it only been three months?

Three months filled with surprise cups of tea in bed, near disasters in the kitchen, constant avowals of love, endless proposals of marriage.

Endless.

And each time, she'd said no. Never directly, never in any way intended to hurt his feelings. Never in any way dismissive.

In truth, she hadn't wanted him to stop proposing. She adored his earnest entreaties—as much as she knew he adored presenting them to her. But something always stopped her from saying "yes." Perhaps it was fear. She and Jeff had loved one another so completely, so deeply and passionately... and then he'd been killed... and a part of herself had died as well.

And now, in spite of all her caution, in spite of everything, she'd lost Mr. Deeley too.

None of what had just happened to him made any sense. Their first meeting in 1825 had seemed almost predetermined. It was meant to be. As was their journey together from 1825 to her present, and a short one after that, to 1848. Was this, their third excursion together, also meant to have happened? Was his life meant to have been extinguished in a random act of savagery from the skies? How could he be dead, when he didn't even belong in this time and place?

Charlie abandoned the gaiety of the Saturday night couples, forcing herself to continue walking. Using the white-painted bottoms of lampposts and the curbs cloaked in zebra stripes, she was able to navigate her way along Haymarket and Cockspur Street, all the way down to Trafalgar Square.

Three months of happiness.

It wasn't fair.

She remembered Mr. Deeley's outrageous foreign accent as

he'd negotiated their release from the Underground. And standing on the platform at Balham station, imagining what was going to happen in three days' time, debating the ethics of saving Thaddeus.

And his kiss, last night, on the upstairs landing… lost in his arms….

And then, she heard the sound. The unmistakable moan of the siren.

Another bloody air raid.

She could see the entrance to Trafalgar Square tube station. There were no exterior buildings—just a set of stairs disappearing down into the ground, with the Underground roundel above them, lit by a low-watt bulb. Charlie raced towards it, the broken shoulder strap of her bag flapping against her legs.

"Come along, my dear, don't dawdle, this way to the platforms." Someone from London Transport was directing her down the steps to the booking hall just under the road.

People were appearing from nowhere, materializing out of the darkness, rushing past her, jostling her out of the way. But something was telling her not to go. Something was niggling her memory…

She stopped.

It was Saturday, the 12th of October, 1940. The night a high-explosive bomb had dropped on the National Gallery, on the north side of Trafalgar Square. She knew this. But she couldn't remember why… her brain was too foggy. And then… yes. The bomb had destroyed the room where Raphael's paintings had hung before they were evacuated to an old slate mine in Wales at the start of the war. On her desk at the museum in Stoneford was her favourite mug, featuring the two quizzical-looking cherubs from Raphael's *Sistine Madonna*. She'd bought it after visiting the National Gallery, where she'd learned about the wartime damage to the building.

She remembered that same night another bomb had fallen on the roadway, immediately above where the station was. It had penetrated the pavement and exploded at the head of the escalators. The blast wave had travelled downwards, collapsing concrete and steel. And the subsequent avalanche of wet earth and gravel and mud and water from a broken main had killed seven people and injured more than thirty others.

Charlie turned around and ran back up to the surface. Over the moan of the sirens she could hear the rhythmic rise and fall throb of approaching German planes. She could see the bright beams of the searchlights on the ground, criss-crossing the dark sky. And now she could hear the *THUD* of a bomb dropping, and then another and another and another.

Racing across the road, she fled east, along Strand, reaching Craven Street just as the first 500-pound explosive fell onto the National Gallery.

The blast deafened her. She felt it as much as she heard it, thundering through her body, shaking the pavement and the buildings on either side of the street, filling the road with smoke and the acrid smell of detonation.

She heard the whistle of the second 500-pound bomb as it was let loose from the overhead Heinkel, soaring earthward. And as it slammed into the roadway above Trafalgar Square, she tumbled to the ground, hitting her head on the zebra-striped curb, and remembering nothing more.

CHAPTER THIRTEEN

It was not immediately apparent to Shaun what had happened. His last clear memory was of the cellar of the hotel, and huddling beneath a table with Mrs. Collins and the gentleman with the fair hair who claimed to be Thaddeus. And then there had been a massive explosion, the lights were extinguished, and the better part of the ceiling had collapsed on top of them. He remembered being thrown out from under the table by the blast, and then, it seemed, that for a few moments, he had lost awareness of what was going on around him.

And now that he had regained his senses, some small portions of time appeared to have gone missing.

He was also aware of a terrible pain in his left arm, the source of which, upon closer inspection, seemed to be a large wound, similar to what might have been caused by a very long, sharp knife. The wound had bled, but the bleeding had been staunched by the application of what looked like several layers of paper towelling.

Shaun took stock of where he was.

He was sitting in an armchair beside a bright and sunny window, and he was alone.

As he attempted to get his bearings, Shaun realized that his armchair was located in the front section of the Bedford Square Hotel.

But the front section of the Bedford Square Hotel was not as he remembered it.

To be sure, the marble floor was the same. But it had been cleaned and polished, and it gleamed spotlessly. The reception desk had been relocated, and behind it stood ladies and gentlemen in black coats and white shirts, tending to well-heeled travellers. The curving marble staircase leading to the upper floors was not so shabby-looking, and its brass banisters had been rubbed to a shine. But one of the two lifts was still not in working order, a sign once again conveying sincere apologies. That had not changed at all.

Shaun got to his feet stiffly. And then he walked across to the restaurant, where they had eaten lunch with the fair-haired gentleman.

Except it was not now a restaurant. The room appeared to have been divided into three, one part given over to an area furnished with more comfortable armchairs and potted plants, a second part fitted with glass walls and a sign which said *Business Centre*, and a third section concerning itself with the selling of many varieties of coffees, teas, and pastries.

Shaun sat down again, in another of the armchairs beside another of the large windows.

It seemed to him that this was most definitely not 1940.

He had been living with Mrs. Collins long enough to know that the clothing these travellers wore, the shop that was selling coffee and tea, and the Business Centre, all belonged to the time that Mrs. Collins had originally come from—or something very close to it.

He located a newspaper upon a small table beside his chair, and consulted its front page.

Monday, October 14, 2013.

He put the newspaper down.

Unaccountably, he seemed to have returned to the present.

He sat for a few more moments in the comfortable armchair, working out what he ought to do next. He supposed it was possible that Mrs. Collins had also been transported into this time, and that they had simply become separated. He might, therefore, stay in this place and wait for her.

That would, however, require money.

Shaun checked his pockets. The coins from that morning were still there. Five pounds and fifty-five pence.

He got up, and approached the Reception Desk.

"Yes, sir. May I help you?"

The young woman seemed to consider his clothing a source of amusement. His long black overcoat was somewhat dusty, it was true. This, he attributed to the fact that it had accumulated a good deal of ceiling plaster when the bomb had dropped. His trousers and pullover and shirt and tie from Betty's father's wardrobe were also rumpled, and far too old-fashioned for this sort of establishment.

"Good afternoon," Shaun said. "Would you be so kind as to tell me the tariff for one night's accommodation?"

This, unaccountably, caused the young woman to smile.

"Certainly, sir. Standard, superior, king deluxe, business class, or luxury suite?"

Shaun fingered the five pounds and fifty-five pence in his coat pocket.

"Standard, I should think."

"Two hundred and forty-five pounds. And that does include a twin or a double bed, as well as complimentary Wi-Fi."

"For just the one night."

"Yes, sir. We do offer an advance booking rate of £214.50, VAT included, if you reserve at least one week ahead."

"Thank you."

He'd had no idea an overnight stay at a London hotel could be so outrageously expensive. Especially at an establishment which, in 1940, could hardly have been termed luxurious.

Shaun briefly considered commandeering one of the comfortable armchairs beside the sunny window for the night, but decided it would not likely be welcomed by the smiling young woman behind the counter, nor by anyone else.

There was nothing for it. He would have to go back to Balham.

"Might I leave a letter for someone who I believe will be staying here?"

"Of course."

"Do you have pen and paper?"

The young woman had obviously not heard of this form of communication, as it took her some time to locate both items. After much searching, she was able to produce a pen with the hotel's name printed upon it, and a blank piece of paper from a printing machine attached to her computer.

Shaun composed a message to Mrs. Collins, advising her that he had survived the air raid and that he had returned to her grandmother's house in Balham, and that he would wait for her there. He folded the paper in two, and wrote her name upon it, and gave it back to the smiling young woman.

"Many thanks."

"And when will Mrs. Collins be checking in?" the young woman inquired.

"I am uncertain," Shaun said. "It may be today. Or tomorrow. Or the day afterwards. Or a week from now. Might you keep the message nearby, in case of her unexpected arrival?"

"Very well," she said, putting it under the counter.

"Many thanks. I bid you a good afternoon."

"Good afternoon, sir."

• • •

Shaun left the hotel, and turned right, and walked along Bloomsbury Street, in the direction of the main road.

The buildings on either side of him looked almost exactly as they had in 1940. But their facades had been cleaned and repainted, their windows washed, their doors replaced. The Bedford Square Hotel's large pavement-side windows were draped in smart blue and white striped awnings. And the road roared with traffic, the likes of which Shaun had never before seen or heard.

There had not been that many cars or buses that morning, when he and Mrs. Collins had walked from Tottenham Court Road to the hotel. But now, Bloomsbury Street was packed with them, three abreast, all of them roaring off in the same direction. The noise they made assaulted Shaun's ears. They squealed, reminding him of Farmer Hopkins's piglets in terrible distress. And they smelled, most unpleasantly.

He reached the corner, and turned right again, onto New Oxford Street.

Shaun knew that if he continued walking in this direction, he would eventually reach the Underground station—assuming it was still there. He focused his mind on the task at hand, blotting out the dreadful sense that he was lost and completely alone in an immense and unfamiliar city.

There. That seemed to be where the station had been that morning, at an intersection which was now dominated by a very tall structure. Shaun stood in awe before it, counting the floors. He had seen such buildings on the television. And he had observed some similarly lofty constructions through the train window, as they had approached Waterloo. But to witness such a thing in close proximity, to look up to the sky and see so many windows....

He imagined the number of steps involved, and then reminded himself that in this present time, steps were no longer needed. There were lifts. Although the conveyances themselves seemed to be singularly unreliable, since they seemed always to be in need of repair.

Perhaps that was why there were always two in any given location, Shaun mused.

The village of Stoneford did not have any lifts.

He brought his gaze back down to earth. There was a great deal of demolition and reconstruction going on around him, all of it hidden behind a long fence painted to look like the sky. What then of the Underground station they'd been in this morning?

Confused, he searched for the familiar round red circle with the blue bar crossing through it, and located, at last, a hole in the pavement with steps disappearing down beneath the road. And there it was: the Underground sign.

That was it, then. Tottenham Court Road.

• • •

The station swarmed with passengers, and this Shaun found most unsettling. His momentary terror on the platform at Waterloo

111

had been genuine. The largest single gathering of people he had ever encountered prior to that had been at the manor at Monsieur Duran's annual summer ball in Stoneford. But Stoneford Manor in 1825 was nothing like London in the present.

And it was not remotely similar to this ticket hall at half past four on a Monday afternoon.

Shaun found a safe place to stand against a wall, and tried to understand what was expected of him in terms of purchasing his fare. Yesterday, the journey to London from Middlehurst had been terrifying for him. But, except for that one brief moment at Waterloo Station, he had not let Mrs. Collins see his fear. She thought him to be courageous, invincible, even heroic. If she could see him now, he thought, she would be utterly disappointed by his deficiencies.

He regretted not paying attention when she had bought their tickets from Waterloo to Balham. And there would be no question of trying to bluff his way through the automated barricades with adulterated Latin, as he had earlier.

He walked across to one of the ticket machines, intending to watch while others used it. This did nothing but confound him. He did not have a plastic card. He had coins, but which coins were required was not immediately clear at all.

Glancing across the hall, he spied a window in a wall, and a person sitting behind the window. An illuminated sign indicated this was where he could seek assistance.

"Good afternoon," he said. "Might I inquire about the fare from this station to Balham?"

The woman behind the window glass was dark-skinned, and perhaps had come from one of the islands notorious for pirates in the Caribbean Sea.

"That's four pounds seventy, my dear."

Shaun placed the sum total of the contents of his pockets on the little shelf under the window.

The woman took most of the coins, and gave him back a few more in exchange, along with a printed ticket.

"There you are, my dear. Through the gates and follow the signs for the Northern Line. You'll want the southbound platform."

Shaun took his ticket and what remained of his money. He observed how his fellow travellers approached the barricades, and inserted their tickets, and collected them again as they went through to the other side.

He did the same, and was mildly astonished to discover that he was able to accomplish this on his own with very little trouble. He turned, thinking he would share his delight with Mrs. Collins. And then he remembered, with a sinking heart, that she was not there.

She *would* be there, though. He had no doubt she had also made the journey forward from 1940, and needed only to check at the reception desk at the hotel for his letter. And then she would also buy a ticket on the Underground, and meet him at her grandmother's house in Balham.

CHAPTER FOURTEEN

It might have been seconds. It might have been minutes.

Charlie was covered in dust, and her ears were ringing, and everywhere she could hear the thunder of London under fire from the sky. The road, already blacked out, was obscured further by a smoky fog. She could see nothing.

But she knew where she was. She knew her name. And she was fairly certain she knew the date and when she'd been born. And she knew she had to find shelter.

She got to her feet and picked up her bag and staggered into an entranceway next to the forecourt of Charing Cross railway station. Half running, half falling down some steps, she found herself, at last, in the booking hall of Strand Underground.

Strand no longer existed in the time she'd come from. It was closed in 1973, and incorporated into the grand restructuring of Trafalgar Square and Charing Cross in 1979. Its surface entrance was no longer there. But it was here now. And downstairs was the Northern Line. And it would shelter her, and a train from here would take her back to Balham.

A man in a uniform stood at the passimeter, checking for tickets.

"I haven't got a ticket. I'm sorry."

"You'll have to buy one, then. Penny ha'penny."

He nodded at a woman selling platform tickets from a little window in the wall.

Charlie was incredulous. There was a bloody air raid on outside, and this man was making sure nobody got past him without paying their way.

She didn't have any money that would buy her a place on the platform. Her coins were from the next century.

But over there was a ticket machine. Several ticket machines, in fact. Nothing like the high tech machines she was used to, but she could see the list of fares, and the fare from this station to Balham was 5d. The machine would accept 6d and 4d and big copper pennies.

Charlie dug her change purse out of her bag and opened it. She made a calculated guess. She'd personally sourced and collected all of the coins in the saucer in the Blitz display at the museum. A little silver sixpence was nearly the same size, weight and colour as one of her new 5p coins.

Nearly, but not exactly.

She picked one out, and pushed it into the slot.

The machine seemed to consider this for a moment, and then rewarded her with one old copper penny in change, and a little cardboard ticket.

Charlie grabbed both, then showed her ticket to the inspector.

"That way down," he said, indicating the spiral emergency steps.

"What about the lift?" Charlie said. She felt dizzy, and her head hurt profoundly.

"No lifts during air raids," the inspector replied. "Down the stairs, if you please."

Wearily, Charlie joined a stream of shelterers negotiating the narrow circular stairwell. Down, down, down... a hundred steps or more. She clung to the handrail, trying to keep her balance, trying not to look at her feet.

Finally. The bottom. And the southbound platform, crammed with shelterers, many of whom had bedded down to sleep in what they were wearing, their hats and coats made into improvised pillows and blankets.

Charlie picked her way past them to the white line that had been painted along the edge of the platform, indicating where passengers could stand and wait. A train was coming. She could hear it, far down in the tunnel, and she could feel the wind as it pushed the air in front of it, like a pneumatic ram.

The driver slowed as he guided the train into the station; it crept to a stop with its nose buried in the tunnel at the opposite end. The guard in the last car opened the doors, and Charlie went aboard a middle carriage. It was mostly empty, and much cooler than the stifling heat on the platform.

She sat down, but almost as soon as she was seated, the guard entered her carriage by way of the door at its far end.

"You'll have to get off, I'm afraid. We're reversing here and going back to Euston."

Charlie's heart sank. "Why?"

"They've shut the floodgates. We don't go under the river during air raids."

"But I've got to get back to Balham."

"Eighty-eight bus then, if it's still running. You can nip round to Trafalgar Square and flag down the driver. But wouldn't you much rather wait down here till the All Clear sounds?"

• • •

"Are you all right?"

Someone had touched her shoulder. Charlie opened her eyes. She'd found an unoccupied bit of space in a cross-passage, and had sat down and leaned her head against the curving wall.

It was Betty's lodger. Thaddeus Quinn. The dark-haired man who had originally claimed to be Thaddeus Quinn, anyway. She wasn't sure who he was now. He sat down beside her, placing the small suitcase he was carrying on the floor between them.

"I'm terribly sorry. I didn't mean to frighten you."

Charlie looked around. She didn't want to be alone with him. Not after what the fair-haired gentleman had told her. There were a couple of men sitting a few feet away, minding their own business. Within safe shouting distance.

"What do you want?" she asked warily. "Why are you here?"

"I saw you last night in Harris Road, talking to Silas Ferryman. And Betty told me that you were coming up to London today to have lunch with a gentleman you'd met when Mrs. Crofton's house was bombed. I put two and two together. My apologies, Charlotte. I've been following you. "

Charlie stared at him. "Silas Ferryman."

"Yes. I recognized him immediately."

"But you're Silas Ferryman."

The dark-haired gentleman was clearly shocked.

"Is that what he told you?"

"Yes."

"The despicable rogue. I suppose he claimed he was me, then?"

"That's exactly what he said, yes."

"I have known the man to be less than honest, but this is outrageous. I hope you dismissed him outright."

"Why should I?" Charlie said, making sure the two men further down the passageway were still there. "He gave perfectly reasonable answers to our questions."

"Then please tell me this. What was his purpose in asking to meet with you?"

"Actually, he wanted to know how well we knew you. He'd been watching Betty's house. He wanted to know what Mr. Deeley and I were doing there."

Betty's dark-haired lodger contemplated the floor, deep in thought.

"I have been searching for Silas Ferryman for the better part of a year," he said, at last, "and now, it seems, he has discovered me first. I had not credited him with such tenacity. I had believed—wrongly, it seems—that he would do his best to simply disappear."

"Go away," Charlie said. "Leave me alone. I don't know what to believe anymore."

She meant it. She was past worrying about the logic of time travelling, and past worrying about which Thaddeus was telling the truth and which one was fabricating it. She wanted to go back to Stoneford, back to her own century, where Mr. Deeley was still alive, and not lying dead on a World War Two stretcher in an ambulance that wasn't in a hurry to go anywhere.

"I understand you being upset. Did he mention the crime I'm supposed to have committed?"

"Yes," Charlie said. "But it's not that. It's my friend, Mr. Deeley. He's been killed."

The word sounded wrong. It was too new, too unfamiliar. It couldn't be describing Mr. Deeley. He couldn't be that. Dead. The memory of it was coming back to smother her, like the dense, smoky fog after a bombing.

And she remembered something else… when she had first met Mr. Deeley, in 1825, he had been accused, unfairly, of arson. He had been beaten and thrown into a prison cell, with the promise of a quick trial, a quick conviction, and a quick dispatch. Arson was a hanging offence. She had wanted to see him desperately, and his jailor had taken pity on her and allowed her to visit him for one hour. And in that hour, she had come to understand that they were meant to be together, inseparable, for whatever time each of them had left.

But time had played a very cruel trick on her. Why allow Mr. Deeley to escape the hangman in 1825, only to be killed three months later anyway? Was it always meant to be? Was it always intended that he should die at this exact moment in his life?

"He was killed in the air raid. In the cellar of the hotel where we had lunch. And I had to identify his body."

"I'm so sorry, Charlotte."

Charlie looked at him. His voice told her he meant it. And his face.

"I liked him. I really did. Such a shame."

He paused.

"I am curious," he said hesitantly, "about the tale that Ferryman has told you. You said he gave you details of the crime…?"

Charlie nodded.

"Did he tell you the year that it happened?"

It was Charlie's turn to hesitate. "Yes," she said, finally. "1849. Christmas."

"And this doesn't confound you?"

Charlie shook her head.

"Then you are not surprised by the suggestion that men and women are capable of travelling from one time, into another...?"

Charlie shook her head again.

"Then you must know, Charlotte, that I was less than honest with you last night, when we spoke about my origins. Betty knows nothing of my life before we met, and I hope to continue to protect her from that knowledge. Before I arrived in London, in December of last year, I was employed as a police officer. In Middlehurst. In the year 1849."

"Yes," Charlie said. "That's what the other Thaddeus said. But he was the police officer. Not you."

"'The other Thaddeus,' as you call him, knows a good many details about me. We grew up in the same village, separated by only a few houses. We attended lessons together as children. He apprenticed as a blacksmith, working for my father. And he married my sister, Matilda. The same Matilda Ferryman who was later found dead with her throat cut. Did he happen to mention the two other murders to you?"

Charlie nodded.

"I considered him to be the most likely suspect in all three killings in 1849. I believe him also to be guilty of two additional killings in the present time. The method he used to dispatch each of his victims is remarkably similar."

"Two more killings?" Charlie said, faintly. "I know about one..."

"There have been two more killings," Betty's lodger confirmed. "The man has a taste for it. Having indulged himself three times in the past, he has found pleasure in repeating the evil, and will continue to do so until he is stopped. Before the sirens went I was observing you and your friend—and Ferryman—in the restaurant. I was careful to stay out of sight, so I couldn't overhear what he was saying to you. But his familiarity with the waitress caused me great concern."

"He invited her to have dinner with him," Charlie said. "She agreed."

"Dinner tonight?"

"Yes. And then dancing. And he promised to see her home safely. Her name's Violet."

The dark-haired gentleman closed his eyes. "I took shelter in the cellar with everyone else… and then, after the ceiling collapsed… I found my way out. I saw the young lady in question. She was uninjured. And I saw Ferryman, also unhurt. But while I was distracted, looking for you and your friend… Ferryman and the young woman disappeared from my sight." He rested his head back against the curving passageway wall. "I may live to regret this day."

"What time is it?" Charlie asked, after a few more moments.

"Just gone ten."

"Has the All Clear sounded yet?"

"No idea," Betty's lodger replied, tiredly. "But the trains still aren't running under the river, and that's usually an accurate indicator of conditions outside. We may be stranded here for the better part of the night."

Charlie struggled to her feet, using the passageway wall for balance. "I've got to get home."

Betty's lodger reached up and grabbed her arm, stopping her. "You can't."

"I don't care. I'll catch a bus. I know they keep running during air raids. I'll find one going to Balham."

"Please sit down, Charlotte. Don't be stupid. You're safe down here. Betty will understand. It's wartime. People are caught out. And we've already lost your friend. I don't want to lose you as well."

Defeated, Charlie slid down the wall. The station was packed with shelterers. Until the All Clear sirens sounded, there was nowhere else she could go.

But it was true. She was safe down here—from the bombs, anyway, and from Silas Ferryman, whoever he was. Strand had been untouched by the Blitz. And if the dark-haired man sitting beside her really was the Middlehurst Slasher, he was hardly likely to draw attention to himself with so many witnesses present.

Charlie closed her eyes and waited. And at some point, she

dozed off again, and then woke with a start as someone walked past, negotiating a path through the outstretched legs and slumbering, prone bodies.

She glanced over at the dark-haired man who Betty believed was Thaddeus. He was asleep, sitting upright against the wall, his jaw slightly open, his breathing verging on a quiet snore.

On the floor between them was his suitcase. It was small and black, with tan-coloured leather reinforcements around its edges and corners.

Why did he have a suitcase with him?

Charlie contemplated this for a moment.

She checked. It wasn't locked.

And then she did something she would never have considered doing at home, in the present, where it wasn't wartime, and life was ordinary, and orderly... and safe.

Curiously, and very carefully, she opened the lid of the case.

She was expecting clothing—shirts and socks and underwear and jumpers. But the case contained only two items. The first Charlie recognized as the yellow and black box belonging to a Brownie Box camera. Nana Betty had one just like it.

The other item was a gas mask. Or, what she at first assumed was a gas mask, but which turned out to be something altogether different.

Inside the cardboard gas mask box was a collection of jewellery.

A locket.

A ring.

A bracelet.

Charlie caught her breath as she realized what she was looking at.

But there was more. A brooch, painted gold, with leaves and three delicate flowers. In the centre of each flower was a tiny glass globe.

A pair of clasp earrings, tortoiseshell imitations, probably Bakelite.

Underneath the jewellery were two cuttings from newspapers, carefully folded.

The first was a story about Angela Bailey, whose body had been discovered on a bomb site, her throat cut, and her brooch missing. The murder that everyone in Betty's road was talking about.

The second story was unfamiliar to Charlie. Deirdre Allsop, a young woman who lived with her invalid aunt and worked in a sweet shop in Balham, had failed to come home after work on Friday, August 23. The aunt was certain her niece did not have any boyfriends, however the manager of the sweet shop reported seeing her with a gentleman several times when leaving work. When Miss Allsop's body had at last been discovered on Mitcham Common, it was determined that her throat had been cut, and that her earrings, which she had borrowed from her aunt, were missing.

Charlie put everything back in the gas mask box, and closed its lid, and then very quickly and quietly closed the suitcase. And then, without disturbing the man snoring beside her, she got to her feet, and, clutching her broken handbag, ran out of the passageway and through the station to the emergency stairs.

• • •

Outside, the night air was cold and damp after the suffocating heat of the tube station, and it smelled of demolition and explosives and burning wood. After her eyes had adjusted to the sudden darkness, Charlie could see smoke rising from multiple fires, pale grey smudges against the red-tinged sky.

But the bombing seemed to have stopped, and the city was quiet.

She had no idea what time it was, or even if there would be a bus. If there were no buses, she would walk. It was about five miles from Strand to Balham. She could manage it in a couple of hours, easily. She rode her bike twice as far as that on summer weekends at home.

At Trafalgar Square, she saw the damage the bombs had caused. There was a rubble-strewn hole in the road across from Nelson's Column. It really didn't look that bad, but she knew the worst of it was below, out of sight in the tube station.

Rescuers were still running up and down the steps beneath

the Underground sign, carrying shovels and bandages. Ambulances waited nearby to take the injured to hospital.

She spied an 88 bus and ran to catch it, jumping onto the open rear platform just as the bus rattled away from its stop.

"Single to Balham Station," she said, to the conductress.

"That'll be five pence, please."

There was barely enough light inside the bus to see properly. Charlie offered another of her little silver 5p coins, which the conductress seemed to assume was sixpence: she received a big brown penny in return, and a very tiny cardboard ticket.

It was a long, slow ride along a blacked-out Whitehall and around the darkened Houses of Parliament. The driver stopped three times to pick up passengers and then crossed over Vauxhall Bridge to the south side of the river. It seemed like hours before the bus reached Balham, with delays and detours, and cautious navigations around holes in the road, and collapsed walls, and puddles of muddy water of unknown depths.

At last she saw the tube station, completely blacked out except for its dimly lit and hooded Underground signs. She got off the bus and, walking quickly, reached Harris Road in a few minutes. She let the knocker drop at the front door of Number Twelve, and waited.

There was no answer.

Charlie's heart sank.

And then she realized that Betty was probably asleep in the shelter at the bottom of the garden. It was well past everyone's bedtime.

Charlie knew there was a little paved lane that ran along the backs of the houses. Here, the wooden fences were all very high, preserving their owners' privacy. She located Betty's gate, and, standing on her toes, reached over its top to release the latch on the other side. She let herself into the garden, then shut the gate, making sure it was firmly latched behind her.

It appeared that the sound of the gate had woken Betty up; she peered out of the shelter's entrance, shining her torch in Charlie's face.

"Oh!" she exclaimed. "It's you! I wondered where you'd got to. What on earth's happened? And where's your friend, Mr. Deeley?"

CHAPTER FIFTEEN

Shaun inserted his ticket in the automatic gate at the top of the escalators at Balham, and the barricades parted to allow him through.

He congratulated himself on this further accomplishment, and then took himself to task for dwelling upon the triviality of such matters. It was only the fact that he had dealt with the entire journey by himself, without the assistance of Mrs. Collins, which made it remarkable. Nevertheless, as he climbed the steps to the street, he made a note in his mind to mention his achievement as soon as he located her.

It was a short walk to Harris Road. He passed the shop that Betty's father had owned, where the fellow who called himself Thaddeus had been employed. It was still a greengrocer, but now it also sold bus passes and travel cards, newspapers, magazines, a book containing historical photographs of Balham, confectioneries, and tins of things, all on display through its large window.

Shaun's footsteps were almost jaunty as he approached Betty's little terraced house. He opened the gate and walked up the path. Then he lifted the brass knocker on the green front door and let it drop against the mail slot.

Mrs. Collins's aunt Wendy opened the door. Shaun recognized her from the Friday before, when he had met her for the first time after Mrs. Collins's grandmother's funeral. He'd thought, at the time, that she was remarkably youthful for someone who had been born seventy years earlier. Indeed, both Jackie—who was Mrs. Collins's mother, and who was seventy-two years old—and Wendy herself could easily have passed for women who were much, much younger.

"Yes?" Wendy said.

"Mrs. Weller."

"Yes?"

"Do you not remember me?"

"No," she said. "Sorry. Should I?"

"But I am Shaun Deeley. Surely you recall our introduction. I live in the cottage in Stoneford with Charlotte."

"I'm terribly sorry," Wendy said, "but I don't know anyone named Charlotte. And which cottage in Stoneford?"

How could this be?

Shaun tried again.

"Your niece is Charlotte," he said. "She is the youngest daughter of your sister, Jackie. She was married to Jeffrey Lowe. He died in a traffic accident. Charlotte lives in the cottage where she grew up. She owns it now. Her parents left it to her when they moved away to Portugal."

Wendy Weller shook her head.

"I really am terribly sorry," she said, "but I don't know anyone named Charlotte, and I don't know anyone named Jackie. And I have no idea who you are. My son Nick lives in Stoneford, but that's as far as my family connection goes. And I'm in the midst of a bereavement. My mother has died. I really must get on…"

She tried to close the door, but Shaun stopped her.

"Wait," he said, "please. I beg of you. Charlotte Duran. You must know the name."

Wendy paused. "Charlotte Duran…?"

"Charlotte Duran," Shaun repeated.

"Yes…" Wendy replied thoughtfully. "Yes… I think I do know the name. Perhaps you'd better come inside."

• • •

The sitting room of Nana Betty's house was dark and cool, and filled with glass-fronted cabinets that held collections of china and silverware, and stockpiles of magazines. A very ancient television, which looked nothing like the enormous flat screen Mrs. Collins had installed in her own sitting room, stood in one corner. Shaun only recognized what it was because he'd watched old films. An upright piano leaned against the wall, and on top of it were piled even more magazines, and books, and newspapers, which reminded him of Mrs. Collins's propensity for collecting items which had long outlived their usefulness.

He had not entered this room on Friday. Instead, he and Mrs. Collins had been ushered into the dining room next door, and from there they had sought solitude outside in the garden.

"Sit here," Wendy suggested, indicating a sofa covered with a pattern of green leaves and red roses. "I'll see if there's some tea left."

She left him alone for a few minutes, and he took off his overcoat, easing the sleeve down over his left arm, which, he noted, had begun to bleed again. He pulled off the paper towels and examined the cut, unable to fathom how he had received it.

Wendy returned from the kitchen, carrying a tray with a teapot and two cups, milk in a jug, and sugar in a bowl.

"Here we are," she said, placing it on a low table in front of the sofa. She saw Shaun's arm, and the little wad of blood-soaked paper he was holding. "What's happened there?"

"In truth," Shaun said, "I do not know. I have no memory of receiving this wound at all."

"Let's have a look."

She switched on a light beside the sofa, and sat down beside him.

"What did you say your name was?"

"My name is Shaun Deeley."

"I trained as a nurse, Mr. Deeley. And this looks very much like a cut from a knife. You really ought to see a doctor."

"Might we not just bandage it, and avoid a complexity I fear I may not be able to explain?"

"Very well," Wendy said. "I think there might be something upstairs in the medicine cabinet. But if that gets infected and you come down with tetanus, I won't be held responsible."

The wound in his arm thus washed, disinfected, and dressed with white gauze held in place by strips of adhesive tape, Shaun at last turned his attention to the tea which Wendy had brought in from the kitchen.

"Milk and sugar, Mr. Deeley?"

"Yes, please."

Wendy added both before giving the cup to Shaun. Then she reached into the pocket of her cardigan and took out a little blue booklet. Frayed and faded though it was, Shaun recognized it instantly.

It was the booklet that Betty Singleton had written upon with her pencil. *War-Time Cookery to Save Fuel and Food Value.*

"My mum died last week. Her funeral was Friday, in fact. I live in Croydon but I looked in on her every day while she was alive. I've just been going through her things. I was emptying one of the drawers in the other room and I found this. Mum's written something on the back. *Charlotte Duran says I am going to have a little girl. And I will name her Jackie. And a sister for Jackie, and I'm going to call her Wendy.*"

"*And,*" Shaun finished, "*she says my house will not be bombed.*"

Wendy stared at him.

"Yes," she said slowly. "And she's put the date on it. October the 11th, 1940. How did you know that, Mr. Deeley?"

Shaun drank his tea without comment.

"I'll show you something else, then."

She gave him a large brown envelope, which she'd carried into the room with the tea tray.

"When I was going through the other drawers in the sideboard, I found that. Mum had paid for the funeral of a young woman who'd perished in 1940. And then she'd paid for her burial plot, and her headstone, and for the ongoing maintenance of her grave. All through the years, up until now, she made sure the payments continued and the grave was tended. Look at the name of the young woman."

• • •

It was the end of time.

It was the end of life itself.

Shaun sat in the passenger seat of Wendy's car. Numb. Not believing.

But it was there in plain writing. Inside the brown envelope were the documents. And a photograph of the headstone, and the number of the plot, so that it could easily be located in the graveyard.

This was where Wendy was taking him now, in her car. The same cemetery he had visited with Mrs. Collins on Friday.

A lifetime ago.

As Shaun sat in the car, staring out of the window at the buildings and buses, it was obvious to him that something had happened to cause a rift in reality. That was the only term he could think of to describe his circumstances. It *was* the present, but not the present he had inhabited before. There could be no other explanation.

He recalled the journey he had undertaken with Mrs. Collins, the one that had brought them both to that time and place. He had abandoned 1825—and certain death for both of them—cradling her in his arms in the pouring rain. He recalled the anguish he had felt at the thought of losing her. And the terror that had accompanied the lightning and thunder, the massive surge of something that had transported both of them, together, from then to now.

And the horrible hours in the hospital after that, when it was not known whether she would ever wake up.

And then…his relief when she had at last opened her eyes. Unaware of where she was—and in what time—she had seen him, and asked, "Are you here… or are you there…?"

And his response, accompanied by a tender and reassuring kiss: "I am here."

In the solid reliability of *here*, he had found shelter and love in her little cottage. His life had been protected in her village by the sea.

I am here.

Suddenly, *here* had become unreliable.

Suddenly, he was lost and alone, and without the knowledge needed to mend the tear in the fabric of time.

"Did your sister not marry a gentleman whose last name is Duran?" Shaun asked, trying again to make sense of what this *here* consisted of.

"I haven't got a sister," Wendy replied. "There is only me."

"But you married Toby Weller. And you have a son, whose name is Nicholas."

"Yes, that's right. And a daughter. Julie."

"And another daughter? Natasha?"

"No," said Wendy. "Just the two. Julie's a TV producer and Nick's a physicist. He lectures at Wandsworth University. And spends his in-between times in Stoneford."

Shaun didn't say anything. Mrs. Collins, who had apparently died in 1940, was the daughter of Wendy's sister, who apparently had never existed. How was it possible?

"Here we are, then," Wendy said, driving the car into a place where they could get out and walk.

"What of your father?" Shaun asked, as they made their way along the paved cemetery road. "What is his name?"

"His name was Peter Lewis," Wendy replied. "He passed away in 1970."

That, at least, had not changed.

They located the grave, using a map from the cemetery office.

"Here we are. Not so difficult to find."

Shaun read the inscription on the little weather-beaten marker.

In Loving Memory
Charlotte Duran
14th October 1940

Carved into stone. Indisputable.

Shaun looked for somewhere to sit and located a bench beneath a tree. As he sank down onto its slatted wood seat, he realized this was exactly the same bench, in exactly the same spot, where he had discovered Mrs. Collins on Friday, contemplating the grave of Thaddeus Quinn.

In fact, the grave marker was exactly the same, but for the name.

How could this be, if she had never existed?

Shaun stared at the ground, trying to work out the logic.

"I'm going to tell you something my mum told me a very long time ago," Wendy said, joining him on the bench. "She didn't like to speak of it, I think… perhaps because it brought back too many bad memories from the war. But I could always coax things out of her with a little neat Scotch."

She smiled, remembering.

"Before I was born… before she was married to my dad, my mum was seeing someone named Thaddeus Quinn. And she fell pregnant. But something happened to him… and to her… and she wouldn't tell me what. And there was a young woman who was visiting her when she was six months along. A friend she'd grown very fond of. And this young woman died. And something caused Mum to miscarry the baby. They didn't have the medical knowledge back then to save very premature infants. So the baby was lost. She would have been my older sister."

"Jackie," Mr. Deeley said, staring at the little gravestone.

"Perhaps. Yes. If we're to believe the note on the cooking pamphlet. And the young woman who died… she never told me her name. But it must have been Charlotte Duran. It all makes sense now."

Shaun digested this. "It does," he agreed.

"A few years ago I decided to do some research on the fellow my mum had been seeing. I had a subscription to one of those family tree sites. I think it's lapsed now. It turned out to be far more work than I thought. I asked Mum for his full name, and she said it was Thaddeus Oliver Quinn. I tried to find Thaddeus Oliver Quinn, and I couldn't. So, just on a whim, I put in a general search, for any year. And then I found the record of his christening. June, 1816. Thaddeus Oliver Quinn. St. Eligius Church, Stoneford. And I found him again in the first English census, in 1841. There he was, living in

Middlehurst. And then, by the time of the second census, in 1851, he was gone. The only Thaddeus Oliver Quinn in existence. Ever. The thing is, I mentioned that to my mum. About how strange it was. And she refused to believe it. She said he was certainly born in Stoneford, and had certainly grown up in Middlehurst. But he was thirty-three years old when she'd met him in 1939. And he'd had his thirty-fourth birthday in June 1940. I suggested that perhaps he wasn't who he'd claimed to be, and that he'd borrowed Thaddeus Quinn's name because he had something to hide. Perhaps he was a criminal, on the run from the law. But she refused to discuss it further."

She paused.

"Do you know anything about Thaddeus Oliver Quinn, Mr. Deeley?"

Shaun thought very carefully before he replied.

"I do," he said. "But first, I will tell you the date of my own birth. It's the 12th of November, 1791. Is this possible for you to understand and accept?"

"The 12th of November," Wendy repeated. "1791. But that would make you more than 200 years old."

"It would," Shaun admitted, "if I had inhabited all of the intervening years, and my life had followed its natural progression. And if I had also somehow managed to circumvent the law of nature, which dictates that we rarely survive beyond our hundredth year. In truth, I will celebrate my own thirty-fourth birthday next month."

Wendy looked at him. And then she stood up. "You're having me on, aren't you? All this business about knowing Charlotte Duran and what my mum wrote on the back of a pamphlet and the sister I never had… who's put you up to this? Nick?"

Shaun shook his head. "I have told you only what I know to be the truth."

"I'm going to strangle him. And so soon after Mum's death. I don't suppose he thought his practical joke would be in such poor taste. You can tell him that, for me."

"Your son has had nothing to do with this," Shaun said, also getting to his feet. "Please believe me."

"How? How can you be more than 200 years old? And how did you end up here, now?"

"A consequence of an oddity in logic and time," Shaun said. "An accidental incident."

"You'll have to do better than that. I know all about Time Lords and TARDISs, in spite of what Nick thinks about my television viewing habits. And how could you know Charlotte Duran?"

"Charlotte is... was... a traveller in time, like myself. She was accidentally sent back to 1825, where she met me. We fell in love. And then she became desperately ill, and it was imperative that she returned, or she would die. It was your son who engineered this, harnessing his computer to the forces of nature. I could not bear the thought of Charlotte leaving me, and so I made the decision to go with her. And then, together, we travelled in time again... to 1940. Which is where she apparently died. And then I travelled again, to the time we are in now. That is why I am here. You may choose to believe me, or to discard my story as fantastical nonsense. But I have no other explanation to offer."

"So if I were to ask Nick about this, he'd say the same thing? He'd know who you were, and he'd confirm what you've just told me about his computer and 1825 and this woman named Charlotte?"

"Yes," Shaun said. "Of course."

He paused, reminding himself that this was not the present that he was accustomed to.

"Perhaps not," he decided, after a moment.

"Yes," said Wendy. "Perhaps not. Thought you might say that. I don't know whether to laugh or cry. You certainly spin a good tale."

"Can you not accept that what I have told you is the truth?" Shaun asked, unhappily, looking again at the little stone marker, his heart filling with despair. "In the time and place that I have come from, Charlotte's year of birth is 1979. She is your niece. And her mother is your sister, Jackie, who was never born. "

"The same Jackie that Mum wrote about on the back of the cooking pamphlet."

"The very same. And the very same Charlotte."

"I don't know who you really are," Wendy said, "and I don't know what you think you're going to accomplish by showing up like this, out of the blue, with your unbelievable story. If you're thinking you might try to extort some money by claiming to be a long lost relative, you've got another thing coming. I'm going to leave you here, Mr. Deeley. And I don't expect to see you again. Goodbye."

And she walked away, leaving Shaun standing alone beside Mrs. Collins's grave, unable to bring himself to run after her, to remonstrate his innocence.

Nothing he might say or do was likely to cause her to change her mind.

He shook his head, as if doing so would cause him to wake up from this horrible, horrible dream.

But nothing changed.

And if he was asleep, then the nightmare was unceasing.

CHAPTER SIXTEEN

It was morning. And it was very cold. Charlie shivered under the blanket and the eiderdown and her winter coat, which she'd dragged over her shoulders in the middle of the night. At home, in Stoneford, her eighteenth-century cottage had been modernized with hot-water heating throughout. On freezing winter mornings, she woke up to warm rooms and warm floors and warm feet.

There was no hot-water heater in Betty Singleton's little house on Harris Road. There were fireplaces, but the only two that appeared to be in regular use were downstairs, in the sitting room and the dining room. And in Betty Singleton's big front bedroom, there was no glass in the windows. The boards that had been nailed over the empty frames were excellent for keeping out the morning light, and even better at letting in the chilly morning damp.

Charlie lay in bed, dreading getting up and making herself even colder. Her feet were freezing, in spite of the two pairs of socks she'd put on, foraged from Bert Singleton's collection in the bottom drawer of the dressing table.

And then the realization that Mr. Deeley was no longer alive came back to her like a thick, suffocating fog. For a brief moment, just now, upon waking, that knowledge had been absent; her mind had been clear and her memories unencumbered. And then, the horrible truth had descended. Nothing was ever going to be the same again.

Outside the boarded-up windows, she could hear morning sounds. London waking up and carrying on. Motor cars. Gates clicking shut. People chatting with one another on the pavement.

There ought to be church bells, she thought. It was Sunday

morning, and the church at the end of the road ought to have been calling people to come in and pray.

And then she remembered that during the war, all of the country's church bells were silenced, to be rung only in the event of an invasion by German forces.

She crawled out of bed at last and looked outside through a gap in the boards. It was a grey, misty day. The kind of day she'd have loved, if she'd been at home in Stoneford. And if....

And if....

If only.

She'd travelled in time twice before, and each of those journeys, like now, had been accidental. Or, at least, beyond her ability to influence and control. And at the end of each journey, she'd been returned to her own time and place as if nothing at all had happened.

Perhaps there was a mechanism, something she had yet to learn about.

Perhaps there was a way to get back home.

On the night she and Mr. Deeley had arrived, Betty had said her next-door neighbour, Ruby, had been expecting them. Ruby was the name of the woman who had visited the museum's Blitz Display, and given her the piece of shrapnel on the station platform at Middlehurst.

Ruby Firth. Who was due home today from Basingstoke.

Charlie put her winter coat on over her nightgown and went downstairs.

• • •

Breakfast was porridge with a little milk, and tea, and was notable for the absence of Betty's lodger.

Charlie was relieved. She'd been dreading seeing him again. She found herself wishing, rather uncharitably, that he would stay away permanently. She huddled in her winter coat, focusing on her spoon and her bowl and the porridge, hoping Betty assumed her numbness to be the result of Mr. Deeley's death.

The numbness was real. She couldn't think, couldn't function. Even recalling what she'd seen last night at Strand Station, after opening Silas Ferryman's suitcase, was an ordeal. She knew she had to tell Betty about it. She knew she had to tell the police. She or Betty could be this man's next victim. But she was unable to summon the strength.

"It's not like him not to ring," Betty said, staring out through the blast-taped windows into the garden. "I didn't see him at all yesterday, or last night. He said he had some business in London. I just hope..."

She stopped.

"I mustn't. It would be too dreadful to contemplate. And here's you, and your poor Mr. Deeley. I'm so sorry, Charlotte."

Charlie raised her head to acknowledge Betty's kindness, but said nothing.

"I'm so glad you got back safely. I went out earlier to see if Thad was about and I ran into Mrs. Lane from down the road. Her husband's a policeman, and she told me another young woman was discovered dead last night. Her throat had been slashed. She was found near the British Museum, on a bomb site. Just like poor Angela Bailey."

Charlie went cold.

"I'll fetch the Sunday papers later. Perhaps it'll be in there."

Charlie continued to eat her porridge in silence, while Betty took an envelope out of her apron pocket.

"I've had a letter," she said. "From Pete. It came in yesterday's post. I haven't seen him since the summer."

Charlie raised her head again.

"He wants to marry me," Betty said, hopelessly, looking at Charlie. "What am I to do?"

• • •

Charlie let the knocker drop on the neighbour's door and waited.

"Coming! Coming!"

The door opened, and Charlie immediately recognized the full-moon face, the very red cheeks and the bowl haircut of Ruby Firth. And, astoundingly, she looked exactly the same as she had when Charlie had first seen her at the museum, and later, on the Middlehurst station platform.

"It *is* you," she whispered.

"It is, it is," Ruby replied. "And I'm so terribly sorry for not being here on Friday. Called away on an urgent mission. But it's all worked out for the best, hasn't it? Do come in."

She stood aside to let Charlie enter, and then shut the door behind her.

"I'm a bit at sixes and sevens today, I'm afraid. Got home to discover Mrs. Crofton's been bombed out and all my front windows smashed by the blast. I've been trying to arrange for someone to come round and mend them, but of course everyone's in the same boat. And I'm confounded by this recipe for potato macaroni pudding."

She held up a slip of paper that looked like it had been printed by the government.

"I might be good at time travelling but I'm a ruddy poor excuse for a cook."

Charlie followed her into the kitchen, where she lit the gas and placed a kettle on the ring for tea, and then into the dining room, which was laid out exactly the same way as Betty's, but all in reverse.

"And, actually, that's not even true. I'm a ruddy poor excuse for a time traveller as well. Still only displaying my L plates, truth be known. Haven't quite passed my competency test. Jolly nice to see you again, by the way. Everything all right? Aside from bombs dropping in the middle of the night?"

Charlie sank down in an armchair to one side of the fireplace.

"No," she whispered. "Nothing's all right at all, Ruby. I've lost Mr. Deeley. He was killed yesterday. In an air raid."

Ruby sat down in an armchair that was the twin of Charlie's, on the opposite side of the fireplace.

"I'm so terribly sorry," she said, leaning forward, her eyes bright.

"Why am I here?"

"Because you're a time traveller, my dear. You have it in your blood. It's inescapable."

"But why this place? Why now?"

"I shall give you the only answer I can. You were always going to come here. Nothing in the world could prevent it. And whatever you undertake while you are here, was always meant to be undertaken. There. Does that answer your question?"

Charlie contemplated the fireplace, which Ruby had swept clean, and which awaited its next instalment of coal.

"No," she said miserably. "Why have I come all this way, only to have Mr. Deeley die? Was that always meant to be?"

"I think not," Ruby answered. She paused. "Are you absolutely positive he's dead?"

"Of course I'm bloody positive!" Charlie answered, her voice filling with anger. "I was there. I touched him. I saw them carry his body away."

She stared into Ruby's back garden, which, like Betty's, had been taken over by rows of vegetables and had an Anderson shelter dug into the ground at its bottom end.

"Why did you come and visit me at the museum, Ruby? And why did you give me that piece of shrapnel?"

"Truth be known, Charlotte, I'm a terrible busybody. I do love poking my nose into places where it really shouldn't be poked. I was impatient. I knew you were going to arrive. I wanted to meet you, in your own time, before you got here. And the shrapnel was a gift. Nothing more, nothing less."

"Well. I hope you were amused. Here I am. Now what? And how did you know I was going to arrive?"

"I belong to a group," Ruby replied. "A circle of travellers. All with different levels of accomplishments and skills. Some tour the realities. Others hop over the years. Some manage both, which is a very special talent indeed. And we've all taken an oath not to interfere with anything that might have a profound effect on anything else. So we tend to tread very carefully. But we have regular meetings, you see, and we discuss things, especially things which affect us personally."

The kettle let off a shrill whistle.

"Back in half a mo'," Ruby promised, disappearing into the kitchen.

She returned with the teapot, and two cups and saucers, and a little milk and sugar, and a packet of Jaffa Cakes. The Jaffa Cakes, in fact, looked rather familiar to Charlie.

"Where did you get these? You can't get them on your ration book, can you?"

"I was going to pop into a shop when I visited you in Stoneford," Ruby said, confidentially, "but then I discovered, much to my horror, that I didn't have the right kind of money. So I asked a very good friend who frequents your time to bring me some instead. I'm quite addicted to them. We shan't tell Betty as she doesn't know about my time travelling."

"And you belong to a group...?" Charlie said. "And you discuss things that affect you personally...?"

"Yes. And last month we had a new fellow join us. He claimed he was an accidental traveller—someone who's ended up in another time, either because of something that happened beyond their control, or because of something someone else did."

"Much like myself," Charlie said. "And Mr. Deeley."

"Quite. Well, my friend, Mr. Jaffa Cakes, first spotted this fellow during one of his excursions back to see me. He's a jolly bloke, really, Mr. Jaffa Cakes, frightfully good at identifying people like us in a crowd. They got talking, and one thing led to another, and my friend brought him along to one of our meetings. And that was when this new fellow introduced himself as Thaddeus Quinn."

"Not Betty's lodger."

"Very much not Betty's lodger. I was astonished, as he had the same name as the fellow, and I told him so. He seemed frightfully surprised, and engaged me in a conversation during which we talked quite a lot about the other Thaddeus Quinn. And when I told him where Betty's lodger was to be found, he couldn't thank me enough. And he then went on to tell me that the fellow was, in fact, a completely unsavoury character named Silas Ferryman who had cut his wife's throat and robbed his father-in-law, and was suspected of being someone called the Middlehurst Slasher."

"So that's how he knew where Silas Ferryman was. He told us he'd only recently been able to find him. He got the information from you."

"Oh! Then you've met him."

"Yesterday," Charlie said. "He invited us for lunch at his hotel in London. That's why we were there. That's why…."

She stopped. If they hadn't met him after Mrs. Crofton's house was bombed… if they hadn't gone up to London… Mr. Deeley would still be alive.

"So, what do you think, Charlotte? Which one's which?"

"Don't you know?"

"Have a Jaffa Cake," Ruby suggested, instead of answering.

Charlie took one from the package, but she wasn't really hungry. "Thaddeus Quinn—whoever he is—will be killed tomorrow night in an air raid."

"Will he?" Ruby mused, pouring milk into their teacups, followed by strong tea from the pot. "Sugar?"

"Yes please. And yes, he will be."

Ruby gave one of the cups a stir, and passed it over to Charlie.

"How do you know he's going to be killed?"

"Because I saw his grave. In the present. My present. Seventy-three years from now. His headstone says he was killed by enemy action on October the 14th, 1940. And I'll tell you what else I know. A bomb is going to drop on Balham tube station tomorrow night at two minutes past eight, and it's going to kill and injure quite a lot of people. And that's where he's going to die."

"Indeed."

"You don't sound very surprised."

"When I first learned about what was going to happen, of course I was terribly upset. The thought of all those mums and dads and little children. We discussed it in our circle, you see. Those who have come to visit us from the future brought it into the conversation. It is all so terribly tragic."

"And even if you know what's going to happen, you won't do anything to prevent people from dying…?"

Ruby shook her head. "We cannot. We've taken the oath."

"Not even if it was someone you knew? Or someone related to you?"

Ruby looked at her. "It can be a terrible thing to have our kind of knowledge, Charlotte. And if supposing… just supposing… we were to interfere… and it all went wrong, we would be left to deal with the consequences, wouldn't we?"

Charlie didn't say anything.

"For instance," Ruby said, "how do you know which fellow is buried in the grave you saw? Is it Betty's lodger… or is it the gentleman you had lunch with in London?"

"Do you know?"

"If I did, I wouldn't tell you. I couldn't."

Charlie stared at the empty fireplace. Ruby's answers annoyed her. But what she was saying was true. If everyone who had advance knowledge acted upon it, the world would erupt into chaos.

"So," Charlie reasoned, "if I take any kind of action to try and prevent Thaddeus—whoever he is—from going down into the tube station tomorrow night, then I'll be guilty of interfering. And I'll be responsible for everything that follows on from that interference. Correct?"

Ruby said nothing, drinking her tea in silence.

"And yet, you've just told me that I was expected here. And that whatever I do while I'm here, I was always meant to do. Also correct?"

"Maddeningly so, but yes," Ruby relented. "And because of that, you must consider your choices carefully, and make your decisions wisely. And you must always remember the Overarching Philosophy. It may be that you were always destined to cause something to happen. Or it may be that you will change the outcome of something. But, perhaps, the outcome of something was never in question at all, merely the means by which it is achieved."

"That's what happened the other night, when the bomb dropped on Mrs. Crofton's house. Mr. Deeley helped to dig out her two children. I told him he'd changed history by saving their lives."

"Or," said Ruby, "perhaps it was always intended that he would rescue them. Or you might have been right, and he did alter history. Or, their lives were always going to be saved—it was just a matter of who came along to do it."

"The Overarching Philosophy," Charlie repeated.

"Yes, We have it written on a board sitting at the front of the room whenever we convene."

Charlie had a thought. "Did your fair-haired gentleman take part in any of your conversations about Balham? Does he know?"

"He does not know. Our discussions took place before he was introduced to the group."

"Then I don't know what I'm supposed to do. I still don't know why I'm here. All I really want to do is go home, Ruby. Back to my life before all of this happened. Back to when Mr. Deeley was still alive. And I don't know how to do it. This is my third time-travelling journey… and each one has been accidental. None of them has had anything to do with what I wanted."

Ruby leaned forward. "Perhaps that's what you think, Charlotte. But in fact, you have more to do with it than you know. A one-time occurrence is accidental. If it happens more than once… then there's something else at work. As for three times…. Well, you've got the touch, as Mr. Jaffa Cakes would say. You've got the means inside you. All you've got to do is learn how to harness it. It's taken me ages to learn how to master mine. And I still haven't quite got the hang of it."

"Then tell me how I can get back to Stoneford, Ruby."

"It's different for each of us, my dear. And you cannot go home now. That I must tell you. You must play your part first. But afterwards… perhaps my friend Mr. Jaffa Cakes will be able to help."

142

Ruby got up and hunted around in a stack of papers on top of the mantle, and then handed something to Charlie: a business card.

"Here you are. He's often to be found at Waterloo Station in your time. But he's here almost as frequently. I'm sure he'll be popping in again very soon. And when he does put in an appearance, I shall introduce you."

Charlie looked at the card.

Fenwick Oldbutter. Busker. Musician. Composer. Contemporary Arrangements. Historical Time Pieces.

At the bottom of the card was a phone number and an e-mail address.

"Oldbutter," she said. "There's an Oldbutter and Ballcock in Stoneford in my time." She paused. "They arrange funerals."

They were interrupted by a *rat-tat-tat* at Ruby's front door. Ruby went to answer it.

"Oh!" Charlie heard her say. "Hello. Speak of the devil. We've been discussing you."

Charlie got up, expecting Fenwick Oldbutter. Or Thaddeus Quinn. She peeked around the dining room door.

It was neither Fenwick Oldbutter, nor Thaddeus Quinn.

Her heart leaped when she saw who was standing in the front hallway, his hands jammed into his coat pockets, looking for all the world like someone who'd just popped round for tea.

"Hello," he said, spying Charlie. "Betty suggested I should find you here."

"Mr. Deeley!" Charlie sobbed, running out of the dining room, throwing her arms around him.

CHAPTER SEVENTEEN

Not knowing what else he could do, or where else he could go, Shaun had walked the several miles back to Betty's house, following the same route Wendy had taken when she had driven him to the graveyard. He stood now with one hand on the front gate, debating his next course of action. Night had fallen, and the streetlights had been switched on. Yet he could not see any illumination shining through the windows of the house, in spite of the curtains being open. And Wendy's car was not in evidence on the road.

Shaun opened the gate and walked up the path, then let the knocker drop upon the front door, three times.

There was no response.

He supposed Wendy must have returned to her own house, in Croydon.

Betty's front door was similar to the front door of Mrs. Collins's cottage in Stoneford. It had no exterior handle. A key was turned in the lock, which released a mechanism, allowing the door to open inward.

Shaun gave the door a perfunctory push. Locked tight. Of course.

He stood on the path, battling weariness. What he required, most urgently, was a place to sleep. And in the morning, with a fresh mind, he would try and sort out what to do next.

He wondered if, in this altered present, Betty still had an air raid shelter at the bottom of her garden. It would be damp and cold, but better than nothing at all.

He remembered, in the other present, seeing a gate in the high wooden fence behind the shelter. That meant there had to be access behind the garden.

Walking to the end of the block, he turned right, and then walked a little farther, until he discovered a small, unlit lane. Trudging along in the dark, he counted gates, finally arriving at the one he determined belonged to Betty. The latch was on the inside. Reaching over, he released it, and was admitted to a garden not unlike the one he remembered from before.

He could just see, in the darkness, an area with paving stones and large fired clay flowerpots. And a patch of lawn, and a path made out of more paving stones. And, nearly hidden beneath an overgrowth of ivy, a shelter.

Common sense told him he should try the garden and kitchen doors of the house first, in case Wendy had neglected to lock them. But she had not forgotten. The house was inaccessible. And Shaun was not of a mind to break a window, lest he be arrested as a thief. He had once been accused, and very nearly been convicted of, a hanging offence. He had no wish to commit a serious crime now.

He walked back to the Anderson shelter and, remembering the Swan Vestas in the pocket of his trousers, took one out, and struck it against the side of the box, the way Mrs. Collins had shown him.

From the outside, the shelter seemed no different.

But standing just inside its half-buried entrance, allowing the flame to burn down to his fingers and then striking another, and another and another, Shaun realized that the inside was very different indeed.

A little staircase had been constructed, containing four steps and a handrail, creating an easy way down from the garden. The whole of the shelter's corrugated walls and ceiling within had been given a coat of white paint. And a carpet lay upon the floor. A rug of oriental origin, Shaun guessed, recognizing a very old Persian pattern he had once seen in Edwin Watts's shop, Antiques Olde and New, in Stoneford.

Upon the back wall of the shelter hung a photograph of a smiling, grey-haired woman wearing a crown and a blue satin sash, and, standing beside her, an elderly gentleman, very tall, wearing a military uniform. The current Queen of England, Shaun remembered, and her consort. The Queen was called Elizabeth, but the prince's name escaped him. He made a mental note to look it up on Mrs. Collins's iPad later… and then corrected himself.

In this time and place, Mrs. Collins no longer existed.

He forced himself to concentrate, pushing to the back of his mind the unreality of a life without her. He was inhabiting this time and place temporarily. He *would* find a way to return to her.

Underneath the framed photograph of Queen Elizabeth was a well-worn armchair, with a cushion, and in front of it, a matching hassock which, he assumed, had given comfort to Betty's feet, allowing her to raise them up from the draughts upon the floor.

Beside the armchair was a small table, upon which were a stack of books and a lamp. Curiously, Shaun tried the switch, and was surprised when it came on. This shelter had been provided with the means for electricity.

He extinguished his match.

Sitting in the armchair, he saw that what Betty had created for herself was a private room, completely separate from her house: a place of contemplation and peace. There was a little bookcase, and its shelves were crammed with all sorts of books and magazines. On top of the bookcase sat the very old device which, in 1940, had provided the music that Betty had been dancing to when he and Mrs. Collins had first arrived.

Beside the bookshelves were a small electrical heater and a chest, and on top of the chest sat a smaller case, which, oddly, seemed familiar to Shaun. He had no idea why. He was positive he had never seen it before.

He got up from the armchair to investigate.

The suitcase was made of some sort of stiffened board, dyed black, with brown leather reinforcements along its edges and corners. It had a brown leather handle, and two latches with locks and leather straps to help keep it securely closed.

Curiously, Shaun unbuckled the straps, then tried the first

latch. It was rusty and stiff, but not locked, and after considerable manipulation, he was able to slide the lock piece sideways and release the mechanism. He applied the same diligence to the second latch, and then lifted the lid.

It was clear the case had not been opened in many years. It smelled of damp and mildew. But the two objects that were inside had been preserved from the elements, and so were virtually untouched.

The first object was a small yellow and black box bearing the legend: *Made in Great Britain. A Kodak Camera. Popular Brownie.*

Mrs. Collins had told Shaun about photography. She had special books that she kept in a cupboard in their cottage in Stoneford, filled with little paper pictures from her childhood. She had explained about film, and had shown him the strips of plastic that contained the opposite images from the ones on the paper. She had shown him the device she had called a camera, too, and had taken it apart to explain how it worked, in the time before people were able to capture pictures on their phones.

The device inside the box did not resemble the camera Mrs. Collins had shown him in any way, shape, or form.

This device was shaped like the box which contained it. It had little glass windows embedded on its front and side, and seemed to be made of some kind of heavy cardboard covered with a fabric resembling leather. It was not leather, however; Shaun knew the difference.

He put the yellow and black box aside, and considered the second article.

This was a cardboard container that he recognized as the receptacle for a wartime gas mask. He had seen them before, in the Blitz display at Stoneford Museum, and again in the restaurant at the hotel where he and Mrs. Collins had eaten lunch, tucked under tables and beside chairs.

Assuming he would find a similar gas mask within, Shaun was surprised when he opened the lid. Inside was a collection of objects, none of which had the slightest thing in common with gas masks.

The first of these objects was a bracelet, constructed of pieces of coloured agate—terra cotta, black, mossy green, charcoal, bisque pink—shaped and polished and joined with silver links.

The second was a ring, of plain silver.

The third….

Shaun stopped, and stared.

The third item was a locket, the kind that might be worn on the end of a chain.

He lifted it out of the box, wondering if he might be mistaken. No. There was no mistake.

It was an oval pinchbeck locket, made to hold a miniature portrait, or a cutting of hair. Its outside case was exquisitely detailed.

He coaxed it open, holding his breath.

The locket had cost him a fortune, but his love had known no bounds. He had given it to Jemima for her twenty-first birthday. Inside, behind the oval of glass, he had included strands of his own hair, a keepsake to which he hoped Jemima might add a snippet of her own.

Three months later, she had forsaken him, and had, instead, chosen Cornelius Quinn.

Shaun had supposed the locket had been discarded, as he had never set eyes on it again. Yet here it was. He knew it was the same locket, because on the back he had arranged to have their initials engraved. *SPD and JEB.*

The initials were still there, testimony to his undying love.

Shaun stared at the little collection of jewellery he had placed upon the Persian carpet, and remembered the conversation he had held with Mrs. Collins, when they were travelling to London aboard the train. The subject of their conversation had been the Middlehurst Slasher. He mined his memory to recall the names of the three unfortunate women. Annie Black… Mary Potter… and Matilda Ferryman.

He investigated further, and discovered a very old folded piece of newspaper. He opened it with care.

The story was immediately familiar to him. It was the unhappy tale of Angela Bailey, who had lived on the same road as Betty in

1940, whose body had been discovered in the rubble left by a bomb just before he and Mrs. Collins had arrived. According to Miss Bailey's mother, she had been wearing a brooch, made of gold, with three small flowers.

Shaun looked in the box. There it was.

And there was a second newspaper story. It concerned the disappearance of Miss Deirdre Allsop, who worked in a sweet shop in Balham and lived with her invalid aunt. Miss Allsop's body was discovered upon Mitcham Common earlier in the year, in August. Her throat had been cut, and her earrings, which she had borrowed from her aunt, had been taken.

Shaun looked once more in the box, and found the earrings. They were not the sort of earrings that women wore in the present, which were poked through holes in the earlobes, the very thought of which made Shaun feel quite unwell. These were the sort of earrings that he had seen for sale in Antiques Olde and New, which were fixed to the ears by means of tiny clasps.

Shaun put everything back inside the gas mask box and closed the lid, and then placed it back inside the suitcase.

How had this case come into the possession of Mrs. Collins's grandmother?

Shaun considered the possibilities, and arrived at the only conclusion which made sense. If, indeed, Silas Ferryman was the Middlehurst Slasher, then the case must have belonged to him. The dark-haired gentleman who was Betty Singleton's lodger.

He placed the suitcase beside the armchair and arranged the pillow so that it would afford him the most comfort for the night. He dragged the hassock under his legs and feet. He switched on the small electrical heater, then took off his long black overcoat and placed it over himself. He turned off the lamp.

He was exhausted, but his mind was at odds with sleep.

From his birth until now, he had never been alone.

He had been born in a little house in Christchurch, and had lived there with his mother and father and six brothers and sisters until his father, made redundant by the untimely death of his aged employer, had found work as head groom at Monsieur Duran's manor in Stoneford. Shaun's entire family had packed up its belongings and moved ten miles to the east to accommodate the arrangement. And after his father had died—the unfortunate recipient of a horse's hoof to the head—Shaun had taken over his position, moving into a room of his own in the manor's servants' quarters, surrounded by maids and a butler, a cook, and a gardener.

He had willingly left them all behind when he had taken up residence in Mrs. Collins's cottage, within sight of the manor, but separated by nearly 200 years.

She had become his family. She was his reason for being.

Here and now, and for the very first time in his life, there was no one who cared whether he came or went, or lived or died.

Here and now, if he were to take the train to Stoneford, and if Mrs. Collins's cottage even existed, he would find other people in residence, and no trace at all of the woman he adored.

Shaun's mind tumbled with questions: what had happened to cause him to wake up in this different future? And when?

Had it occurred in those forgotten moments between the time that the bomb had dropped near the hotel in 1940, causing him to lose consciousness, and his coming back to awareness, sitting in the comfortable armchair in the hotel's lobby in the present?

He had no idea.

And now his mind was flooding with memories of Mrs. Collins. Her fright at discovering that he had placed the plastic kettle upon the fire in order to boil water for tea. The way she'd opened all of the windows and doors to let the pungent smoke escape. Their excursion to the shop to purchase a new kettle, and also two new and very fine saucepans, which Shaun had convinced Mrs. Collins were the accepted signal of betrothal between a gentleman and his intended in 1825… until she had looked it up on her iPad.

But she had not returned the saucepans to the shop.

She had used them immediately, and had invited him into the kitchen to help, her patient instructions concerning cookery in the twenty-first century always accompanied by a loving embrace and a reassuring kiss.

Their last embrace, at the top of Betty's stairs, after the bomb had dropped on the house across the road.

The last kiss they had shared, its sweetness and its passion.

He shut his eyes, and in the silent darkness, could not prevent himself from weeping.

• • •

He did not own a timepiece, but he knew, instinctively, that his sleep had been brief and troubled. And now, he was wide-awake again. Something had woken him up. Something urgent. Perhaps it had been a dream. He wracked his brain to try and remember the ephemeral images that had fled like naughty children the moment he had opened his eyes.

Yes. *There.* He closed his eyes again and focused his mind on the very end of the filmy dream-thought, fixing it, preventing its dissolution.

It had not been a dream. Dreams melted away with wakefulness.

What had woken Shaun up was a fragment of memory, sparkling like a bright shard of glass. And now he was aware of more glittering pieces, large and small, scattered about him, that he could pick up and fit together to construct a complete pane, a window into his mind.

He remembered.

He was in Balham Underground Station. He was on the northbound platform and he was running. He could see the big old-fashioned clock, and its hands....

It was two minutes past eight.

Behind him, he heard the sound of a massive explosion, and the tunnel roof collapsed in an avalanche of mud and water and gravel and sewage. The platform plunged into darkness. All around him, he could hear the screams of women and children, and the roar of water and gravel and pieces of the roadway above falling through the hole in the top of the tunnel.

And then… suddenly, he was no longer trapped in the collapsing station. It seemed as if he had blinked and everything had changed. The memory was there, as clear as if he had lived it, all over again.

It was no longer nighttime, but day, and he was standing on the pavement outside a building, and the noise from the traffic on the roadway beside him was deafening.

He recalled staring, bewildered, at the modern cars and the streamlined buses and the men and women who were walking along the pavement, going about their daily business, texting and talking on their clever devices.

He remembered turning around to face the building behind him, with its large pavement-side windows draped in smart blue and white striped awnings.

And he recalled the realization that he was standing directly outside the Bedford Square Hotel, and that it was no longer 1940, and that his arm was dripping blood, and that he was absolutely alone.

Had his own accidental abilities caused this to happen? Shaun was unsure. He had travelled in time twice before, each excursion at the behest of something or someone else. This was different. This had *felt* different. As the lights had arced out on the station platform, he recalled that he had wished himself away… *willed* himself away… and the last thing he remembered picturing in his mind was the Anderson shelter in Nana Betty's back garden, with Mrs. Collins, on the day they had arrived in Balham for the funeral.

He had most certainly *not* been thinking about that hotel, in the centre of London.

Whatever machinations or influences he had drawn upon to deliver himself there had drained him. He remembered his head spinning, his arm hurting, and that he felt very faint.

"You all right, mate?" a stranger had asked him.

"I fear," Shaun had said, leaning upon the man, "that if I do not soon locate a seat, the pavement will shortly become acquainted with my face."

"Come this way," the fellow had replied, guiding him through the hotel's front doors and into the lounge, just off the lobby. "Sit here."

Shaun had sunk into one of the chairs, and was immediately attended to by a gentleman in a waistcoat with stripes that matched the awnings outside.

"Can you get him some water?" the helpful man had asked.

"Certainly, sir. A bottle of San Pellegrino?"

"A glass of ordinary water will suffice," Shaun had said. "From the tap."

"As you wish."

The gentleman in the striped waistcoat had seemed somewhat less attentive as he'd delivered Shaun's request to a nearby barman.

"You've got something nasty going on with your arm there. Hang on." The helpful man had disappeared and was back, moments later, with a wad of paper towels, some wet, some dry. These, he had applied to Shaun's wound. "Just keep pressing down with your hand to stop the bleeding. You'll be OK, yeah?"

"I believe so," Shaun had said. "Many thanks."

"Not to worry. I'll be off. I'm sorry to have to leave you but I'm late for an appointment. Take care of yourself. See a doctor."

"I will," Shaun had said.

And it seemed to him now, thinking back, that he had drifted off into a kind of sleep, and when he had opened his eyes, he had found himself alone in the lounge, with absolutely no recollection of anything that had come before.

And so some of the glittering shards were, at last, glued together. Not all of them. But enough to give him an idea of how he had come to be inhabiting this new reality. It was like staring through a pane of cracked glass at an unfamiliar room.

He could remember the ceiling of Balham Underground station collapsing behind him as he ran... but nothing before that. His last memory prior to the Underground was of seeking shelter in the cellar of the Bedford Square Hotel, and of a bomb dropping. And then... nothing more.

CHAPTER EIGHTEEN

"You must forgive my untidy manners," Mr. Deeley said in between gulps of tea and hungry mouthfuls of hot soup. "I have not eaten since lunchtime yesterday."

"We'll forgive you anything, Mr. Deeley," Charlie said, sitting beside him at the table in Betty's dining room, holding onto his hand, never wanting to let go of it again. "What happened? I could have sworn you were dead. You weren't breathing. You *were* dead."

"I cannot say for certain," Mr. Deeley replied, pausing midspoon. "I have no recollection of anything beyond the noise of the bomb outside, and the ceiling collapsing on top of me. When I woke up, I was lying upon a very hard table. And this was attached to my wrist."

He took a slip of brown cardboard out of his pocket, and held it up so that Betty and Charlie could see. It was like a luggage tag, with a bit of string going through a hole at one end. All of the particulars concerning where and when he had been found were written on it, including the state he had been found in, and his name. The words DEAD BODY were quite prominently printed across the top.

"And I was exceedingly cold, and my head hurt profoundly. My only thought was to locate a place with more warmth. And so I climbed down from the table, and I let myself out. It seems to me that I then walked a considerable distance, along hallways and up stairs and then down again, until I found another room, into which there had been placed a number of chairs, occupied by people, the majority of whom seemed unwell or injured or otherwise indisposed.

And that is where I sat, largely unnoticed, until I was able to return to a more sensible state."

Mr. Deeley paused to finish his soup. Charlie poured him another cup of tea.

"I recall hearing, at a great distance, the sound of an air raid warning. And then also, at a great distance, the noise of more bombs. And the room where I was sitting shook a little. But those who surrounded me seemed unperturbed, and so I determined that I was safe there, for as long as I remained. I recall that a woman wearing some sort of uniform inquired whether I was well, and I replied in the affirmative, and then she left me to tend to a gentleman with a bandage on his hand. And then, after the bombing ceased, and the All Clear was sounded, I left the room and discovered a door which took me upstairs, and outside. It was, by that time, quite dark. I located a police constable, and asked him for directions to Balham. I believe he found me somewhat amusing. But he provided instructions, which I followed. And here I am. Slightly the worse for wear. But alive, nonetheless, and in very great need of a bed."

"You may have your bed," Betty replied, "and you may sleep to your heart's content. We are both very glad of your safe return."

Mr. Deeley paused once more, and placed his hand over his heart.

"This aches. It feels much like the time I was kicked by one of Monsieur Duran's more disagreeable horses."

"Chest compressions," Charlie said. "I was doing CPR on you, until they dragged me away. I'm sure that's what brought you back to life."

"What on earth is CPR?" Betty inquired.

"Something I learned in a life-saving course in Stoneford. Cardiopulmonary resuscitation." Charlie paused. "It's quite a new technique."

"It sounds jolly useful, however it's done," Betty said.

"I shall forgive you for the pain you inflicted," Mr. Deeley said with a smile, "as it appears to have achieved what you intended.

You held my heart in your hands, Mrs. Collins, and for this, I love you impossibly."

He raised her fingers to his lips, and kissed them, with great tenderness.

"I love you impossibly, too, Mr. Deeley," Charlie said, clasping his hand between her own.

"You two planning on getting married then?" Betty inquired.

"Yes," Mr. Deeley replied, without hesitation.

"I'm definitely thinking about it," Charlie added.

"Ah," said Mr. Deeley. "Progress. I should arrange to die more often."

Charlie laughed.

"Forgive me—I am overcome by weariness. Mrs. Collins, will you assist me up the stairs? I fear my legs may not have any strength left in them."

Charlie helped him to his feet and stayed close behind him as he climbed the narrow staircase, one hand on his back, steadying him with a gentle push.

"The big bedroom," she said, steering him through the doorway. "I don't want you to have anything more to do with that little room over the stairs."

"Because it belongs to Silas Ferryman?" Mr. Deeley guessed.

"Exactly," Charlie replied, plumping up a pillow on the big double bed.

"Are we in agreement, then, that the that the fair-haired gentleman who met us for lunch is the real Thaddeus Quinn? And that the man who was introduced to us as Betty's lodger is the impostor?"

"I believe we are, Mr. Deeley."

"I noticed he was not present downstairs, which I think peculiar, as the grocery shop where he is employed is not open on Sundays."

"I don't know where he is," Charlie said. "Though I did see him yesterday. He followed us up to London, Mr. Deeley. He saw us talking to Thaddeus in the road outside Mrs. Crofton's, after you'd rescued her children. And then, after the hotel was bombed, he followed me all the way to Strand and down into the tube station. He was very anxious to know what Thaddeus had said to us in the restaurant."

"And did you tell him?"

"I did. But I wasn't in any state of mind to think properly, Mr. Deeley. And then he said another young woman had been killed, before Angela Bailey. And this morning, Betty told me about a third murder, last night. I'm so afraid it was Violet, the waitress. Her body was found on a bomb site near the British Museum… which is very close to the hotel where we had lunch."

Charlie plumped up a second pillow.

"And he had a suitcase with him, Mr. Deeley. He fell asleep while we were waiting for the air raid to end. I looked inside it." She swallowed. "There was a box. And inside the box was some jewellery…." She paused, and then listed the items from memory. "A locket. A ring. A bracelet. A brooch. And a pair of earrings."

"A locket," Mr. Deeley said, thoughtfully. "And a ring… and a bracelet…."

"The jewellery missing from the victims of the Middlehurst Slasher. And Angela Bailey's brooch was stolen from her body. And the other woman who was killed…her name was Deirdre Allsop. Her earrings were taken. And there were two newspaper clippings in the suitcase—one about Angela, the other about Deirdre."

Charlie stopped. She was shivering uncontrollably.

"Will you report Betty's lodger to the police?"

"I ought to. I don't have to mention the 1849 killings. The two current ones are enough."

Mr. Deeley fell back upon the two plumped-up pillows, closing his eyes.

"Three," he corrected, tiredly.

"Yes, three…."

"He has no inkling that you discovered what was inside his case?"

"No. He was asleep. I was very careful not to disturb him."

"Ah," said Mr. Deeley. "Good." He smiled a little. "An

afterthought, Mrs. Collins. If this lodger, the father of Betty's child, is indeed Silas Ferryman, then we may arrive at the conclusion that he is not my son. And therefore, Mrs. Collins, we may also arrive at the very happy conclusion that you are no longer my great granddaughter."

"That is a happy conclusion," Charlie agreed. "But then… I wonder who's buried in the grave that we saw, Mr. Deeley? Is it the real Thaddeus… or is it Silas Ferryman?"

"Indeed, we might ponder this…." Mr. Deeley said, his voice drifting away into sleep. "Will you stay with me, Mrs. Collins?"

"Always, Mr. Deeley. Always."

She knelt by the side of the bed, watching him, afraid that if she looked away, he would disappear again.

She removed his shoes and put them underneath the bed. She unknotted his already loosened tie, and pulled it off, and placed it beside him on the pillow. He'd fallen asleep on top of the sheets and blankets, so she manoeuvred the eiderdown out from underneath his legs, and gently covered him with it.

And then, still kneeling beside him on the floor, she kissed him, and kissed him again, and rested her head upon his chest, and closed her eyes, and stayed that way for long minutes, listening to his strong, even breathing.

• • •

Betty was standing in the doorway to the little kitchen. "I suppose I should think about supper," she said as Charlie came downstairs. "I might attempt that spiced beef recipe from the cookery pamphlet, as I've managed to dig up the last two potatoes from the garden. Will you two be staying here for tonight, do you think, Charlotte? Has Ruby got herself sorted yet?"

"She's still a bit disorganized," Charlie said apologetically. "And she hasn't been able to get anything over her broken windows yet. I think just one more night with you, if you wouldn't mind? And then, I promise, Mr. Deeley and I will go home. We'd only really intended to stay the weekend… but everything got mixed up after we lost our suitcase and got caught in the raid."

"I don't mind at all," Betty said. "In truth, I've been glad of the company. I shall miss you when you're gone. We must stay in touch."

"We must," Charlie agreed, as the front door knocker went *rat-tat-tat* and, moments later, she heard the sound of the key in the lock.

"Thad!" Betty shouted, rushing out of the kitchen to greet her dark-haired lodger. She kissed him, and gave him a hug. "We've been ever so worried about you! Where on earth have you been?"

"I'm so sorry, my love. I was caught up in London. I'd have rung, but everywhere I tried, the telephones were either not working, or nowhere to be found."

Charlie stayed where she was, beside the staircase. As he shut the door, she noted that he did not have his suitcase with him.

"Well come in and have a cup of tea," Betty said. "And sit down. You look thoroughly worn out." She went back into the kitchen to put the kettle on.

"I worried about where you'd gone last night, Charlotte," Ferryman said. "I must have dozed off, and when I came to, you'd disappeared."

"Sorry," Charlie said. "I just wanted to get out of there. The bombing had stopped. I caught a bus."

"Well, I'm very glad you got back safely. I'd never have forgiven myself if something had happened to you."

"Thank you," Charlie said. "I suppose you know another woman was found with her throat cut on a bomb site quite near to the hotel where Mr. Deeley and I had lunch."

The lodger's face hardened. "Yes. He did kill again. It is as I feared. It was the waitress, Violet. And a string of pearls was taken from her body."

"How do you possibly know that? It only happened last night."

"I was a police constable in Middlehurst," he said quickly. "I am not without the means of investigation." He paused. "I didn't say anything to you about it last night, Charlotte, but I am better equipped to travel in time than you—or Ferryman—may know.

My journey to this time was accidental. But since my arrival, I've discovered the means by which I can go back. And I have done so, on several occasions. After each of these visits, I was able to return here. And after completing each journey, my confidence has grown. I merely need to place my hands upon Ferryman, and ensure he doesn't escape, and he will be removed to 1849 to face a judge and jury."

"Why do you keep coming back? Why don't you just go back to 1849 and arrest Silas Ferryman before he can get away?"

"I don't seem to be able to. I seem only to be able to return to a time that follows our departure."

"Then why don't you do that? Just go back to 1850. Then no one from this time will be able to find you."

In the kitchen, Betty was humming the Artie Shaw tune that had been playing on the Marconi radio when Charlie and Mr. Deeley had first arrived on Friday night.

"Because of her," the lodger replied simply. "And our child. I love them both."

"Well, if you do manage to arrest Ferryman and return him to 1849, you'll be saying goodbye to Betty, won't you?"

"I will. And it's not something I want to dwell on, believe me. I don't know how I'll reconcile that. Perhaps my stay in 1849 will not be permanent."

"Lucky Betty."

"You still doubt who I am."

"Wouldn't you?"

"I would," Betty's lodger replied, not unkindly. "You saw the suitcase I was carrying last night…?"

Charlie nodded.

"It belongs to Ferryman. I removed it from his hotel room while you and Shaun were having lunch with him. Before the raid. Inside that suitcase is everything I need to prove he is, indeed, the Middlehurst Slasher. It contains his trophies. All of them, from 1849 and from now."

"If he is Silas Ferryman," Charlie said, "why doesn't he just go somewhere else—some time else? Why is he still here?"

"I can't say for certain, Charlotte, but I don't believe he's able to go into another time. I believe he's more or less stranded here. He's arrived here because of me. And because of that, I believe his only recourse, if he wishes to remain free, is to do away with me. That's why I've gone into hiding. I hope you understand."

He took a piece of paper out of his coat pocket and handed it to Charlie. Upon it was written an address and a telephone number.

"What's this?"

"It's where I'm staying now, The Slug and Cauliflower. It's a pub, but it has lodgings above. I'm entrusting it to you, Charlotte. If Ferryman puts in another appearance, would you ring the pub? The proprietor will fetch me immediately, and I can be here in fifteen minutes."

"Of course," Charlotte said.

"Thank you. And I'm still so dreadfully sorry about the loss of your friend."

Charlie was about to correct him, but he turned and walked briskly to the front door.

"I must be off, Betty!" he called, over his shoulder. "Urgent matters!"

Betty came out of the kitchen. "But I've just made tea...."

"Terribly sorry, my love. I'll make it up to you." He blew her a kiss. "See you tomorrow. Promise."

And he was gone.

CHAPTER NINETEEN

It was morning. Shaun could see daylight through the doorway of the shelter, and some of that light was spilling inside. He yawned, and stretched, feeling all of the discomfort of having slept in his clothes, semi-upright, in an armchair never designed for such a purpose.

In spite of the electric heater, the shelter was still chilly, and very damp.

Unkinking his arms and legs and back, Shaun could see that a good deal of blood had seeped out of the place where he had been wounded, and had dried on the bandage overnight. The pain was tolerable, but worse than yesterday.

He switched off the electric heater and got to his feet.

• • •

Shaun knocked on the garden door, but there was still no answer from within.

A young man with a beard poked his head over the wooden fence on Shaun's right.

"Are you looking for Wendy Weller?"

"I am," Shaun confirmed.

"I haven't seen her since yesterday. She mentioned she'd probably be late today. Something to do with her granddaughter's school."

"Do you know Wendy's son?"

"I know *of* him," the young man replied. "Nicholas, isn't it?"

Shaun was in two minds how next to proceed. If Wendy did not recognize him, then it was highly likely he would receive the same reaction from Nick. However, while Wendy was a sceptic of the highest order when it came to time travelling, Nick had made it his preoccupation.

"I am Shaun Deeley," he said. "I am an old friend of Nick's, however I have not seen him in some time, and I thought I might surprise him with a visit."

"Andy Wiggins," the young man replied, extending his hand over the fence.

Shaun shook it. "Do you know where Wandsworth University is located?"

"I've got a good idea."

"Excellent." Shaun paused. "Might you have at your disposal a means of transportation...?"

• • •

Andy Wiggins was a professional photographer. In fact, he had produced the book Shaun had seen in the window of the shop that had once belonged to Betty's father. The pictorial history of Balham. The seats of his Audi were packed with copies in cardboard boxes.

"A personal project," he explained, making room for Shaun. "I published it myself. I'm very fond of the past."

He gave Shaun a small piece of cardboard. One side was a replica of the cover of the picture book, showing Balham Underground Station. The other side contained information about how to locate Andy by telephone and e-mail, and also directed people to his website.

"And here we are," he said, stopping outside Wandsworth University and calling up the directions he had researched on his clever phone. "Through the main gates, across the quadrangle, down the little lane beside the main library, and there's your physics building."

He showed Shaun the map.

"Dr. Nicholas Weller, Professor of Theoretical Physics. 541B. I'd hazard a guess his office is on the fifth floor. If you get lost I'm sure someone will point you in the right direction."

"In theory," Shaun said, humorously.

"Oh, ha ha! Very good! You'll be all right on your own?"

"Yes. Many thanks for your assistance."

"Not a problem. If I see Wendy I'll tell her you were looking for her."

Shaun, wisely, refrained from further comment and climbed out of the car.

• • •

The office door was slightly open, and he could see that Nick was sitting behind his desk, working at his computer. He was as Shaun remembered him, down to his habit of wearing brightly patterned shirts which had their origins in a South Sea island known as Hawaii. And there was a walking cane propped against the wall.

Shaun knocked upon the door. Nick looked up from his screen and then beckoned him inside.

"Good morning," Shaun said.

"Morning. How can I help you?"

"Do you know me, sir?"

"I don't think so. Should I?"

"Perhaps not," Shaun said, treading carefully. "I am Shaun Deeley. Is the name, at least, familiar to you?"

"It isn't, I'm afraid. Are you a student here?"

"I met your mother yesterday. I had harboured a hope that she might have mentioned me to you."

Nick looked amused. "Sorry," he said. "Any particular reason why she would...?"

"In the time and place that I have come from," Shaun said, "you and I are very well-acquainted.... And in that time and place, you are much interested in the theories of travelling in space and time, and also the habits of sprites and tachyons and massive electrical charges."

"Yes, that is the main focus of my research. But... sorry... in the time and place that you've come from...?"

"Yes. Stoneford. In the present. But it is not the present you and I currently inhabit. Certain individuals are... missing. Your aunt, for one. Jackie Duran. And her daughter, Charlotte. And your sister, Natasha."

Nick leaned back in his chair and observed Shaun with a quizzical look.

"Either you've been put up to this by one of my students... and I have my suspicions who... or...." He paused. "What is it you actually want?"

"I wish to return to my time and place," Shaun said. "And I had hoped you might assist me."

Nick seemed to be assessing the information Shaun had provided to him.

"I would not blame you if you dismissed me outright," Shaun added. "Your mother had much the same reaction yesterday."

"And you and I are well-acquainted in this other universe...?"

"In fact, you and I are the closest of friends. You are the first cousin of Charlotte Duran. You were friends, also, with her husband, Jeff Lowe, who was killed in a traffic accident five years ago. The accident damaged your leg, and rendered you lame."

"I was injured in an accident five years ago, and Jeff Lowe was driving the car... and he was killed. But he wasn't married to anyone called Charlotte Duran. He wasn't married at all, in fact." He paused. "That traffic accident was widely reported. Anything else that might convince me you've come from a parallel universe?"

Shaun thought for a moment, then put his hands into the pockets of Bert Singleton's best Sunday trousers and withdrew the box of Swan Vesta matches and the three used bus tickets.

"I am wearing the clothing that belonged to your great-grandfather, Bert Singleton," he said. "These trousers were loaned to me by his daughter—your grandmother, Betty—in the year 1940. Her father smoked a pipe, and these are the matches he used to light it. It seems he also undertook at least three journeys by bus... and here is the proof. These are not articles from the present."

"They aren't," Nick agreed, examining the bus tickets, and the box of Swan Vestas. "They're not really proof, though, either... are they? You could have picked these up anywhere. They could be very good replicas...."

"I assure you, they are not."

"Assuming your story is real... sorry, what did you say your name was?"

"Shaun Deeley."

"Assuming your story is true, Mr. Deeley, my research is all theoretical. I've never met anyone from the past—or the future—and I've certainly never been able to influence travel to or from anywhere, other than the old-fashioned kind involving timetables and trains. Or planes and cars. And occasionally ships. It would take me months to try and work out a way to help you."

• • •

"You again," Wendy said, opening Betty's front door in response to Shaun's urgent knock. "I thought I'd made it clear—oh. Hello Nick."

"Morning," Nick said. "Can we come in?"

Wendy paused, and then stood aside.

"I must confess to you," said Shaun, "that I spent last night in the air raid shelter at the bottom of your garden. I know I was trespassing. However, I had no means to pay for lodgings. I hope you will forgive me."

"I'm surprised you didn't just fly away—or whatever it is you do—back to your own time."

"I am, alas, unable to 'fly away,' Mrs. Weller. I would gladly do so, however I am without knowledge of the mechanism that might accomplish it."

"And you believe him?" Wendy said, to her son.

"I've given him the benefit of doubt," Nick answered. "He tells me there's something in the shelter we ought to see."

• • •

"Here we are," Shaun said, placing the suitcase upon the dining table.

He removed his overcoat, easing his injured arm through the sleeve.

"That looks worse than yesterday," Wendy said, seeing the bloodstained bandages. "Let me change the dressing for you."

She went upstairs.

"A nurse first and foremost," Nick said. "Even if she does believe you're Doctor Who's evil cousin. How did that happen?"

"I do not know," Shaun said. "And this confounds me greatly."

Wendy came back with fresh bandages and a bottle of antiseptic, which she placed on the table beside the suitcase.

"Sit down," she said, going into the kitchen for a bowl of warm water. "And I'll have that case on the floor, if you don't mind. It's covered in mildew."

Shaun placed the suitcase under the table, and then Wendy gently stripped away the blood-soaked dressing, bathed Shaun's arm, and applied the antiseptic.

"I've never met a time traveller before," Nick said, sitting across from Shaun.

"Oh, well," Wendy said, busily. "Something to tell your grandchildren, then. This one comes from 1825. Where he apparently fell in love with Charlotte, who is the daughter of the older sister I never had. And apparently, you saved both of their lives."

"Did I?" Nick said. "How did I manage that?"

"By facilitating our journey from 1825 to the present," Shaun said. "As I recall, it was your knowledge of the atmosphere which became paramount. Specifically, the employment of a lightning strike to recreate the conditions which had resulted in Charlotte's original journey from the present, back through time."

"Interesting," Nick replied. "A focused electrical charge, then."

"Among other things, which I cannot pretend to understand."

"And what was it like?" Nick said, sitting forward on his chair. "What did it feel like, to be transported like that?"

"It was the most terrifying experience of my life," Shaun

answered. "And, to be honest, it is not a journey I am anxious to repeat."

"But how did you arrive here?"

"In an instant. Without any lightning strikes whatsoever. And previous to that, I—we—travelled to the year 1940. Again, without any sort of electrical interference at all."

"So what, then, do you think caused those journeys?"

Shaun thought for a moment.

"I believe the travel back to 1940 was precipitated by a lump of metal. It was a relic from the war, given to Charlotte by a woman called Ruby Firth, who once lived in the house next door to this one."

"I remember Ruby," Wendy said, finishing the bandaging on Shaun's arm. She snipped one last piece of adhesive tape from the roll and pressed it into place. "There you are. Much quicker than A&E at the hospital." She gave him a highly suspicious look. "And no questions asked."

"I am indebted to you," Shaun replied.

"Ruby was great friends with my mum when I was growing up. But I haven't seen her in years. Her grandson lives in the house now. Andy Wiggins."

"I have met him," Shaun said. "He drove me to the university this morning. I had no idea he was Ruby's grandson. Perhaps he could shed some light on the lump of metal."

"Oh yes, that'll go down well," Wendy said, collecting the bandages and tape and antiseptic. "Mention you were born in the eighteenth century while you're at it. He'll love that."

She went back upstairs.

"And what's in the suitcase?" Nick hinted.

Shaun opened it, to reveal the two boxes within. And then he opened the gas mask box, and arranged the jewellery and the newspaper clippings on the table.

"Is any of this familiar to you?"

"I've not seen any of it before," Nick said. "Why do you ask?"

"Have you never heard of the Middlehurst Slasher…?"

Nick shook his head. "Should I?"

"I suppose not."

Shaun picked up the locket, and held it, delicately, in the palm of his hand, to show Nick. "I gave this to Jemima Beckford to celebrate her twenty-first birthday, in 1815." He paused, to try and gauge Nick's reaction. But if Nick doubted him, he did not, this time, betray any scepticism.

"If you were to research the Middlehurst Slasher on your computer, you would learn that he killed three women in 1849, in the New Forest near Southampton, and that he took from each of them an item of jewellery. One was a bracelet—here. And another was a silver ring. Here. And the third was this locket, stolen from Jemima's daughter, Matilda."

"And how did these come to be in my grandmother's air raid shelter?" Nick said.

"Again, this is something I do not know. Although I have developed a very good theory." Shaun paused again, smiling.

Nick laughed. "Go on."

"I believe that the Middlehurst Slasher was a traveller in time, like myself. Two similar murders were committed in 1940—here you see the jewellery that the killer collected. And here are two stories from a newspaper from that time, detailing the killings. And everything was put here in this gas mask box. I believe this suitcase belonged to the man who is responsible for all five of these foul acts."

"That is intriguing," Nick agreed. "But still no explanation for their presence in my grandmother's air raid shelter."

Wendy returned from her excursion upstairs.

"You'd have noticed it, wouldn't you, Mum? That suitcase in Nana's shelter?"

"Not me," Wendy said. "I was never allowed near the place when I was growing up. And neither were you or your sister when I brought you to visit. It was Mum's private domain. She used to disappear down there for hours at a time."

"You ought to show Nick the blue cooking pamphlet," Shaun said.

Wendy retrieved it from the drawer in the sideboard, and placed it on the table in front of Nick.

"The note on the back was written by your grandmother in 1940," Shaun said. "I knew exactly what it said, as I was there during the conversation."

"That's true," Wendy said. "He did know. To the word. And I don't know how he could have come by that knowledge, really, unless he'd seen the pamphlet before."

"Not likely," Nick said. "And still you dismissed him as a fantasist?"

"I'm not one of your scholars, Nick. I did my degree in nursing. It's very down-to-earth and factual. My experience with self-professed time travellers generally involves medication and a psychiatric evaluation."

"I apologise on behalf of my mother," Nick said to Shaun, lifting the camera out of its yellow and black cardboard box. "You used to have one of these, didn't you, Mum? I remember playing with it when I was small."

"I did," Wendy replied, taking it into her hands. "That's the lens. You point it at what you want to take a picture of, and you look down into the little window on top to see what it's seeing. You push the lever down here and that's what takes the photo."

She looked through the second little window.

"And there's still film in it."

• • •

Andy Wiggins opened the door.

"Hello again!" he said, seeing Shaun. "Is this the famous Professor Nick Weller?"

"It is," Shaun replied. "And once again, many thanks for your kind assistance. I have only just learned that you are the grandson of Ruby Firth."

"That would be me," Andy said.

"Does she still live in this house?"

170

"In memory only, I'm afraid. She passed away three years ago."

"Ah," said Shaun. "A shame. I knew her. My condolences."

"Andy," Wendy said, holding out the camera. "Look what we've found."

The young man's eyes lit up. "Excellent," he said. "That's an antique. 1937, I should think. Or 1938, judging by the packaging. Instruction booklet and everything. You could get a nice little sum for this if you decided to sell it."

"You interested?" Wendy asked with a laugh.

"I might be. I've got quite a collection of cameras upstairs."

"It's still got film in it. Can you work your magic and develop it?"

"Absolutely. It's 620, the same size as 120. Got a tank that'll take it, got the chemicals. An hour to develop, fix, rinse, and dry. Another hour for the prints. And I've got an old ferrotype dryer I can use to give them a nice glossy shine."

• • •

Wendy had made a late breakfast in Betty's kitchen: toast with butter and ginger marmalade, and scrambled eggs with grilled tomatoes and sausages. In the dining room, she'd set out three Blue Willow cups and saucers, a little jug of milk, and a bowl of sugar. She carried the teapot to the table, covered with one of Betty's striped knitted cosies.

Shaun dug in hungrily.

"I remember Nana loved this ginger marmalade," Nick said.

"Indeed. In 1940 it was the only marmalade that was available," Shaun replied.

"This is what I don't seem to be able to get my head round," Wendy said. "To be able to travel from the nineteenth century to the twenty-first, and then back again to 1940... and then forward once more... as easily as getting on a train and riding off to Brighton for a day beside the sea."

"It is nothing at all like riding on a train," Shaun said. "I only wish it were."

"And," said Nick, "to actually meet someone who has come from a different reality. And who personally knows another version of me! Am I much different?"

"You are very much the same," Shaun assured him. "I would not, in truth, be able to tell you apart from your other good self." He looked at Wendy. "Nor you. But in the other time that I've come from, a woman exists whom I love more constantly than anyone else in the world. And that is why I must find a way back."

"I do understand," Wendy said. "Well, I can't *really* understand, because it hasn't happened to me. But I understand the feeling of being disconnected and isolated. I spent a little time in South Africa after I married Toby, and before you were born, Nick. It was a terrible time for the country, and we lived in a gated community. I had no friends there, and I couldn't go out without Toby worrying about me, so it was easier just to stay at home. It was the best day of my life when Toby was transferred back to England."

The sound of the front door knocker interrupted their conversation. Wendy got up to let Andy Wiggins in.

"Here we are," he said, following her into the dining room, handing over a large brown envelope.

Wendy pulled out eight black and white photographs and eight pieces of thin plastic.

"Negatives," she said, showing them to Shaun. "You don't see these anymore."

Shaun examined the pieces of plastic. They were much larger than the little strips with the perforated edges that Mrs. Collins kept in her photograph books. And they were black, without colour.

"I'd guess that all eight photos were taken during the war," Andy said, "which would have been quite a feat, as film was notoriously difficult to get hold of back then. Whoever took those must have known someone in the business."

Wendy spread the photographs out on the table.

The first picture showed a copse of trees and wild grasses. A landscape, with no particular beauty or point of interest. The second, a collection of rubble, the remains of a building. In the background Shaun recognized the telltale signs of a bombing—the insides of rooms missing their walls, with dressing tables and beds and chairs exposed to the elements. The third photograph was similar—a bomb site—but in a different location. And the fourth showed a row of brick arches, atop which ran railway tracks, judging by the presence of a train, driven by steam, crossing from the right side of the picture to the left.

The fifth photograph was of a young woman with fair hair. She seemed unaware that her picture was being taken, as she was not facing the camera. She was walking out of what looked like a sweet shop.

The sixth was of another young woman, again seemingly oblivious that the photographer had singled her out as a subject of interest as she approached the entrance to Balham Underground Station. Something on the collar of her coat was catching the sun... was it a brooch?

The seventh picture caused Shaun to pause. It was the waitress from the restaurant in London. Violet. She was wearing her black and white uniform, and the picture had, once again, been taken without her knowledge.

Shaun stopped cold as he saw the eighth and final photograph. It was Mrs. Collins.

She was standing in the road, looking at the devastation caused by the bombing of Mrs. Crofton's house. It was morning... the same morning, Shaun realized, that they had travelled up to London to have lunch with the fair-haired gentleman. Mrs. Collins was still wearing her skirt and blouse from their other present time.

Shaun could not stop staring at Mrs. Collins's face. If the person who had taken these pictures was Silas Ferryman... and if the first two women were Deirdre Allsop and Angela Bailey... and if the first photograph was Mitcham Common... and the second, the bombed house where Angela Bailey's body had been discovered....

He shook his head, realizing why Ferryman had photographed a different bomb site, and the railway arches.

"Do you know who any of these lovely young women are?" Nick asked his mother.

"Not a clue," Wendy replied.

"This," Shaun said, showing them the photograph of Mrs. Collins, "is Charlotte Duran."

"Oh!" Wendy said. "Well, there's a mystery cleared up, anyway... Are you all right, Mr. Deeley? You look like you've seen a ghost."

• • •

He was not all right at all.

He had placed the photograph of the fair-haired young woman with the picture of the copse of trees and wild grasses and then matched both pictures with the tortoiseshell earrings, and the newspaper story about Deirdre Allsop. There. Complete.

Then he placed the photograph of the second young woman, approaching the entrance to the tube station, with the picture of the bombed building, and then the brooch, and then the second newspaper story, which had been about Angela Bailey. Complete again.

And then he matched the photograph of the second bomb site with that of Violet, the waitress. And the last two pictures... the railway arches... and Mrs. Collins.

He placed these last two photographs with the brown envelope that contained the receipts from the cemetery confirming payment for Mrs. Collins's grave, and the photograph of her headstone.

He had a dark and dreadful feeling, like a dagger tearing into his soul. He knew why Mrs. Collins had died. And by whose hand. And, very likely, where Ferryman had left her body.

He picked up the gas mask case, thinking he would replace the jewellery and the newspaper stories.

Something inside made a tiny rattling sound.

Shaun investigated, wondering what he had missed, and how.

His blood ran cold.

Nestled at the bottom of the box was a slender silver chain. And upon the silver chain was a pendant which said: MRS. COLLINS.

• • •

"The shrapnel seemed to have some sort of... energy," Shaun said. "It had the ability to make the hands of a timepiece travel backwards. And it became hot, entirely of its own volition. Charlotte was holding it in her hand when we were taken back to 1940. And she kept it in her bag while we were there."

"Mum paid for her headstone and the upkeep of her grave," Wendy said. "So it stands to reason that no one else identified or claimed her body... so Mum must have done it."

"So," Nick reasoned, "if Nana claimed her body, then her personal effects would have been given to her as well. Might we assume that would include her bag?"

"I think so," said Wendy.

"Then all we need to do is find Charlotte's bag," Nick said. "And we'll find the shrapnel. And you know Nana, Mum. She never threw anything away."

"It is made of leather which has been dyed black," Shaun said. "It has a long carrying strap, and many small compartments."

"I'm positive I haven't come across any handbags that sound like that," Wendy said. "Twenty-three others, yes. But all brown. And one faux alligator. Nothing at all in black leather."

She paused.

"But I haven't looked in the air raid shelter."

• • •

They stood inside Betty Lewis's private domain, considering what was there: the armchair and hassock, the bookcase, the table, and the chest.

"If you were Nana," Nick said, "and you wanted to keep something secret and safe for a long, long time... where would you put it?"

"In here," said Shaun, kneeling down in front of the chest.

It was very old. As old as a similar chest he had seen in Monsieur

Duran's manor, where he had worked in the first decades of the nineteenth century. It was constructed of wood, with a curved lid surfaced with embossed tin, and three reinforcing wooden straps. Its latches and locks were of metal, quite tarnished, but without rust.

He tried the lid, but it wouldn't budge.

"Key," Wendy said, thinking. "Where would you keep the key if you were my mum?"

"The sideboard in the dining room?" Nick guessed.

Wendy left the shelter, and was back five minutes later, with a Cadbury chocolate tin filled with keys.

Shaun tried them all, unsuccessfully, until there was only one left.

He inserted it… and the lock clicked.

He lifted the creaking lid.

Inside were boxes of games: Scrabble and Monopoly and Cluedo. And plastic action men, and toy motor cars and train engines, and an entire family of dolls in various states of undress.

"Our toys," Nick said. "We used to play in Nana's sitting room. I can't believe she kept everything."

Wendy lifted each item out of the chest and placed it carefully on the shelter's carpeted wooden floor.

"We had so many toys," Nick said. "One lot at home. One lot here. I don't think kids today would know what to do with half of these things. No computers. No Xbox."

"You were Mum's only grandchildren," Wendy reminded him. "She loved to indulge you."

The chest had been emptied.

"Not there, obviously," she said, starting to put everything back again.

"One moment," Shaun said.

He felt around the inside of the chest until his fingers located a nearly invisible slot along one edge. And then another, on the opposite side.

"There," he said with satisfaction, lifting the false bottom up to reveal what was beneath.

"Oh!" Wendy exclaimed.

"Oh, indeed," said Shaun.

Nestled in the cavity were three items.

The first was a little black and white photograph, old and faded.

"Thaddeus Quinn," Shaun said. "Or rather, the man Charlotte and I believed to be Thaddeus Quinn."

The photograph showed him perching, with great nonchalance, atop the Anderson shelter. He had the same dark hair and the same expression upon his face that Shaun remembered. And he was wearing similar clothing: the same coat and trousers, the same tweed flat cap, and very nearly the same tie and shoes.

Wendy turned the picture over.

On the back someone—likely Betty—had written: *Thad, July 1940.*

"Any further doubts about Mr. Deeley's time travelling abilities?" Nick inquired.

The second item was wrapped in tissue, but Shaun recognized the pattern showing through the thin paper immediately, even before Wendy had lifted it out.

"That is a knitted pullover," he said. "It has a V-shaped neck and no sleeves, and it has a peculiar repeating design, worked in brown and deep orange and yellow, and green and blue. When I saw this pullover in 1940, it was unfinished. You may also find a knitting pattern."

"Unfinished," Wendy confirmed, unwrapping the tissue, and holding the front and back pieces up. A pattern, a page torn from a magazine, fluttered onto the floor. "I believe you, Mr. Deeley. I'm so sorry I doubted you earlier."

The third object was a mud-stained black leather handbag.

"I'll be damned," Nick said.

His heart aching, Shaun carefully unzipped all of the compartments. He found Mrs. Collins's leather wallet, which held all of her plastic cards. The packet of tablets she had shown him at the breakfast table in Stoneford. Her phone and the cord that plugged into the wall, which could restore its functions when the battery had run out.

"None of these things existed in 1940," Nick said. "Further proof, as if we needed it."

At the bottom of the bag was a curious card Shaun had not seen before:

Fenwick Oldbutter. Busker. Musician. Composer. Contemporary Arrangements. Historical Time Pieces. With a telephone number printed at the bottom, and an address where he might be contacted by e-mail.

He turned the card over and saw that Mrs. Collins had written something in pencil on its back.

Call about time travel. Mention Ruby.

He put the card in his pocket.

And there, at last, was the lump of shrapnel.

"Are you all right, Mr. Deeley?" Wendy asked.

"I believe," Shaun said, "that I am in need of a telephone."

CHAPTER TWENTY

It was Monday morning, and it was the 14th of October, and something had woken Charlie up.

She reached across the double bed to reassure herself that Mr. Deeley was still there, and not dead.

Still there. Still sound asleep.

She'd climbed over him the night before, and joined him, very chastely. She wore her great-grandmother's flannel nightgown, leaving him fully dressed and lying on top of the sheets, covered only with the eiderdown. And she'd slept deeply, and contentedly, comforted by the knowledge that the person she loved more than anyone else in the world was beside her, safe and very much alive.

Until the German planes had flown over, the throb of their engines and the blast from their bombs—and the return fire from the ack-acks on Tooting Bec Common—ensuring nobody got any more sleep at all.

But a sound had woken her up now, and she was sure it wasn't the bombing.

As her mind settled back into consciousness, she realized she knew exactly what the sound was. It was a woman's voice. It was Betty. She was downstairs.

And she had screamed.

Charlie clambered over Mr. Deeley and listened at the closed bedroom door. She had taken the precaution of locking it the night before, hiding the key under her pillow. She dared not unlock it now.

She heard nothing else. There was silence downstairs.

She rushed to the dressing table and looked out what was left of the bedroom window. Through a gap in the wooden boards she could see that the garden gate was open.

Charlie was positive it had been closed last night.

"Mr. Deeley," she said, urgently, running back to the bed. "Mr. Deeley—wake up!"

• • •

There was no sign of Betty downstairs.

But she had been there. She'd eaten breakfast—a boiled egg and perhaps toast. The plate sat in the sink, ready for washing up. And she was going to make tea. The tea leaves were in the pot. The kettle was boiling on the stove.

Charlie switched the gas off and removed the kettle from the ring. The handle was burning hot. There was very little water in the bottom.

In the dining room, one of the Blue Willow cups lay smashed on the floor next to its saucer.

And the front door was wide open.

"What's happened, Mr. Deeley? Where's she gone?"

Mr. Deeley studied the front door. "I think Betty either ran from the house, or she was made to leave, against her will."

Charlie shivered. "Silas Ferryman."

"I agree, Mrs. Collins. And the knowledge of this fills me with a very great fear."

As they stood in the front garden, Ruby Firth came out of her house, pulling the door shut behind her by its knocker.

"Oh!" she said, spotting Charlie and Mr. Deeley over their common brick wall, which was low and nearly obscured by a hedge. "Hullo! Just on my way to the shops. And then a man's coming to bang something over my windows. You look unhappy. What's happened?"

"Did you hear anything, Ruby? Someone screaming? A commotion?"

"Not at all, I'm afraid. I've been in the back garden, sorting out the last of the vegs."

"Betty's missing. We think she's been forced to go with someone. She left the kettle boiling on the stove."

"And the front door wide open," Mr. Deeley added.

"Oh dear," Ruby said, her face suddenly looking very grave.

"Was this meant to happen, Ruby? Please tell me you didn't know this was going to happen."

Ruby didn't say anything. And then: "You most definitely must do what you can to bring her back safely."

And then, she opened her own garden gate, and stepped out onto the pavement, and closed it again behind her.

"Ruby!"

"I trust you will," she replied. "In fact, I know you will."

She walked away briskly, carrying her shopping bag.

"That bloody woman," Charlie said.

"You are here with me now," Mr. Deeley reasoned. "Therefore, nothing untoward will happen to Betty. She will give birth to your mother, who will, in turn, give birth to you. This stands to reason."

"I don't know, Mr. Deeley... something doesn't feel right." She shivered again. She was still wearing her great-grandmother's flannel nightgown, with just her thin winter coat thrown over top. "I'm so cold, Mr. Deeley."

Inside the house, in the front hall, the phone was ringing.

Charlie rushed to answer it. "Yes? Hello?"

"Is that Charlotte?"

"Yes."

"It's Silas Ferryman, Charlotte. Are you surprised to hear from me?"

"What's happened to Betty?"

"She's quite safe. Not terribly happy, but unharmed."

"Why have you taken her? I don't understand. You told me yesterday that you loved her."

"I did, didn't I," Ferryman mused, after a moment. "I suppose I must, then. What else did I tell you?"

"That you'd stolen Silas Ferryman's suitcase from his hotel room. I didn't believe that, either. You knew I'd seen you with it at Strand Underground and you had to come up with an explanation. I looked inside it, by the way. While you were sleeping. I know what you've done. I know who you are."

"This is excellent news," Ferryman replied. "Well then, if you know so much, perhaps you might help me locate Thaddeus Quinn."

"Why don't you try the Bedford Square Hotel in London?"

"Oh, I did, Charlotte. But he was bombed out. The hotel is uninhabitable. He's taken lodgings elsewhere. And I've grown impatient. I'm tired of waiting."

"If anything happens to Betty, I'm going to the police with what I know about your suitcase. And Mr. Deeley knows, too. So that's two of us."

Ferryman laughed. "You aren't really in any sort of position to be laying down the law to me, Charlotte. I might, for instance, assure you that if you go to the police, something very unfortunate will most definitely happen to Betty."

"And you're supposedly in love with her. And the father of her child. You're despicable. I feel so sorry for Betty. What do you want?"

The man on the other end of the telephone line paused. And then: "I should have thought that was obvious, Charlotte. I want my suitcase back."

Charlie stared at the telephone.

"But you have it."

"No," Ferryman corrected, patiently. "Thaddeus Quinn has it. He removed it from my room while you and I were having lunch. And you met him at Strand, where you've just told me you saw what was inside. And you've also just told me that you spoke to him yesterday. So… I think you very definitely must know where he is… and therefore, you must know where my suitcase is too."

"You're the fair-haired man we had lunch with," Charlie said slowly.

"Clever clogs," Ferryman replied. "I must admit I was

congratulating myself at having carried it off. I thought I was quite convincing as Thaddeus Quinn. But, needs must. The disappearance of my suitcase has forced me to play my hand. Thank you for confirming who took it. I hope you'll now assist me in arranging for its return...? Let's set a meeting time and place. Perhaps... this afternoon? There are two public air raid shelters on the north side of Tooting Bec Common. They're along Emmanuel Road—you can't miss them. I shall meet you outside the second one, at the northeastern end, opposite the old Hyde Farm estate, at half past two. I hope you'll be bringing me good news."

"But I don't know where Thaddeus Quinn is," Charlie said.

"Oh, I don't think that can be true. I'm sure you know exactly where he is. Goodbye, Charlotte."

And he rang off.

• • •

"Perhaps," said Mr. Deeley, "we might telephone Thaddeus at The Slug and Caterpillar, and let him know what has happened. That would be a beginning."

Charlie looked through her bag for the slip of paper that Betty's lodger—the genuine Thaddeus—had given her.

"BAT," she said, frustrated. "That's how the phone number starts. What's a BAT?"

Mr. Deeley studied the dial on the front of the telephone.

"228," he said. "Each hole in this dial has letters and a number. The same as the letters and the numbers on your clever mobile."

Charlie picked up the receiver and listened. She heard the dial tone—a low-pitched purring sound.

"I've never actually used one of these before," she said. "Not with a dial. I think you do this."

She inserted her finger in the "2" hole, and dragged the dial around, then released it, then did the same thing again, and then the "8" hole.

She waited.

"I'm getting a high-pitched buzz," she said.

Mr. Deeley found the little stack of directories stored on a shelf underneath the table that held the telephone. There were two for London—A to K and L to Z. He pulled out one of them and flipped through it until he found a page with dialling instructions.

"You are advised to depress the receiver rest for at least two seconds, again listen for the dialling tone, and then redial your number. If the same continuous buzz is heard once more, the number is unobtainable."

Charlie dialled once more, and again heard the high-pitched buzz.

She replaced the receiver, defeated.

"What now?"

• • •

There had been an inn on the site of The Slug and Cauliflower for nearly two centuries, although the most recent establishment had really only been in existence for forty years. In the 1880s, trams had terminated at The Slug and Cauliflower, and the horses that drew them were put up in a stable behind it. At the turn of the century, an imposing new building had replaced its derelict predecessor, and had become a destination board on buses travelling south from Central London: *Clapham, Slug and Cauliflower.*

Charlie recalled that in the time she and Mr. Deeley had come from, the building had met a somewhat ignominious fate: closed down in 2010 in the wave of pub failures that had swept the country, it had emerged, after a restorative facelift, as a mini-supermarket. She'd seen a story about it on Facebook, lamenting its loss as a historical public house.

Here and now, in 1940, the public house was flourishing as it had been designed, with a ground floor constructed of red brick, and an upper floor of white stucco, with black trim around its windows. An imposing sign over the entrance read, in gold Victorian script, *Slug and Cauliflower Hotel.*

And just down the road was the reason why its telephone number had been unreachable. A bomb had fallen in last night's air raid, landing squarely in an intersection. The public house, however, was undamaged and open.

Having been summoned by the proprietor, Thaddeus Quinn joined Charlie and Mr. Deeley in the wood-panelled saloon, which was infused with the smell of warm ale and cigarettes.

"I'm very surprised to see you again, sir," he said, to Mr. Deeley, appropriating a table beneath a row of leaded glass windows, around which were arranged wooden chairs with plush red cushions. "Charlotte told me you were dead!"

"I was dead," Mr. Deeley replied. "However, as you can happily discern, I am dead no longer. I do not recommend it, as it is uncommonly uncomfortable, and plays merry havoc with one's internal humours."

"Silas Ferryman's kidnapped Betty," Charlie said. "We don't know where he's taken her. But he knows you have his suitcase. And he wants it back."

A shadow passed across Thaddeus Quinn's face. He looked momentarily alarmed. And then, his training as a police constable seemed to take over.

"How do you know this?" he asked.

"He rang us. I really thought he was you... I'm so sorry, Thaddeus. I told him everything... Strand, what I saw in the suitcase...."

"Where I'm staying...?"

"No," Charlie said.

"And he did not follow us here," Mr. Deeley added. "We made certain."

"And he wishes to meet?"

"At the public air raid shelter on Emmanuel Road. At half past two."

"If Ferryman wishes to meet with me at all, it will be for one reason only, and that is to do away with me."

"But if you give him the suitcase," Charlie said, "he won't

have any reason to kill you. You won't have the proof of his guilt anymore. He'll let Betty go and then he can just…disappear."

"You're too generous in your assumptions," Thaddeus said with a grim smile. "I very much doubt he would just 'disappear.' Not while I'm still alive and able to pursue him."

He paused.

"Here is what I propose."

CHAPTER TWENTY-ONE

The parade of shops that Betty had listed in her ration book as the suppliers of her meat and butter, cooking fats and sugar, was at the end of Harris Road. Long queues of women, many with young children in tow, stretched out along the pavement. There was a butcher and a grocery—not the one owned by Betty's father; that was closer to Balham tube station—and a bakery; a hardware store and a clothing store; and on the corner, a newsagent's, which offered, as well as the daily papers, glass jars filled with sweets, and cigarettes.

Farther on, Charlie and Mr. Deeley reached the top end of Tooting Bec Common, a triangle of green defined by Emmanuel Road on one side, and the railway line which ran down to Crystal Palace on the other.

There was the first air raid shelter, at the park's western edge, dug into a trench in the ground and covered over with earth.

The big anti-aircraft guns that they'd heard in the night were not in evidence, but Tooting Bec Common was an immense area, subdivided by more railway tracks and several roads. Charlie suspected they were located in the wider section, farther south, along with the searchlights that sought out the German planes as they flew over the city.

They walked along farther, past an ARP post and then a barrage balloon, looming silver against the afternoon sky. And then red brick and white stone trimmed houses, with steeply pitched roofs and distinctive porches. Two of the houses were fractured and crumbled from a recent bombing, the wood from their interiors splintered and scattered across the ground like tumbled matchsticks. A family of five was retrieving its possessions from the remnants of their home and loading them into a van.

"There were a great many wars fought during my other lifetime," Mr. Deeley said, thoughtfully, "the most well-known of them being the ones waged against Napoleon. But these were distant adventures, and when we received news, it was also distant, like a story narrated from a book, a great excursion abroad. And when the soldiers returned from their battles, some were scarred, others missing arms and legs... and such tales they told of swords and rifles... and launching cannonballs at fortress walls... but nothing, Mrs. Collins, nothing, was like this. I cannot imagine spending years living in terror of certain death arriving from the skies as I sleep. The sight of this poor family fills me with such sadness."

"And me, Mr. Deeley."

They had reached the collection of houses which made up the Hyde Farm estate.

"It is not a farm," Mr. Deeley said, with some disappointment.

"It used to be," Charlie said. "In fact, it was still a farm in the time you came from... all of this area was very rural. It was made over into houses beginning in the 1890s... and a lot of these homes were set aside for soldiers who'd fought in the Boer War and the First World War."

"It's a pity the pilots of the planes which drop the explosives are not mindful of all this careful preservation," Mr. Deeley observed. "But there is the second air raid shelter, on the corner, and there, I believe, is the gentleman who has summoned us."

It was indeed the fair-haired gentleman from the Bedford Square Hotel, standing in front of the shelter, under a tree, smoking a cigarette.

"This is one habit I find wholly distasteful," Mr. Deeley said, within earshot of the man. "It makes the air disagreeably foul. As if the bombings and coal fireplaces of London did not corrupt the atmosphere enough. Good afternoon, sir. "

"Good afternoon," Ferryman replied. "I do not see my suitcase."

"You did not request that your suitcase attend this meeting," Mr. Deeley replied. "You only requested news. We are here to deliver it."

"Where's Betty?" Charlie said.

"You did not request that Betty attend this meeting," Ferryman countered. "She's safe."

"Unharmed?"

"Unharmed," Ferryman replied. "For now."

"We've spoken with Thaddeus and he proposes to exchange your suitcase for Betty," Charlie said.

"He furthermore proposes to arrange a truce," Mr. Deeley continued. "He will agree to shake hands with you, and bid you goodbye. A gentleman's agreement, if you will, predicated upon the fact that you and he have arrived at a stalemate, which neither of you can profit by."

"And Mr. Deeley and I will be there as your principal witnesses, to seal the agreement."

Ferryman laughed.

"An admirable proposal," he said, "but I draw the line at shaking hands. It's a cunning suggestion, the outcome of which is, no doubt, to spirit me back to 1849 to face a judge. Where is this exchange to take place?"

"Clapham South Underground Station," Charlie said. "Tonight. At half past seven. It's very public, and there will be no shortage of witnesses in case you're tempted to do something stupid."

"The tube station's a rather large place," Ferryman replied, finishing his cigarette. "Anywhere in particular?"

• • •

Clapham South Underground station was just up the road from The Slug and Caterpillar and, like Balham, was a preferred shelter for hundreds of men, women, and children each night as the Luftwaffe returned to rain bombs down on London.

It was twenty-five minutes past seven when Charlie, Mr. Deeley, and Thaddeus descended to the southbound platform. It was

189

already filled with shelterers and their bedding, their flasks of tea, their suitcases and books, their knitting and chess games, packs of cards, and household keepsakes. It was very hot, and the pungent smell of too many people in need of a wash and a change of clothes was overpowering.

Standing by the edge, studying the length of the station tunnel, they could not see Silas Ferryman. Or Betty.

A train arrived. No one got off.

A handful of children scampered aboard, presumably to ride to the end of the line, at Morden, and then come back again on a northbound train. An evening's entertainment.

The train clattered out of the station.

"Perhaps," said Mr. Deeley, "we ought to look on the other platform."

They crossed over to the northbound side of the station, which was as crowded as the first, but they did not see Silas Ferryman.

Charlie looked up at the clock that hung from the station ceiling. It was twenty-five minutes to eight.

Another train arrived, this one coming north from Balham, on its way into London.

A few people got off and picked a path through the shelterers, to the Way Out, and the escalators.

A small boy, aged about eight, in a knitted pullover and short trousers, tugged on the sleeve of Charlie's coat.

"Are you Charlotte?" he asked.

Charlie looked around, and down.

"I am," she said, not recognizing him at all. "Where've you come from, then?"

"I've come on the train from Balham," the small boy said. "Mr. Ferryman sent me to find you. He said to look for a man with a suitcase, and a woman with brown hair and a green and white dress, and a tall man wearing a long black overcoat."

"Mr. Ferryman is meant to be here," Charlie said, with another glance at the clock. Twenty minutes to eight.

"I'm to tell you that he won't be coming, as he isn't happy with your arrangements. But he will be at Balham if you'd care to meet him there."

"Whereabouts in Balham?" Thaddeus asked.

"In the tube station. On the southbound platform."

Charlie looked at Mr. Deeley, and then at Thaddeus.

"Then to Balham station we must proceed," Thaddeus decided.

"Stay here," Charlie said to the child. "Don't move from this platform. Promise me."

"But my Mummy and Auntie will be looking for me."

"What's your name?" Charlie asked, kneeling down, so that her eyes were level with his.

"Arthur Barry."

"Right then, Arthur Barry. I want you to stay here, on this platform, until I come back and tell you it's all right to leave. Understand?"

Arthur nodded.

"Good. See you in a little while, then."

She got to her feet, and caught up to Thaddeus and Mr. Deeley at the cross-passage that led back to the southbound tunnel.

"Thaddeus," Mr. Deeley said. "You cannot proceed to Balham. Not now. I beg of you."

"Whyever not?"

Mr. Deeley looked, in desperation, at Charlie.

"It may be," Charlie said, remembering what Ruby had told her, "that we were always destined to cause something to happen. Or it may be that we will change the outcome of something. Or, the outcome of something was never in question at all, merely the means by which it will be achieved."

She looked at the clock. Fourteen minutes to eight.

And there was a train coming. She could feel the wind. She could hear its peculiar muffled roar, far down the tunnel.

"Thaddeus," she said, lowering her voice to a whisper. "There's an air raid in progress. And a bomb's going to drop on Balham High Road at two minutes past eight. It'll explode at the north end of the station, above the cross-passage between the northbound and southbound platforms."

Thaddeus took this in, the look on his face grave.

"The tunnel roof will collapse and rubble and water and sewage and gas will pour into the station. Nearly seventy people are going to be killed."

"And this bomb will destroy both platforms?"

"Only the northbound side. The southbound side will be virtually untouched."

"Then I will go," Thaddeus decided. "I'll be safe on the southbound platform."

The train emerged from the running tunnel and rattled to a stop. The guard in the last carriage pressed the button to open the doors.

Thaddeus stepped aboard the first carriage. He placed the suitcase on the slatted wooden floor and sat down beside it.

Mr. Deeley looked at Charlie. "We must go with him. Who knows what Silas Ferryman might do? You said it yourself, Mrs. Collins. It may be that we will change the outcome. That is why we are here. It is to save Betty. And perhaps Thaddeus, too."

He followed his son aboard the train, then turned around.

"Will you come with me?"

• • •

The train drew into Balham Station, slowing as it passed the rows of shelterers, some sleeping, some sitting with their backs against the curving platform wall, chatting or reading.

Charlie checked the clock again as she stepped onto the platform with Thaddeus and Mr. Deeley. Twelve minutes to eight.

She made note of the openings in the platform wall, which mirrored the ones on the northbound platform. Here, at the south end, was a cross-passage. And then midway along were the two exits to the Way Out, protected by heavy watertight doors, leading to the escalators and the stairs. And then, at the north end, another cross-passage. *The* cross-passage.

One of the two watertight doors at the Way Out had been pulled shut. Charlie remembered the reasoning behind their installation. There were water pipes buried under the roads around the station, and the fear at the start of the war had been that if those pipes were damaged, the water would cascade into the booking hall and down the escalators, and flood the lower level and the tracks.

They had not considered what would happen if the roadway itself collapsed onto the platform, on the other side of the watertight doors.

She glanced at the clock.

Eight minutes to eight.

A few last-minute stragglers were making their way onto the platform from the booking hall upstairs. Someone wearing a London Transport uniform was pulling the last watertight door closed.

And then she saw them. Silas Ferryman. And Betty.

They were standing just beyond the cross-passage at the other end of the platform, almost at the mouth of the running tunnel.

"Mr. Deeley!" Charlie said. "Thaddeus!"

Six minutes to eight.

They ran down the perilously narrow free space along the edge of the platform, Thaddeus in the lead.

"This man told me you wanted to see me," Betty said, looking confused. "He said you had a message of vital importance. And then he dragged me out of the house and locked me in a shed. I don't understand what's going on, Thad."

"Forgive me for not introducing myself earlier," the fair-haired gentleman said to Betty. "I am Silas Ferryman. You may have heard of me."

"I swear I have not," Betty answered, close to tears, gasping for breath, holding her middle. "And if you do not allow me to sit down, Mr. Ferryman, I shall faint. I am carrying a child, in case you failed to notice."

"Sit down then," Ferryman replied. "Your usefulness to me is at an end."

193

Betty sank onto the platform, bracing her back against the white-tiled wall.

"And so," Thaddeus said, to the fair-haired gentleman, "we meet again at last, sir. Face to face. I have brought your suitcase."

"Put it there," Ferryman directed, indicating the spot on the platform where Betty was sitting.

Two minutes to eight.

Thaddeus placed the case at Betty's feet.

As he did this, the fair-haired gentleman pulled from his coat pocket a very large knife. In one swift movement, he drew it across Thaddeus's neck, slashing arteries and veins, causing a gush of blood to spray out and splash the white tiled wall red.

Betty screamed as Thaddeus staggered and crumpled to the platform. And in that same moment, Silas Ferryman seized Charlie's arm and dragged her through the cross-passage, into the northbound side of the station.

"You'll do instead of Betty," he said. "Thank you for being so helpful. You may now assist me in making my escape."

He pulled her along to the edge of the platform, past the shelterers, the knife held to her throat.

"Please let me go," Charlie pleaded.

She could see Mr. Deeley following close behind her, unable to act. One wrong step to their right would mean certain death on the electrified tracks.

"The watertight doors are shut. The trains aren't running under the river. You can't go anywhere."

She could also see the big old-fashioned clock, with its Roman numerals. Eight o'clock.

"We're going to die," she said, quietly, desperately. "In two minutes a bomb's going to drop on the roadway above. The tunnel's going to collapse. Everything that's up there—sewers, water lines, ballast, earth—will come crashing down here and nearly seventy people will be killed. Please. Please, Mr. Ferryman. Let me go."

Silas Ferryman stopped, looked at her, and then smiled. "If you know this will happen," he said, "then surely we can employ your time travelling skills to extricate ourselves." He tightened his grip on her arm. "Do it. Now!"

"I can't! I don't know how!"

Charlie saw a look of doubt pass across Ferryman's face and then... she felt his fingers loosen. She twisted away from him. And then Mr. Deeley was behind her, pushing her along the platform.

"Run!" he shouted. "All the way to the other end! Now!"

Charlie ran. Halfway to the Way Out sign, she heard screams and a commotion. She stopped and spun around, aware that Mr. Deeley was no longer behind her. Far, far down the platform, she could see that Silas Ferryman had tumbled into the pit beneath the railway tracks. And that Mr. Deeley was racing as fast as he could towards her, but he was holding his arm, and it was dripping blood.

She turned to run back to him.

"No!" he shouted. "Leave me! Save yourself!"

His voice was lost in the thunder of a cataclysmic explosion. The lights flashed out. And then the station was filled with hysterical shouting and the sound of gushing water and the smell of gas and sewage and the thunder of cascading earth. In the utter darkness, panicking shelterers pushed and shoved Charlie, desperate to escape. She fell, and was immediately stepped on, not once, not twice, but many times, so that the breath was trampled from her body. She tried to crawl away but her hands met wet earth and gravel and then her arms were buried by it, and then the top of her head, and then the weight of it pressed her face onto the concrete platform and her nose and mouth were filled with it... and then... and then....

CHAPTER TWENTY-TWO

Wendy had given Shaun enough money to pay for a ticket on the Underground, there and back again, and a little bit extra, just in case.

She and Nick had offered to come with him but Shaun had politely declined. It was a journey he wished to undertake on his own.

It was a journey he needed to undertake on his own.

He stood on the northbound platform at Balham tube station, waiting for his train, reading the huge trackside ads for travel to Bournemouth, and extending a mortgage, and brewing a delightful and very special green tea.

Walking a little further to the north, he could see that there was a gap where no ads were pasted to the curved white wall at all. Indeed, the wall itself was discoloured and peeling, with black cracks and water stains showing through the plaster. The dark stains seemed to mimic almost perfectly the outline of the iron rings from which the Underground tunnels were constructed.

Turning around, he saw that he was standing directly in front of what might have once been a cross-passage to the other platform. Except the opening had been blocked off and a locked doorway installed, with signs warning about the need for caution when entering the electrical switch room, and dangers of shock.

A man wearing a London Underground tie and a navy blue pullover was standing nearby.

"Interesting, that," he said, to Mr. Deeley, noting his interest in the wall. "This tunnel was badly damaged by a bomb in World War Two. You can clearly see the repair works, where the paint is lifting, due to water ingress. And that cross-passage was blocked by the rubble. It was never re-opened."

Mr. Deeley looked at the wall again. And then, he followed one of the black stains up, and up, to the curved ceiling of the tunnel.

And then.....

...He remembered.

The same way he'd recovered the fragment of a memory earlier that morning.

Except that this was the part before the fragment.

He could see the clock suspended from the roof of the platform tunnel.

One minute past eight.

And he could see Mrs. Collins, trying to reason with the man who had deceived him, and who had killed his son, cold-bloodedly and without any remorse.

He heard her tell Ferryman about the bomb that was about to drop from the sky, and he heard Ferryman demand that she use her time travelling abilities to remove them from the station. He heard her response. And then he saw Ferryman pause, and a look of doubt cross his face. And he saw, in that moment, that Mrs. Collins had pulled herself free from his grasp.

And, in that moment, Shaun raced to her side, and dragged her away, and pushed her along the platform.

"Run!" he shouted. "All the way to the other end! Now!"

Driven by the knowledge of what was about to be, she fled. Shaun prayed she would have enough time to reach the southern end of the platform, far away from the devastation. But Ferryman now had hold of Shaun's arm, and the two of them were in very great danger of falling over the edge of the platform.

"What about you, then? What are your time-travelling skills like? Surely you can get us out of here?"

"I cannot, sir. My ability to travel in time is as hopeless as Charlotte's. There is nowhere you can run. She told you the truth. We have only moments to live."

"Now then!" said a man in a uniform, who had been alerted by the commotion on the other platform, and had come through the passageway after Ferryman. "Now then... let's not have any of this! We've got Germans trying to kill us outside. We don't need you down here helping them! Put that knife down."

"I dare you," Shaun said, to Ferryman, "to use that knife against me. Go on. Show me how much courage you have now. You have achieved what you wanted, the death of the man who pursued you in the name of justice. The death of my son. My grief and anger know no bounds. I am consoled by the fact that you will be dead in less than a minute yourself."

"Then you shall have your wish," Ferryman replied, raising the knife.

Shaun heard screams as he deflected the knife with his free arm, its blade slicing into his skin. But the deflection caused Ferryman to let go. Shaun pulled away, at the same time kicking Ferryman backwards, tumbling him over the edge of the platform.

"Don't move!" the man in the uniform shouted at Ferryman, who had slipped into the pit underneath the electrified middle rail. "For God's sake—the tracks are live!"

Shaun raced after Mrs. Collins, his arm dripping blood. He saw her stop and turn towards him.

"No!" he shouted. "Leave me! Save yourself!"

• • •

Fenwick Oldbutter was where he promised he would be, occupying the buskers' pitch at the foot of the escalators in the tube station at Waterloo. He was a little man, about fifty years of age, with round, wire-framed spectacles. He wore black trousers and an old-fashioned pullover vest, underneath which was a white shirt with rolled-up sleeves.

Shaun waited while he finished his hour, playing a battered fiddle with exceptional skill, his violin case open on the floor in front of him for the collection of coins. And there was a rather large collection. The music sounded Celtic, very old, and would not have been out of place, Shaun thought, in a tiny Irish pub with impossibly low ceilings and rounds of Guinness on its tabletops.

"There we are," Fenwick said, at last, transferring the day's take into an old-fashioned drawstring bag, into which he added the musician's ID card issued by London Underground Limited. He laid his fiddle lovingly into its case and closed the lid. "You are Mr. Deeley, I presume?"

• • •

Fenwick Oldbutter's lodgings were in Belsize Park, in north London. He occupied a very large house on a tree-lined road, the sort of house that would have suited a renowned actor or a member of Parliament, or perhaps a distant member of a less auspicious branch of the British royal family.

"Independently wealthy," he said, almost apologetically, unlocking the front door and disarming the alarm. "All inherited. Old money. I love the busking, which is why I do it. I donate all the takings to charity. Tea? I've got a very nice Special Gunpowder you might like."

Tea was served in a sunny, glass-walled conservatory filled with potted palms and exotic artefacts from distant times and very distant lands. A life-sized porcelain tiger sat beside a wicker fan-backed chair, and both were overseen by a tall wooden statue, perhaps of some south seas warrior, spear in hand, a look of ferocity blazing from his mother-of-pearl eyes.

"Now," Fenwick Oldbutter said at last, "how may I assist?"

"I wish," Shaun said, "to reverse an injustice. Two injustices, in fact. Two deaths. Both of which occurred as a result of an unfortunate tampering with history."

"Ah," the gentleman said, pressing his fingertips together. "Yes. A consequence of meddling. You must know, of course, that the circle of travellers to which I belong has undertaken a vow never to knowingly interfere with anything which has occurred, or which has yet to occur. For precisely the reasons you have just described."

"I did not know," Shaun replied.

"Well. Now you do. There also exists an Overarching Philosophy.

One, you were always destined to cause something to happen. Two, you may change an outcome, altering what had occurred previously. Three, the outcome was never in question at all, merely the means by which it was achieved."

"If that is the case, sir, then I propose we apply our intelligence to the second option. And it is also my contention that the offering of advice does not, in itself, constitute an interference. Are you in agreement?"

"I might well be."

"Therefore, sir, I may act upon your words, or ignore them. You will have nothing to do with my decision, other than to make me aware of my choices."

"A sound philosophy," Fenwick agreed. "Let me ask you this, then. If you were able to return to a specific point in the past, in order to reverse this perceived injustice… how would you accomplish it?"

"I do not know," Shaun replied. "That is why I have consulted you."

"But you have travelled before. Several times, in fact. You told me this in our telephone conversation. How were these journeys undertaken?"

"By accident," Shaun replied, "with no deliberate intent on my part."

"And your most recent excursion, from 1940 until now. You willed yourself to travel?"

"I may well have. But I recall only that my last thought was to escape, and to be somewhere else. Anywhere else but in the northbound tunnel at Balham Underground Station at two minutes past eight on the 14th of October."

"I shall impart some knowledge to you, Mr. Deeley. You were, in fact, chosen for the journey you undertook from your present to 1940. You and your friend, Charlotte Duran."

"But, in the process, both Charlotte and my son lost their lives. I fail to see the advantage."

Fenwick Oldbutter pressed his fingers together again, in contemplation.

"Might I suggest that there was more than one purpose to your journey? That the actions you undertook served the past, as well as the future?"

"Whose past?" Shaun said. "And whose future?"

"I cannot say."

"You can say, sir. You simply choose not to."

Fenwick offered a slight movement of his shoulders. It might have been a shrug. It might have been a tacit agreement. "I will share what I can say, then. I had a sister. Her name was Beryl Allsop. Do you recall the surname?"

"I do," Shaun said, after a moment. "Deirdre Allsop worked in a sweet shop in Balham."

"My niece."

"And she disappeared in the summer of 1940. Her body was discovered lying upon Mitcham Common, with her throat cut, and without her earrings."

"The very same. And does your very excellent memory allow you to recall a further name... Mary Potter?"

"A brick-maker's daughter," Shaun said, "who set off to visit her cousin in June of 1849... but she did not arrive. Her body was located under a bridge... and her throat had been cut... and her silver ring had been taken."

"An ancestor of Ruby Firth's. Rather closely related. And one further name... Matilda Quinn."

"The sister of my son."

"Indeed. And so you see, Mr. Deeley... all of us have something in common. Justice has been served... has it not? Silas Ferryman did not survive the bombing of the tube station."

"And Charlotte Duran?"

Again, Fenwick raised a slight shoulder.

"Perhaps not so much a connection to the past... as a connection to the future. Why not wait and see?"

"Because in this future, this future we are now inhabiting, Charlotte Duran no longer exists. She died seventy-three years ago. And furthermore, sir, by your very admission, you and Mrs. Firth have already meddled, by conspiring to dispatch Charlotte and myself back to 1940."

"Have we?"

Shaun removed Mrs. Collins's lump of shrapnel from the pocket of his overcoat.

"This was given to us by Mrs. Firth, on the platform of the railway station at Middlehurst, before we came to London."

Fenwick took the shrapnel and turned it over and over, examining all of its ridges, all of the places where the heat had seared it and caused pockmarks and cracks.

"She told me about this," he said. "Oh yes. *Yes*. Interesting."

"You may note," Shaun said, "that your timepiece has reacted to this item in a most peculiar manner."

Fenwick consulted his wristwatch, which was of the old-fashioned variety, with springs and cogs inhabiting its insides, resulting in the need for a nightly wind-up.

"Indeed," he replied. "How intriguing. And you think this is what propelled you and the young lady from your present into the past?"

"I do."

Fenwick returned the lump of metal to Shaun's custody. "Smoke and mirrors. Magicians' props. This one is able to generate heat and reverse the hands of a clock, but I daresay those are its only party tricks. Nothing to do with time travelling."

Shaun looked at Fenwick. "What, then, is your explanation for our relocation?"

"Power of suggestion," Fenwick said. "Your young lady had, like you, the ability, the skill. Her imagination was engaged. You encountered Ruby, in the first instance, at the museum. She further encouraged you by meeting you at the railway station with this piece of shrapnel, revealing how she found the object lying in a field, a relic from the Second World War. And then, at the young lady's grandmother's house, you entered the air raid shelter. You were surrounded by reminders of the war. It was your own imagination which took you back. Nothing more, nothing less."

Shaun drank the Special Gunpowder tea and met the shining eyes of the porcelain tiger.

"Did you know that I would come to you, upon this day, to request your assistance?"

"I cannot say."

Shaun gave him a look.

"You, sir, are as vexatious as Monsieur Duran the Lesser, who, I am told, came to a very poor end at the bottom of the Caribbean Sea."

"I remember him well. I had, upon occasion, attended his Grand Summer Ball at Stoneford Manor."

"It is a shame I did not see you there, as I was also in attendance, for a good many years."

"You may have overlooked me, Mr. Deeley, as the ballroom was unfailingly filled to overflowing, and the attendees were merry and danced until midnight. I certainly remember you."

"Do you?" Shaun was unimpressed. "Will you help me, sir?"

"My advice to you, Mr. Deeley, is much the same as the advice Ruby Firth gave to the young lady. You must think very carefully about that which you seek to undo. For instance, if you seek to prevent the death of someone, you should endeavour to return yourself to a point in time where you might influence that person to be somewhere other than where his or her life will be extinguished. But you must be very certain that by undoing something, you do not effect a result that is worse. And another word of warning. You can never be absolutely certain that the death will not still occur. What was always intended may be impossible to overcome."

"I understand," Shaun said. "But if you knew in advance that I would visit you today, then I am certain you *will* decide to assist me, in one way or another. And the outcome of your assistance, in whatever form it takes, was always meant to be. No more, and no less."

Fenwick Oldbutter chuckled.

"Your intelligence does you credit, sir. What is your wish?"

"I wish to prevent the murder of my son. And I wish to prevent the death of Charlotte Duran."

"If that is the case, Mr. Deeley, I therefore advise you to simply return yourself to your parallel present. To the time from which you and your dearest friend originally came. Think upon it, and it will be. You cannot return to a time which you already inhabit— otherwise there would be two of you. But you may return to a time immediately following that. Indeed, you may return to a time one second past the point where you departed on your journey. You can trust me on this. And, once you have affected your return, steer clear of all temptations that would cause you to imagine yourself in the past. Abandon the air raid shelter at the bottom of the garden. Leave immediately. Go back to the museum in Stoneford and dismantle the war exhibit. And if you should be approached by a woman offering you a souvenir of her adventures during the Blitz, send her away without so much as a second thought."

"What about my son? He will still meet his end in the Underground station. I have seen his grave."

"Will he…?" Fenwick inquired, with a slight smile. "Perhaps that is something about which we ought to wait and see."

CHAPTER TWENTY-THREE

Nick was tapping urgent, last-minute observations into his mobile. Wendy was not happy.

"You must go, of course," she said. "If things need to be put right, then you must try and right them."

"I wish, so much, that I was able to go with you," Nick said. "What an opportunity! To be able to prove everything that I've spent my life researching."

"I would gladly take you with me... but I have no idea how you might return."

"You must promise," Nick said, "that once you've got the hang of this, you'll come back and visit me. Us. And perhaps stay a little longer. There are so many unanswered questions...."

"I promise," Shaun said. "And I am indebted to you both for everything. But I am inhabiting a time and a place where I do not belong. It is a terrible whim of fate. I must go back."

Wendy took both of Shaun's hands in her own.

"Even though I've never met her, I know your Charlotte means a lot to you."

"She means everything."

"I shall miss you."

"And I shall miss you," Shaun said truthfully. "There is another you in the other reality whom I hardly know at all. And another Nick who will be as curious as his present counterpart to hear about my travels. You have shown me utmost kindness, Wendy, in spite of your earlier misgivings. And for this, I will be forever grateful."

"Come on, then," Wendy said, summoning a smile.

She gave him a hug, and kissed his cheek.

"What's involved? Do you have to click your shoes together and whisper some kind of magical incantation? Do you need a whirlwind? A wicked witch?"

"If I am to believe the wisdom of Fenwick Oldbutter, I require nothing beyond my imagination. And something to aid its focus."

"Then I'll count you in," Wendy said, impishly.

"Do so, then. And... goodbye."

Shaun closed his eyes and thought of the air raid shelter at the bottom of Mrs. Collins's grandmother's garden. And he thought of the time before that, and Mrs. Collins's little cottage in Stoneford, and making tea, and picking autumn-flowering Clematis from the garden, and their conversation concerning happy conclusions. It seemed a lifetime ago.

It was.

He forced himself to think, again, about the air raid shelter, and about the single second following the moment when he and Mrs. Collins had discovered themselves in 1940.

"Goodbye, Mr. Deeley..." Wendy said, taking a deep breath. "Three... two... one!"

• • •

He could see the clock suspended from the roof of the platform tunnel.

One minute past eight.

And he could see Mrs. Collins, trying to reason with the man who had wholly deceived him, and who had killed his son, cold-bloodedly and without any remorse.

This was not the air raid shelter at the bottom of Nana Betty's garden. This was not the present reality he had wished for.

Fenwick Oldbutter's warning had come true. *You must be very certain that by undoing something, you do not affect a result that is worse.*

This was worse.

This was the worst result possible.

He heard Mrs. Collins tell Ferryman about the bomb that was

about to drop from the sky, and his suggestion that they employ time travelling to escape, and her response. He saw Ferryman pause, and the look of doubt cross his face. And he saw Mrs. Collins pull herself free from his grasp.

Shaun raced to her side, and dragged her away, and pushed her along the platform.

"Run!" he shouted. "All the way to the other end! Now!"

She fled. But Ferryman now had hold of Shaun's arm. And both of them were in very great danger of falling over the edge of the platform.

"What about you, then? What are your time-travelling skills like? Surely you can get us out of here?"

"Not me," Shaun said, thinking quickly. "But look behind you. Thaddeus! Arrest this sorry excuse of an impostor!"

Ferryman spun around. And in that moment, Shaun pulled his arm free. Driven by rage, he kicked Ferryman backwards, tumbling him over the edge of the platform.

There was the man in the uniform. "Don't move!" he shouted, as Ferryman rolled into the pit underneath the electrified middle rail. "For God's sake—the tracks are live!"

Shaun bolted after Mrs. Collins. He saw her stop and turn towards him.

"No!" he shouted. "Leave me! Save yourself!"

Behind him, the tunnel exploded. The platform plunged into darkness, and all around him he could hear the screams of women and children, and the roar of water and gravel and pieces of the roadway above falling through the hole in the top of the tunnel.

But he had bought himself precious extra seconds.

And now he had caught up to Mrs. Collins and he had hold of her hand.

And someone was grappling with the watertight doors. One of them slid open. And then they were being pushed through by the forward stampede of shelterers, desperate to escape the sweeping wash of rubble. Someone switched on a torch, and its meagre beam showed them the stairs, and the way to safety.

The escalators were stopped. Shaun ran up the wooden steps, dragging Mrs. Collins with him, up to the growing chaos in the booking hall, and then up again to the surface.

There, huddled in the shelter of the concrete blast wall, he held Mrs. Collins safe in his arms. He could see the strong white beams of the searchlights on Tooting Bec Common, scanning the sky. And he could hear the drone of the bombers from Germany. He could hear the whistles and the *thuds* of the explosives as they found their targets. He could see the fires in the distance, and billows of smoke, tinged red and white. The ground shook and pieces of shrapnel from the ack-ack guns on Tooting Bec Common rained down, bouncing off the pavement and clinking into the gutter.

A little distance to the north Shaun heard shouting and was aware of frenzied activity. He saw torches shining on a gaping crater that had opened up from one side of the road to the other. An 88 bus was slowly sinking over the edge, headfirst.

Ambulances were pulling up now, their bells trilling, and legions of people were running into the station to assist those still trapped below. And still the shelterers staggered out into the night air, covered in mud.

There was Betty, soaking wet, sitting on the pavement, while a woman in a Salvation Army bonnet tended to her, bringing her a cup of tea, a biscuit, and a blanket.

Shaun wrapped his arms tightly around Mrs. Collins. He drew her close, kissed the top of her head, and, without words, laid his own head upon hers and closed his eyes.

CHAPTER TWENTY-FOUR

The air raid shelter was damp, and it smelled of earth and mildew and the history of ages. And it was uncommonly still, and as quiet as a grave.

"Are we dead, Mr. Deeley?" Charlie whispered.

"I think not, Mrs. Collins."

Mr. Deeley disengaged himself from her arms, and took quick stock of their surroundings.

What was left of the afternoon's sunlight shone wanly through the small open doorway. An old wooden bunk bed lay along one curving, corrugated steel wall, a single bed along the other. The homemade shelves were in a very poor state of repair. He saw a folding chair, a spade, a rake… and a very large red tin watering can.

"We're in Nana Betty's shelter," Charlie said. "We're back where we started."

She scrambled up the ladder, followed by Mr. Deeley. They looked at the garden.

There was the little paved area with its large flowerpots, and the tidy patch of lawn, and the two rock-rimmed fishponds, and the border of ivy along the two wooden fences, and the path made out of flagstones.

Through the net curtains in Nana Betty's windows, Charlie could see her mum and Auntie Wendy, standing in the middle of the dining room.

"We're very definitely back in the present," she said. "No onions and cabbages where the grass ought to be. And it *smells* like now. Car exhaust and wet earth. Not burning houses and coal and explosives. We're home."

• • •

"Oh!" said Charlie's mum. "Where've you two sprung from? We thought you'd gone back to Stoneford."

"Without as much as a goodbye hug," Auntie Wendy added, pointedly.

They were surrounded by an accumulation of Nana Betty's things: papers and books, boxes and baskets, ornaments, lost items of jewellery—now found…random bits of stuff that had been saved for reasons known only to her.

"We were… distracted," Mr. Deeley replied. "We undertook an adventure. Our utmost apologies."

"What day is it?" Charlie asked.

"You really have been distracted," said her mum. "It's Tuesday. You've been gone since Friday."

"We went up to London."

"Shopping for vintage clothing?" Auntie Wendy inquired. "I like that outfit, Charlie. Very 1940s. Is it the real thing?"

Charlie realized she was still wearing Betty's olive green and cream crepe de chine dress, the one she'd loaned her the morning they'd met Silas Ferryman for lunch at the Bedford Square Hotel.

"It is absolutely the real thing," she replied. "In fact, the woman who'd originally owned it was the one who gave it to me."

"She must have been very old," her mother remarked. "Mum's age, at the very least."

"She didn't look it," Charlie said.

"We're just packing up for the night," said Auntie Wendy. "Mum collected so much stuff, it's unbelievable. I can run you over to Clapham Junction if you're thinking of catching a late train back to Middlehurst…."

Charlie glanced at Mr. Deeley.

"Would you mind if we spent the night here instead?" she said. "I'm exhausted. I don't think we could face a two-hour train journey."

"We don't mind," said Charlie's mother, "and I'm sure Mum, wherever she is, won't mind in the least. Although she was always a bit funny about the idea of men and women co-habiting without the benefit of a marriage certificate. Ironic, really, when you stop to think about how I got my start."

"Separate beds!" Auntie Wendy warned, not entirely seriously, waggling her finger at Mr. Deeley.

• • •

Dinner was Chinese, collected from the takeaway down the road, eaten at Nana Betty's big antique dining room table and washed down with a bottle of plonk from Naveed's Wines and Spirits on the corner.

Mr. Deeley had discovered some long beeswax candles in a drawer in the walnut sideboard and placed them in a pair of silver holders from the mantle over the fire. He'd lit them with the Swan Vestas from his trouser pocket; they now flickered romantically on the dining table, illuminating their meal.

"And you say I was dead?" Charlie mused, in between mouthfuls of king prawn chow mein. "Actually dead?"

"For the better part of seventy-three years," Mr. Deeley replied. "And it is only through my dogged determination that you are sitting here now, enjoying a glass of wine and a conversation with your most excellent supper companion."

"I don't remember being dead."

"Your death was in the other 1940. A parallel universe, as Nick called it."

"And there was another Nick, and another Auntie Wendy...?"

"Indeed. However, your mother was not there. Wendy had no brothers or sisters."

"How peculiar. And you actually saw where I was buried?"

"I did, Mrs. Collins. Your grave was located in the very same place as the grave belonging to Thaddeus. I might venture a guess that it might have been the very same headstone, although the name which had been carved there was your own, and not that of my son."

"No," Charlie said. "No, I definitely don't remember anything about being dead. Although I'm not quite sure what a memory of death should be like. I remember Silas Ferryman. He had hold of me and he dragged me off onto the northbound platform… and I remember trying to reason with him… and then you arrived… and I remember you giving me a shove and shouting at me to run. And then… were you injured? Did Ferryman cut you with his knife?"

"He did."

Mr. Deeley rolled up his sleeve to show Charlie his bandaged left arm.

"Poor you. Does it hurt?"

"I am in utter agony."

"Have another king prawn, then." Charlie speared one with her chopstick, and fed it to him across the table. "They're well known for both their healing and their anaesthetic properties."

"Do you have a memory of an enormous explosion?"

"Yes, and the lights went off and people were screaming and scrambling to get out… and after that I don't remember anything at all except you grabbing my hand and the two of us running up the stairs to the road. And then… we were here."

She paused.

"When was it that I actually died?"

"In that moment between the enormous explosion and the ensuing darkness, and my reaching for your hand, Mrs. Collins. It was but a few seconds… but contained within those few seconds was a span of more than seven decades."

"And Thaddeus died too?"

Mr. Deeley nodded, his eyes filling with sadness. "Silas Ferryman cut his throat. He bled to death on the southbound platform. To have known him so briefly… and to have delivered him to such an unjust end…."

He contemplated the dancing candle flames.

"If there was a purpose to our journey, I am unaware of its providence. We have ended up in exactly the same place that we began. Nothing has changed."

"Are you sure? Silas Ferryman did face a kind of justice because of what we did. Because of what you did, he was buried under the tunnel when it collapsed."

Charlie investigated another of the Chinese food containers, then transferred a helping of stir-fried vegetables onto Mr. Deeley's plate with her chopsticks.

"And anyway, you were dead too."

"I have no recollection of that at all. In fact, I have no memory of anything that happened between the moment the ceiling collapsed in the Bedford Square Hotel, and the moment Thaddeus was stabbed in the tunnel at Balham. I recall the wretched act by Silas Ferryman, and what happened next. But nothing before. I have no idea what caused us to be there."

"Then we've a good deal to catch up on," Charlie said. "And I'm awfully glad you visited Fenwick Oldbutter. Because if you hadn't decided to interfere the second time, imagine what might have happened to us."

"I would rather not," Mr. Deeley replied, trying to arrange the chopsticks with his fingers, so that they worked. "You must convince me of the advantage in using these implements, Mrs. Collins. They are altogether hopeless with fried rice."

He put the chopsticks down and instead picked up a spoon.

Charlie smiled, opened her bag, and found her mobile. She switched it on. "Absolutely dead," she said. "Unlike me." She dug out her charging cord and plugged it into the wall socket beside the walnut sideboard, and then looked inside her bag again.

"Where's my shrapnel?"

"Ah."

Mr. Deeley got up, and disappeared into the front hallway, then returned, lump of metal in hand.

"Overcoat pocket," he replied, giving it back to Charlie. "Take good care of that, and do not allow it to influence your imagination. Therein lies the secret of its power, according to Fenwick Oldbutter."

"I'm not even going to ask how it came to be in your pocket."

"Therein lies a further paradox," Mr. Deeley replied. "I discovered it in your bag—the same bag which contained the card that directed me to Mr. Oldbutter. The same bag which was buried in the mud with you, in the wreckage of the Underground station, and which was returned to Betty when your body was dug out weeks later, and identified. And yet, as you can see, you have your bag with you now, undamaged by time or catastrophe."

Charlie sipped her wine.

"And one further paradox. Silas Ferryman cut my arm during our first encounter. When I went back the second time, I pushed him over the edge of the platform before he could use his knife upon me. And yet... the injury persists."

"Too many paradoxes," Charlie decided. "They're making my head ache." She paused. "I wonder whatever happened to that suitcase."

• • •

It was not in the air raid shelter.

"It wasn't there when we first arrived, either," Charlie said as they climbed out and stood in the garden, which was now lit by the moon. "We'd have seen it. And anyway, my brother and sister and I never saw a suitcase in all the years we played in there when we were kids."

"But it was there in the other reality," Mr. Deeley reasoned. "And quite well preserved. Betty's only daughter was forbidden entry. The shelter remained a chamber of utmost privacy."

"Did you look inside? And did it have the same things in it that I saw, in 1940? A camera and a box of jewellery? And a couple of newspaper cuttings?"

"It did," Mr. Deeley confirmed. "And the camera still had film in it, and we took it to the gentleman who lived next door—Mrs. Firth's grandson—and he developed the photographs."

"That's interesting," said Charlie. "What did they show?"

"The places where Silas Ferryman left the bodies of his victims. A copse of trees and wild grasses. The remains of two bombed buildings. A row of brick railway arches."

"That's four," Charlie said. "I thought he only killed three women in 1940."

"He had taken pictures of all of his victims, without their knowledge. Angela Bailey. Deirdre Allsop. Violet." Mr. Deeley stopped, and looked at her. "The last photograph was of you. You were standing in the road, observing the damage to Mrs. Crofton's house. It was the morning we travelled up to London for lunch."

Charlie shivered. "Oh God," she said. "I was next. After Violet."

"I believe you would have been, yes."

Mr. Deeley stopped, and put his hand in his trouser pocket.

"This belongs to you," he said, placing the silver necklace with the pendant that said MRS. COLLINS in her hand. "I discovered it at the bottom of the gas mask box, with the other jewellery. I was certain that Ferryman had killed you, and taken that as his trophy."

Charlie reached up to her neck.

"It must have dropped into the box when I was looking inside it at Strand. The clasp's broken. See?"

She showed him.

"I shall arrange for it to be mended once we return to Stoneford," Mr. Deeley promised.

"So," Charlie reasoned, "in *that* 1940—in that parallel universe—Thaddeus, Ferryman and I all died at Balham station. But in the 1940 that belongs to *this* universe, our present reality, I didn't die. You rescued me. So how can we be certain Thaddeus and Ferryman didn't escape as well?"

CHAPTER TWENTY-FIVE

"Morning, sleepyheads!"

It was Charlie's mum, calling up the stairs from the front hallway.

"We're in here," Charlie said, poking her head out from the dining room.

Auntie Wendy closed the front door, and carried the box of cleaning things she and Charlie's mum had brought with them, into the kitchen.

"We've been up for hours. We're having breakfast. And we slept in separate beds."

"I was joking," Auntie Wendy said.

"Mr. Deeley was on his best behaviour," Charlie assured her, as her mum joined them in the dining room, and sat down at the table.

Mr. Deeley poured her a cup of tea.

"Does the name Thaddeus Quinn means anything to you?" Charlie asked carefully.

"Nothing at all," her mother replied. "Should it?" She turned in her chair and addressed the serving hatch in the wall. "Did you ever hear Mum talk about someone called Thaddeus Quinn?"

In the kitchen, Auntie Wendy shook her head.

"Unusual name though," she said. "I quite like it. Is he well-known?"

"In some circles," Charlie replied. "Can we borrow your car, Auntie Wendy?"

• • •

"I haven't driven in ages," Charlie admitted, starting the engine of Auntie Wendy's Ford Fiesta. "Not since Jeff died, anyway. We won't be saying anything about that to Auntie Wendy, will we?"

"Perhaps I should be sitting in the back," Mr. Deeley replied.

"If it were up to you we'd be going by horse and cart. Put your seatbelt on, Mr. Deeley. My motoring skills are excellent. It's the other drivers I don't trust."

The cemetery was ten minutes away, and the midmorning traffic was relatively easy to navigate. Charlie ignored Mr. Deeley's feigned fear each time she overtook a bus or a slow lorry, and admonished him severely for letting out an unearthly shriek as she sped through an amber traffic signal.

She parked Auntie Wendy's car close to the cemetery gates, and together they walked along the path that had taken them, on Friday, to the place where they had discovered Thaddeus Oliver Quinn's grave.

There it was. Charlie recognized the bench under the tree. She knelt down on the damp grass and brushed away a mound of brown oak leaves.

"Look," she said,

Mr. Deeley knelt down beside her.

"There's nothing there," he said. "The grave marker is gone."

• • •

Mr. Deeley was sitting with Charlie in Nana Betty's garden. Charlie had brought out two deck chairs from the cupboard under the stairs so they could take advantage of a pale noon sun. Inside the house, her mother and Auntie Wendy were conferring over what to make for lunch after their morning's work scrubbing the kitchen.

"So," said Charlie. "No gravestone for Thaddeus…."

"And no gravestone for you," Mr. Deeley said, with some relief.

"You do know what this means, don't you? We have, in fact, changed the outcome. That grave marker *was* there on Friday. So perhaps Thaddeus didn't die, after all."

"If we have indeed returned to the same reality," Mr. Deeley reasoned, "then perhaps we ought not to assume anything at all, Mrs. Collins."

"I believe I might be able to help you."

Charlie and Mr. Deeley both turned around. The voice had come from behind them, from the other side of the wooden fence which separated Nana Betty's garden from the one next door. There was nobody there. At least, not anyone that they could see.

They stood up, walked to the fence, and peered over it.

Sitting in a wheelchair was an ancient woman, her cheery face filled with wrinkles, with a shock of straight white hair that looked like an overturned bowl on top of her head.

"Ruby!" Charlie shouted.

"Gosh yes. Jolly good. Lovely to see you two again. Very pleased you turned up alive in the end, Mr. Deeley, and not dead."

"Not as pleased as me," Mr. Deeley replied.

"And me," Charlie said, slipping her arm around his waist.

"Would you like to come and have a word in the sitting room? I enjoy over-the-fence chats as much as the next person, but at my age it's jolly windy round the old joints, and I'm prone to catching a chill if I spend too much time out of doors. No point in tempting the Fates."

● ● ●

Ruby's sitting room had been adapted for sleeping, with a comfortable-looking bed and cupboards, and all manner of things to assist an elderly person in her day-to-day living.

"Have you been here all along?" Charlie asked, suddenly aware that in all of the years she'd been coming to visit Nana Betty, she had never once set eyes on Ruby Firth.

"Oh yes," Ruby supplied. "But, you know, I have been travelling rather a lot. I've had to give it up now, of course. I'm far too indisposed to manage the wherewithals. But I've had some jolly good adventures." She leaned over. "I got much better at it over the years. Less of the accidental popping in, unannounced. More of the landing as intended."

"Does a gentleman named Andy also live here?" Mr. Deeley inquired.

"Andy? Yes, yes, of course. My grandson. He takes very good care of me. He's the one who arranged to have the extension built on the back. It's got a lovely little washroom for me… and a darkroom for himself, so he can indulge in his favourite hobby. All the mod cons."

"In the other present that I have just come from," Mr. Deeley said, "Andy informed me you had died some years ago."

"Did he?" Ruby mused. "Have a Jaffa Cake."

She offered a plate, and then, without further comment, wheeled herself out of the room, and into the hallway.

Charlie could hear her rummaging around in the cupboard under the stairs.

"Here we are," she said, coming back in. Across her lap lay Silas Ferryman's black and tan suitcase. "I think you might be wondering about this."

"We were," Charlie said. "Where did you get it?"

"Betty gave it to me a few weeks after the tube station tragedy. She wanted me to keep it safe. And she never mentioned it again. Let's have a go at opening it."

Mr. Deeley placed the case on Ruby's bed, unbuckled the straps and flipped the latches.

Inside were two boxes—one a cardboard carrying case for a gas mask, the other a yellow and black carton which was the packaging for a Brownie Box camera.

Charlie opened the yellow and black box, and lifted out the camera.

"It's still got its roll of film inside," she said, looking through the little glass window.

"My Andy'd be jolly interested in that," Ruby said. "I'm quite certain he could have a go at developing it for you."

"I believe we ought to," Mr. Deeley replied, "although I am positive I know what the pictures will show."

"I shall give it to my grandson the moment he comes in. What's inside the other box? Is it a gas mask? You could put that on display in your museum."

Mr. Deeley unfastened the cardboard lid.

Inside were two newspaper cuttings, brown with age. He unfolded them carefully, knowing exactly what each was going to tell him.

The first was the story of Angela Bailey, whose body was discovered on a bomb site, her throat cut and her brooch missing.

The second was the story of Deirdre Allsop, the young woman who had lived with her invalid aunt and worked in a sweet shop in Balham.

"Fenwick Oldbutter's niece," Mr. Deeley said, holding the fragile slip of newspaper up for Ruby to see.

"Poor Deirdre," Ruby replied. "Yes. And wicked, wicked Silas Ferryman."

At the bottom of the box were six pieces of jewellery. A ring. A bracelet. A brooch, painted gold, with leaves and three delicate flowers. A locket. And a pair of clasp earrings, tortoiseshell imitations.

"And those are the earrings she was wearing. Borrowed from her Aunt Phyllis, who, I'm told, always had an excellent eye for fashion, in spite of her gamey legs."

There was a brisk *rat-tat-tat* at the front door, the sound of the knocker dropping against the metal mail slot.

"I took the liberty of making some inquiries on your behalf last night," Ruby said. "Once I was aware that you'd returned, and I was quite sure it *was* you. I hope you don't mind."

"Why would we mind?" Charlie asked.

"Go and see who it is, would you? I think you'll be frightfully pleased with my efforts."

Charlie got up, and went into the front hall, and opened the door.

On the path stood a gentleman in his midthirties. His dark hair was neatly combed, and he wore trousers and boots, and a shirt and coat that seemed to have come from a much earlier time. But it was the same face that Charlie remembered from the night of October the 14th, 1940, the last time she had seen him, sprawled on the platform at Balham Underground Station, his blood gathering beneath him in a dark and ominous pool.

"Thaddeus!" she shouted joyously, throwing her arms around him. "Mr. Deeley! It's Thaddeus!"

• • •

"And so," Thaddeus said, setting down his teacup, "I was saved—in the first instance, by the quick thinking of an off-duty midwife who was sheltering nearby, who staunched the bleeding. And in the second instance by the swift actions of others, who carried me out along the platform after the bomb fell on the other side of the station. Rather than the afterlife, I was dispatched to the nearest hospital to have the damage repaired. And that is where I spent the next fortnight recovering."

"And what of Betty?" Mr. Deeley asked, curiously. He had not stopped smiling since Charlie had called him to the door. "Did she not show an interest in your improving good health?"

"She did," Thaddeus recalled. "She visited me daily. But unbeknownst to me, while I recuperated, the other man in her life proposed marriage, and she accepted. She broke my heart, Mr. Deeley, but I do not begrudge her decision. Because of me, she had very nearly been killed herself. And she had our child to think of, and her own happiness. Peter Lewis was discharged as a pilot after he was injured while flying. Betty made her choice. He took my place in her father's grocery shop."

Charlie held Mr. Deeley's hand tightly.

"It seems this kind of history has a habit of repetition," Mr. Deeley said. "I have undergone the very same heartache as you. If we reflect upon this, and upon the outcome, perhaps we might reach the conclusion that these decisions were for the better."

"At the time, I thought not," Thaddeus replied. "But after some consideration, and the advantage of distance, I am of a mind to agree with you, sir. The day before I was released from the hospital, a gentleman called Fenwick Oldbutter visited me. Are you acquainted with him?"

"I am," Mr. Deeley said.

"I sent him, of course," Ruby added. "We agreed it would not be an interference, but rather, a small nudge."

"Mr. Oldbutter assisted me in returning to Middlehurst," Thaddeus said. "And near enough to the time I had departed, in 1849. To those who were familiar with me, I had been gone only a matter of days, which I was able to explain with ease, and a touch of imagination."

"But the crimes of the Middlehurst Slasher remained unsolved," Charlie said.

"Unfortunately so. But I'm secure in the knowledge that Silas Ferryman did, indeed, pay for his evil acts with his life. Thanks to you, Mr. Deeley."

"I take no joy in having sent a man to his death," Mr. Deeley replied.

"Nonsense," said Ruby. "It was either you or him. If you hadn't pushed him off the platform, you'd have died along with him. And so would Charlotte."

"How do you *know* all this?" Charlie said.

But Ruby merely smiled.

"His body," she said, "was eventually recovered, but it remained unidentified and unclaimed. And his personal effects remained with the police, who were intrigued to discover, in his coat pocket, a string of pearls which had lately belonged to a young waitress, whose own body had recently been found on a bomb site."

"There," said Thaddeus, "is your justice. And before I forget...."

He rummaged around in his own coat pocket, and withdrew a tiny packet of tightly folded paper. He placed it in the palm of his hand, and held it out, inviting Mr. Deeley to look.

"Ruby asked me to bring this to you."

222

Charlie watched as Mr. Deeley delicately, and with hesitant fingers, unwrapped the paper. Inside was a snippet of dark brown hair.

Wordlessly, he turned away, and lifted Matilda's locket out of the gas mask box.

"Look," he said, showing it to Charlie, and Thaddeus, and Ruby. "See the engraved initials. *SPD and JEB.*"

"Yes," Thaddeus confirmed. "That belonged to my sister. And before that, it had belonged to our mother. Of course, I know that JEB are my mother's initials. Jemima Elizabeth Beckford. But we— my brothers and I—have never known who SPD was. And if Matilda was aware of this person's identity, she never let it be known."

"Shaun Patrick Deeley," Charlie said.

Thaddeus looked at Mr. Deeley. "You," he said.

Mr. Deeley nodded. "I was engaged to marry your mother. I gave her that locket to celebrate her twenty-first birthday."

"And she kept it safe, sir. Even though she married another. I shall vouch for that. That locket contained that snippet of hair for as long as my mother was alive, and then, for many years after her death, until my sister was of an age to appreciate its significance. My sister was the one who removed it, wrapped it in paper, and put it away, knowing that it could not be from our father, as our father's hair was fair, and had been for all of his life."

Mr. Deeley was still holding the locket, and now, also the paper bearing the cutting of his hair. "She did not tell you, then."

"Tell me what?"

"Six months after your mother's wedding to Cornelius Quinn, she gave birth to you. Have you never wondered why you have dark hair, while both of your parents are fair?"

"I had wondered, yes." Thaddeus paused. "You...?"

Mr. Deeley nodded.

"This is an unexpected development. I may require some time to digest it."

Mr. Deeley offered him back the locket, and the folded square of paper.

"These are rightfully yours."

"Not at all, sir. They belong to you."

Mr. Deeley gave Charlie a questioning look.

"You must keep them," she said. "I've still got all of Jeff's things. How can we possibly object to anyone from the time before you and I knew one another? They were our first loves. And both are dead. And have been for a long time. Life goes on, Mr. Deeley. But we keep the memories of those we've loved safe."

. . .

They were, at last, on their way home.

"You're sure I can't offer you a lift to Clapham Junction?" Auntie Wendy checked. "What are you looking for, Jackie? I've packed everything up for the day."

"My bottled water," Charlie's mum said. "Posh fizzy stuff. Could have sworn I'd left it in the kitchen."

"Didn't see it," Auntie Wendy replied. "Have some of mine. Not posh and not fizzy. Sorry."

"I think," Charlie said, "that we'd rather go the long way round. Back to Waterloo by Underground. Mr. Deeley seems to be fascinated by the Northern Line."

"Did you tell him about the World War Two bomb at Balham? There's a bit of history for you, Shaun. Toby's cousin Arthur lost his mum and two sisters down there that night. He'd have been killed too, except he'd got on a train and ridden it up to Clapham South to deliver a message to someone. And the lady he delivered the message to asked him to stay put until she came back to tell him it was all right to leave. But he never saw her again. And by the time Arthur decided to go back to Balham... the bomb had fallen and the tunnels were flooded."

"Bloody hell," Charlie said.

"He grew up to be a fireman. Helped rescue people in the Kings Cross Underground fire in 1987. He'd be about eighty now. Wonderful man."

Auntie Wendy kissed them both goodbye, as did Charlie's mum.

"Lovely to see you again… even if it was under such sad circumstances."

She gave Charlie a nudge with her elbow.

"He's a keeper, that one," she said, nodding at Mr. Deeley. "Go on then, off to London with you."

• • •

At a florist next door to Balham Underground, Charlie and Mr. Deeley each bought a perfect white rose. The station, at half past ten in the morning, was nearly deserted. They rode the escalator down in silence.

At the bottom, they turned left and walked through the short passageway to the northbound platform, where they stood for a few moments, again not speaking.

"I can still see all the people," Charlie said at last. "In my memory. All the mums and little children, and the grandmothers and grandfathers… sitting on this platform, making up their beds… getting ready to sleep… thinking it was the safest place on earth."

"And I," Mr. Deeley said quietly. "We were here with them, and would have shared their fate, if it were not for our exceptional good fortune."

They walked together to the north end of the platform, past the big old-fashioned clock, to the place where the earth and gravel and rock had filled the station tunnel up to its ceiling. On the trackside wall, the black marks from the water damage were still there, marking the repairs from seventy-three years before.

"Here, I think," Charlie said.

"Yes," Mr. Deeley agreed.

They placed their roses on the platform, laying them gently against the glazed tiles, beside the blocked-up cross-passage. And then, they stood for a moment longer, remembering those who had lost their lives on that horrible, terrifying night.

A lifetime ago.

Yesterday.

CHAPTER TWENTY-SIX

"How was London?"

It was Reg Ferryman, first through the door of the Stoneford Village Museum after Charlie had opened it the Saturday following her return.

"Not you again," Charlie said. "I understand the Village Council voted you down. You won't be getting your hands on the Old Vicarage after all. What a shame."

"I'm not giving up on my Hampshire House of Horrors," Reg replied. "I've still got the Old Stable, next door to the pub. I'm having new plans drawn up as we speak."

"You do that," Charlie said. "We'll start with Silas Ferryman, shall we? One of your close relatives? I've heard a rumour that he was an infamous cutthroat, who dispatched his wife and absconded with the family fortune. I've heard a rumour that he was actually the Middlehurst Slasher. It'll make a marvellous display, anyway. You can sign replica blood-stained tea towels for punters in the gift shop on their way out."

"You," Reg said, "are a menace. And where's your proof? That's all it is, a rumour."

"Did you specifically want something, Reg, or did you just pop in to see how annoying you could be?"

"Dropping off some leaflets," Reg said, producing a little stack of printed papers. "Introducing traditional amusements at The Dog's Watch. Devil Among the Tailors. Nine Men's Morris. Ringing the Bull. And we're negotiating with a troop of mummers for a performance during the Christmas season. Obliged if you'd put their adverts on display somewhere."

"Free drink in it for me if I say yes?" Charlie inquired, taking the leaflets.

"One," Reg replied.

"Frightfully generous of you. I'll leave them on the counter."

"Many thanks," Reg said. "Good morning."

. . .

Opening the bright blue front door to her cottage, Charlie collected the letters that had been dropped through the mail slot. Most of it was rubbish. Another leaflet from Reg; a postcard from Oldbutter and Ballcock, offering a special rate for advance funeral planning; and a slick brochure from Quinn Motor Services, featuring free Michelin wiper blades with every oil change.

There were two letters, however, which were not rubbish.

One was from Auntie Wendy, posted a few days earlier.

Charlie carried it through to the sitting room, where Mr. Deeley was immersed in a continuing investigation of his family's history on her iPad.

"You were never this interested in where you came from before," she said. "What's changed?"

"The discovery that I have a son," Mr. Deeley replied. "And, I suppose, a certain curiosity about my brothers and sisters, and aunts and uncles and cousins. I left them behind in 1825. It has been a fascinating undertaking to discover whatever became of all of them."

Charlie smiled. She had earlier discovered that Thaddeus Oliver Quinn had not, in fact, disappeared from the face of the earth following the 1841 census. In fact, he was now present in the 1851 census, and that of 1861, and in every census following, all the way up to 1911, which was the last one that had been made available for public viewing.

And Charlie was quite happy for Mr. Deeley to continue his research, without sharing the details. She'd deliberately avoided looking up when Thaddeus Oliver Quinn had eventually died.

Just as she'd deliberately avoided checking for marriage and birth records associated with his name after 1849. She was saving that for another day.

And some other things had definitely changed as a result of their journey back to 1940. For one thing, Mr. Deeley was no longer afraid of the cooker. He'd become quite adept at making scrambled eggs. And he'd made a point of going online to research the mysteries of eggs Benedict, which he'd promised for the following Sunday's brunch.

Charlie sat down at her desk, and opened the letter from Auntie Wendy. It was in a very big brown padded envelope, the sort of package that you knew right away was going to contain interesting things.

> *Your mum and I found this tucked away in a drawer in Nana's dressing table. It's addressed to you, so we thought we'd best forward it unopened. Do let us know what's inside—we're both terribly curious!*

Inside was a second big brown envelope, sealed, with Charlie's name written in Nana Betty's familiar hand on the front. Charlie opened it carefully to find a little blue booklet: *War-Time Cookery to Save Fuel and Food Value.*

"Mr. Deeley," she said. "Look."

She turned the booklet over and read aloud what Nana Betty had written in pencil on the night they'd arrived.

> *Charlotte Duran says I am going to have a little girl. And I will name her Jackie. And a sister for Jackie, and I'm going to call her Wendy. And, she says, my house will not be bombed. October the 11th, 1940.*

She looked at Mr. Deeley.

"Nana Betty really did meet us in 1940. And she never mentioned anything to me, not in all the years I was growing up. Me, Charlotte Duran, with the same name as she's written here... me in 1940, looking exactly like me now. She never said a word to anyone."

228

A piece of notepaper drifted out of the pamphlet, decorated with pansies and violets, and smelling faintly of Nana Betty's lavender scent. It was dated July 11th, 2011.

My darling Charlotte. I have thought many times of giving this to you, but have stopped myself, as I believe it would cause too much confusion. Instead I'm putting it away, until a time when I'm no longer here. And after I'm gone, I'm hopeful it'll be forwarded to you, unopened, to do with as you wish. I remember your 1940 visit so well. At first I thought it a fantastic coincidence, your name and the name of the woman who was Ruby Firth's friend being the same. Charlotte Duran. But as you grew older, and began to resemble my memory of that young woman more and more, I realized that it could not possibly be coincidence, and that it really must have happened. I have yet to discover whether you will meet your very pleasant young man, Mr. Deeley, but if history has anything to say about it, I'm almost certain you will. I do not know what ever happened to Thaddeus. When he was in the hospital, I went to see him every day. But Pete wished to marry me, and I felt he would be a far better choice for our future. And so Thaddeus went away. I never mentioned him to your grandfather, and I will leave it up to you as to whether you wish to tell your mother and Auntie Wendy. I had always thought there must be something like time travelling that we might aspire to, something I know Nick is investigating very keenly. I don't have any familiarity with it, but you have obviously discovered how it's done. If you're reading this now, it means I am no longer with you. But perhaps we can and will meet again, darling, if you find the means to take yourself back into my time.

All my love, Nana Betty.

Charlie wiped her eyes.

"Oh, Mr. Deeley," she said. "She knew. All along."

"This letter is very precious," Mr. Deeley said. "And you must keep it very safe."

"I will."

"What else has the post brought?" he asked, spying another very official-looking white envelope on the desk.

Without comment, Charlie opened the envelope from the private firm that did DNA testing, and read what was inside. Then, she handed him the letter.

"Now you know why I absconded with the teacup Thaddeus had been drinking from—Ruby's idea, by the way—and why I stole my mum's bottle of posh fizzy water. And why I wanted a swab from the inside of your mouth."

"Why?" Mr. Deeley inquired.

"Read on," Charlie suggested.

He did.

"If I am correctly interpreting these results," he said, "then Thaddeus Quinn is definitely my son."

Charlie knelt down beside the comfy armchair where Mr. Deeley was sitting.

"He is," she confirmed.

"But your mother and Thaddeus have no DNA in common at all. Therefore Thaddeus Quinn is definitely *not* your mother's father."

"Which means Nana Betty was wrong. Pete Lewis was my grandfather all along. She must have miscalculated the dates."

"Or perhaps, she knew the dates perfectly, but preferred not to acknowledge them."

"Perhaps," Charlie said thoughtfully.

She took the letter from Mr. Deeley's hand, removed the iPad from his lap, and placed both on the floor beside the armchair.

"You do know what this means, don't you?"

Mr. Deeley's tender and amazing kiss confirmed the fact that no further explanation was needed.

"Mrs. Collins," he said.

"Mr. Deeley…." She paused, summoning her courage. "Will you marry me, Mr. Deeley?"

Mr. Deeley smiled.

"Ask me properly," he said. "Charlotte."

Charlie got to her feet and, ignoring Mr. Deeley's questioning look, ran into the kitchen. She returned, just as quickly, with two saucepans.

"Shaun," she said, getting down on one knee, "will you marry me?"

Mr. Deeley smiled, and kissed her again. He took the pots from her hands, and helped her to her feet.

And then, together—and with no further words required—they climbed the stairs, at last, to bed.

Keep reading for

EASY WHEN YOU KNOW HOW,

an exclusive short story
from Winona Kent set in the
world of *In Loving Memory*!

EASY WHEN YOU KNOW HOW

"It is mornings like this," Mr. Deeley said softly, "which I longed for. The rareness of being able to lie in my bed, listening to the birds, who have been awake since before sunrise, chattering to each other, exchanging gossip and scandalous stories concerning families in the next village."

Charlie laughed. She snuggled closer to Mr. Deeley, into the hollow between his armpit and his chest, resting her head on his arm as his hand cradled her shoulder, drawing her close.

"Did you not have any chance at all for a lie-in?" she inquired.

"Never. The horses needed to be cared for, and although there were stable boys, they were notoriously unreliable. For this I blame the lesser Monsieur Duran, as he had a hand in their hiring, and would never allow me to make sensible decisions. In any case, the servants of the manor were expected to rise at the appointed hour. And as I was not keen to be dismissed, I embraced the expectations."

"Well," Charlie said. "You're in my world now, and in my world, you're allowed to lie in bed for as long as you want. Provided, of course, that we put in an appearance at the museum before lunchtime. Expectations, and all that."

Mr. Deeley smiled, turned a little, and kissed her. It was a gentle kiss, a good morning kiss, for although they, like the sparrows in the apple trees outside her bedroom window, had been awake for hours, they had not been sleeping. And so it was a kiss that reaffirmed the goodness of everything that had gone on that morning, and the night before, and every day and night before that, since the moment they'd first met on the Village Green.

She was wearing a nightgown that he had bought her. She had

no idea where he'd found it. It was very old, and very simple…a fine white cotton, almost see-through but not quite…the old-fashioned term for it was *batiste*. It had a plunging neckline and short sleeves, and it was trimmed at the bottom with beautiful Ile d'Aix lace—she'd looked it up.

He had presented it to her one afternoon, after he'd mysteriously disappeared for two hours, without any sort of explanation.

"It is French," he had said simply. "Worn by the Empress Josephine herself."

Charlie had laughed. "That would make it an absolute antique, Mr. Deeley. And incredibly valuable. What did you do—slip into Napoleon's chateau yourself and steal it from her wardrobe?"

She'd meant it as a joke, but in retrospect, Charlie wondered if she had guessed at the truth—or something very close to it.

Mr. Deeley, like herself, was a time traveller—more accidental than by design. But, unlike her, he had been practicing. She was hesitant to experiment; Mr. Deeley was filled with the sense of adventure, and had no qualms about trying out his fledgling wings… much to Charlie's consternation.

"What would happen if you weren't able to come back?" she'd asked. "What would happen if you got stuck in whatever time you landed in? At least let me know when you're going to go flying off to whenever…so Nick and I can launch a search party for you if you don't come back!"

Mr. Deeley had laughed it off, but Charlie couldn't dismiss his random adventures so easily.

"We really should get moving," she said, kissing the special place on his bare chest that tickled him and made him laugh in the most delighted and wonderful way.

"I shall make breakfast," he decided. "Is what we eat for breakfast now the same as what they ate for breakfast in the time of your new display?"

"Somewhat the same," Charlie said. She slid out of bed and watched as he climbed out of bed too, fully naked but still a little bit shy about showing her his body, even after so many months of sharing her bed. Old attitudes from 1825 were very hard to break. "But in the Swinging Sixties they were still going to work on a boiled egg…they didn't have the variety of food that we have now. And especially not Honey Nut Crunch with Milk Chocolate Curls."

"My favourite," Mr. Deeley said, looking at her as she slipped out of her nightgown and, she knew, very much admiring what he saw. "Why was it called the Swinging Sixties, Mrs. Collins? Was there some sort of…suspension involved?"

"Suspension of old attitudes and beliefs, perhaps, Mr. Deeley," Charlie said. "It was a time of incredible change in England. All the children who were born during the war, or just after it, had grown up and were looking for something new, something different. My mum was just the right age. She worked in a boutique. She kept a lot of her clothes from that time. She's sending me a genuine Mary Quant mini-dress. And I've got some of her other things… some old magazines and newspapers, and a lot of her vinyl records. Albums and 45s."

Mr. Deeley was pretending to understand, but Charlie was certain he had no idea at all what she was talking about. The Swinging Sixties display at the Stoneford Village Museum was still only in the planning stages.

Her mobile rang.

"Leave it," Mr. Deeley suggested, giving her another kiss. "I am impatient for my Honey Nut Crunch."

"I must answer it," Charlie said. "It's Giles Jessop."

• • •

"And who is Giles Jessop?" Mr. Deeley inquired. He had put on a pair of very worn jeans, and an Italian cotton knit jumper, and he was barefoot. Charlie thought he looked amazingly sexy as he poured milk into their cereal bowls, and tea into two mugs.

"A very famous singer from the 1960s," she said. "He was born in Stoneford and was part of the British Invasion of America. He had a band. Brighton Peer."

"Named after the very famous pier?"

"No, though it's a play on that. His dad was an earl who was originally from Brighton. So, you know…a peer. Of the realm."

"Why did he ring you?"

"Because he's heard about my exhibit and he'd like to help out," Charlie said. "I'm quite chuffed, really. He's asked us to come to London to see him."

• • •

Charlie studied Mr. Deeley's boots. They were a lovely light brown, scuffed and creased and generally well worn-in. They were cut low so that they ended just above his ankles, but the foot was close enough in design to the sort of boots he had worn in 1825 that he felt at home in them. And they went perfectly with his jeans. And his white cotton shirt. And his tailored summer jacket. And his long, somewhat untidy, hair. He was, indeed, a man of many ages.

They were on the tube, riding from Waterloo to Piccadilly Circus, a short journey but faster than walking—their train from Middlehurst had been delayed, and they were late for their appointment with Giles Jessop.

It was Wednesday, and on Wednesdays Mr. Deeley was not required at the museum, where, three times a week, he provided horse-drawn cart rides around historical Stoneford for the tourists.

It was almost a year to the day since he'd arrived from 1825 and become such an integral part of Charlie's life that she was no longer able to imagine it without him. She remembered his first ride on the Underground—how terrified he'd been. But he'd acclimatized himself quickly after that. He had mastered the cooker in her kitchen—and she no longer lived in fear that he would try to use the fireplace to boil water for tea. He had appropriated her iPad and completely embraced the Internet, employing it to research his ancestors and his descendants, as well as hers; to buy clothes; to listen to music; to watch videos; and even, she suspected, to dip his toes into the curious world of social networking. She wondered if he had a Facebook account, and made up her mind to ask him when the subject next came up.

They surfaced at Piccadilly Circus, then walked up behind the old London Pavilion, once a music hall, then a cinema, now completely gutted inside and made into a shopping centre. Their route took them, in a few minutes, to Great Windmill Street, and Giles Jessop's £4-million flat, accessed by way of a completely unobtrusive door beside an Indonesian restaurant.

"Very apropos," Charlie said, as they walked up the stairs. "He's right round the corner from Ham Yard, which is where the Scene Club was."

"And the Scene Club was…?" Mr. Deeley inquired.

"Well known in the early 1960s for its mod subculture. The Rolling Stones used to play there. And The Who."

"Who are The Who?"

"Look them up," Charlie suggested, amused. "Roger Daltrey. *Tommy*. There's a posh hotel around there now."

• • •

Giles Jessop was 73 years old. He had a white shock of hair which had once been bright red, and a cheeky look on his face which was the same as it had been in 1964, when Brighton Peer was climbing the pop charts with songs about unrequited love and the heartache of summer goodbyes.

His flat was equally cheeky—a guest bedroom on the first floor, a kitchen and sitting room on the second, an immense master bedroom and en suite bath on the third floor, and the entire fourth floor comprised of an open air terrace planted with exotic palms and giant plants that would have been at home in any convenient jungle. The flat itself had bare brick walls that showed off the age of the narrow little building that housed it, an abundance of black and white furniture, and maple wood accents.

"I was 23 in 1964," Giles said as they sat in comfortable canvas chairs on the open terrace. "Barely out of nappies. 'Course, we thought we knew it all. More than our parents, at any rate. We were kids in the war, which was one big bloody adventure, truth be known. Bits of hot shrapnel in the road after a raid and barrage balloons up in the sky. Our parents were so worn out and so old-fashioned. We grew up in the '50s and by the time the '60s came round we were ready to break all the rules and rewrite everything to suit ourselves. Which is what we did, of course. Have another slice of Battenberg. And some sausage rolls. More tea?"

"Yes please," Charlie said.

"And then, of course, there was Marianne."

"Marianne Faithfull?"

"A wonderful friend. But another. Marianne Dutton. We very nearly married. She had a boutique. In Carnaby Street. Full of all sorts of rubbish and old tat."

"Of course," Charlie said. "Marianne's Memory. My mum worked there. Jackie Lewis. She's about the same age as you."

"Jackie Lewis. Lovely girl. Whatever happened to her?"

"She married my dad—Justin Duran."

"Ah, yes," Giles said, "I was at school with Justin. Of course. How could I forget?"

"It was the 1960s," Mr. Deeley said humorously. "What is the famous quotation? If you remember it, you weren't there?"

"Truer words were never spoken," Giles replied. He paused, and then looked very keenly at Charlie.

"You have an older sibling."

"Yes. Two of them. Abigail. She was born in 1975. And an older brother, too. Simon. 1971."

"No darling, before them. Before your mum and dad were ever married. She had a child." Giles leaned forward, conspiratorially, and whispered: "Out of wedlock. 1964-ish. 1965."

Charlie stared at him, shocked into silence. Mr. Deeley was staring too.

"Admired her for going through with it. Things were very dodgy back then if you wanted to terminate. But she couldn't keep the child. Wouldn't. Said it would be for the best if she gave it up for adoption."

"Did my grandmother know?" Charlie asked, still stunned.

"'Course she did, darling. Jackie was sharing a flat with Marianne, but she was round her mum's all the time for tea. How could she not have known?"

"Who is the father of this child?" Mr. Deeley inquired.

"Don't know. Never did know. Don't think she ever said."

"Didn't she have a regular boyfriend that she was seeing?"

"Not then," said Giles.

"Most interesting," said Mr. Deeley.

"Yes, we all thought so too. Well. We've had a lovely lunch, and I promise if you come back next week I'll have a compendium of things for your museum display. I'll ask my mates—the ones that are still alive, at any rate—for some donations as well. Hang on and I'll give you something for the road."

He got up stiffly, favouring an arthritic hip, and collected a tiny silver box from a table just inside the door to the terrace. He opened the lid and presented it to Charlie.

"There you are."

"A plectrum," Charlie said.

"Imitation tortoiseshell. From 1964. I nicked it from John Lennon. I reckon it's worth a few thousand quid. Saw one just like it for sale at Christie's a few years back. This one doesn't have Lennon's initials on it but I can swear to its authenticity."

"Thank you," Charlie said, holding the little silver box in the palm of her hand. "If you're sure..."

"'Course I'm sure. I've had it for decades...could never think of what to do with it. Now I know. Keep it safe, darling. Put it on display and don't let on who it used to belong to. Our secret. Will you take some Battenberg with you for your journey...?"

• • •

"Where is this Carnaby Street located?" Mr. Deeley asked as they stood outside the Indonesian restaurant, attempting to get their bearings again.

"A bit further north, I think," Charlie said, consulting the map on her phone. "Yes, there. Closer to Regent Street. Would you like to see it?"

"I would," Mr. Deeley replied. "Would it look much the same after the passage of fifty years?"

"I'm not sure, Mr. Deeley. I imagine the buildings are still the same, but I think most of the original shops and boutiques are long gone. They've done it up for the tourists now. The Swinging Sixties really only happened over a couple of years. It's the idea that's survived. The music and the films and the fashion."

They negotiated the narrow back streets of Soho, traversing the history of Brewer Street and Bridle Lane, and Beak Street.

"You're very quiet, Mrs. Collins."

"I'm still in shock, Mr. Deeley. To be told that you have a brother or a sister you didn't know about...and my mum's never said anything to any of us. And my Nana—she knew about it too. Nothing."

"Perhaps it was not something that could be spoken about. Perhaps to spare the feelings of your father. And of you, and your other sister and brother."

"Back then it wasn't spoken about, you're right. But after all this time... I wonder if he or she's been trying to find us."

They had reached the bottom end of Carnaby Street, which had been blocked off to traffic.

"It seems very..." Mr. Deeley paused as he watched the tourists walking along the red brick paving stones, phones, and cameras in hand.

"Ordinary?" Charlie guessed.

"Yes. Ordinary. A very apt description." He looked up. "But for this archway welcoming us to Carnaby Street, I might be forgiven for mistaking this for any other shopping precinct in England."

"Perhaps it's a bit more...exciting... at the other end."

And so they walked, with the tourists, to the upper stretch of the famous street, and the other curved welcome sign.

"It is still very ordinary," Mr. Deeley judged, obviously disappointed. "I see nothing which convinces me this was once the hotbed of unbridled sixties swinging."

Charlie laughed. "I do love you, Mr. Deeley," she said. "Try to imagine these little shopfronts fifty years ago. There was a road running down the middle, with lots of cars. And a narrow pavement on both sides. All the women wore little Mary Quant mini-dresses, with Vidal Sassoon hair and Twiggy eyes. All the men had long hair and tight trousers and the latest jackets and boots from John Stephen." She assessed her companion. "A bit like what you're wearing now, in fact."

"Perhaps you should install me in your museum display," Mr. Deeley replied humorously. "Where is it that your mother worked?"

"I'm not entirely sure about the address. I know it was up this end…mum once showed me a picture of it."

She paused in front of a tiny shopfront painted bright blue, with wide display windows on either side of a narrow little doorway. Above the windows and door was a wide lintel, out of which was growing a mass of greenery. And above the greenery rose three floors of dwellings, two windows per floor, all of the brickwork painted a pale grey and the window frames white. The sign above the doorway, and below the greenery, read: Easy When You Know How.

"I think that might be it," Charlie said. "Change of name…and I'm not entirely sure what they're selling these days…but yes. There. Shall we go inside?"

• • •

The interior of the shop smelled of patchouli and ylang-ylang, and there was a glass wind chime hanging near the door, which tinkled with the passing breeze. Just inside the door was a table covered with spectacles: wire-framed grannies; huge plastic glasses, of the sort Deirdre Barlow wore when she first arrived in *Coronation Street*; monocles and diamante cats-eyes; and all different colours of lenses.

Spreading aspidistras and huge ferns stood on shelves and plinths, and hanging underneath those were neckties, scarves, and shawls from every age known to fashion.

Against one wall hung women's clothing, salvaged from time and second-hand shops: Victoriana, and flapper, and wide 1950s skirts that demanded crinolines and white ankle socks, and mod mini's and cotton shifts from the 1960s. Against another wall, gentlemen's apparel: military uniforms and velvet trousers, and silk shirts and flare-legged denim jeans. Dickensian coats. Leather flying jackets with sheepskin collars. Floral prints and exquisite double-breasted tailoring.

A giant silk umbrella, fully open; a two-wheeled bicycle; and cooking pots, overflowing with silk flowers were suspended from the ceiling.

There was a large sofa against the back wall, and a very ornate mirror, and a single dressing room separated from the main shop by a row of hanging glass beads.

And there was music, which seemed to be emanating from a vintage jukebox beside the mirror. Charlie recognized the song immediately.

"*House of the Rising Sun*," she said to Mr. Deeley. "The Animals. 1964."

"What a noise."

"It's a classic, Mr. Deeley!"

"Might I be of assistance?"

A woman had appeared from a room at the back. She seemed to be in her forties, or perhaps her fifties. She had long blonde hair with a full fringe and she wore a mauve frock, which might have come originally from a turn-of-the-century brothel.

"We're just looking around," Charlie said. "My mum used to work here. In the 1960s. When it was called—"

"Marianne's Memory," the woman finished. "Yes. I know. It was famous! It all rather fell into hard times after the 1960s though…

it sat empty for ages…and then it was a poster shop…and then a touristy souvenir sort of place, maps and flags and t-shirts and mugs…A shoe store. A place that sold mobile phones. And then it was empty again…I've tried to make it as much like the original as possible."

"Why Easy When You Know How?" Mr. Deeley inquired. "Why not Marianne's Memory?"

"Marianne wouldn't let me."

"Oh!" Charlie said. "So you've been in touch with her."

"She's my mum," the woman said. "She's in her seventies now. She was going to marry that pop star, the one in Brighton Peer. Giles Jessop. But she called it off at the last minute and ran off with his brother, Jeremy, the racing car driver. My dad. They live in the south of France, where I grew up. Anyway I asked her if I could use the name and she said no, and I'm dreadful with naming things and so I asked her, what should I call it then? And she said, just imagine something. And I said, I haven't got much of an imagination for things like that. And she said, well, it's easy when you know how. And that's how the shop got its name." She paused. "And you say your mother used to work here?"

"Yes," said Charlie. "She was friends with your mum. They shared a flat together, too. And I work in a museum—I'm putting together a display of the Swinging Sixties and I can see some of the clothes you've got here would look amazing in it. Can we look around?"

"Yes, of course. I'm Sue. If you want any help, just ask."

• • •

"Giles failed to mention his very famous brother, Jeremy," Mr. Deeley said as he and Charlie investigated the racks of frocks and jackets at the front of the shop.

"I wonder why," Charlie mused. She lifted out a black mini-dress with a trumpet flare, printed all over with bright pop petal flowers, with a white collar and white cuffs. "I love this. And these."

She showed Mr. Deeley a pair of white opaque tights on a nearby rack full of stockings and leg coverings.

"And the correct shoes," Mr. Deeley said thoughtfully, examining some shelves beside the sofa. He held up a pair of white t-bar leather Mary Janes.

"Salvatore Ferragamo," Sue supplied. "Genuine leather, made in Italy. Kitten heels. Perfect with that frock. You have an excellent eye for fashion."

"I should love to see you wearing these things," Mr. Deeley decided. "Might you change into them, to show them off...for me?"

"What, now?"

"Indeed," said Mr. Deeley. "My curiosity has been aroused."

Charlie laughed.

"You too, then," she decided, selecting a mod-looking tie from the rack, in a floral and paisley pattern of red ochre, goldenrod yellow, bright aqua, and muted pink.

"John Stephen," Sue said. "Very nice. Would go with this, I think."

She produced a wool suit, dark grey, beautifully tailored.

"Hardy Amies. You can't do better than that."

"The waistcoat only," Mr. Deeley decided, removing it from its hanger. "Thank you. I shall retain my own trousers and boots."

• • •

They emerged from the single dressing room together, and stood in front of the large, elaborate mirror.

"The very picture of a trendy 1960s couple," Sue judged. "Mum would have hired you on the spot."

Charlie laughed as Mr. Deeley made final adjustments to his tie. It was a skill he'd only recently acquired.

"We'll take them," Charlie said.

"Shall I put them in bags for you...?"

"Yes. Unless you want to wear your new togs on the train, Mr. Deeley?"

"I think I might."

"Well, I think I might change back into my own clothes. This frock is lovely but it's far too short to be practical. I don't know how they managed back then, reaching up for things, bending over…"

"I should imagine the view was breathtaking," said Mr. Deeley, admiring Charlie as she turned to go back to the dressing room. Sue totted up the sale and wrote it out on a vintage receipt pad.

"Mr. Deeley." It was Charlie, calling from the dressing room. And then, more urgently: "Mr. Deeley!"

He stepped through the beaded glass curtain.

"What is it, Mrs. Collins?"

Charlie was still wearing her mini-dress. "I feel…peculiar."

"What sort of peculiar?"

"I've felt it before. It's…" She grabbed her bag and her original clothing, then thrust Mr. Deeley's jacket into his hands and grabbed onto his arm. "…the feeling I get when something's about to happen…"

• • •

They were still standing in the dressing room. And it looked more or less the same, down to the glass beads shielding it from the main part of the shop. And the shop still smelled of patchouli and ylang-ylang and there was still music blaring from the jukebox at the back.

But it was not the same.

This was evident as soon as they stepped through the curtain of glass beads.

The shop had changed. In fact, it was nothing like the shop they entered. This shop had clothes hanging from racks and neatly folded on tables, yes, but it was crammed full of other things: guitars, and portable record players, cardboard record album covers, framed photographs, and posters. Two birdcages, each containing a large stuffed parrot, sat at opposite ends of the room. A grandfather clock stood in the corner. Hats and caps and boots and lots of umbrellas hung on racks around the walls.

247

There was a counter, and behind the counter were two young women, one a blonde, one a brunette, both with masses of long straight hair and fringes. The woman with the blonde hair was dressed in a simple green dress with large white flowers, its hem ending just above her knees. The brunette was slightly more daring, in a pink skirt that was somewhat shorter, and a matching sleeveless knitted top with a high neck.

"It's Mum," Charlie whispered. "I've seen photos of her when she was in her twenties. The one with the dark hair."

"Then the other must be Marianne," Mr. Deeley reasoned. "Have we arrived in the fabulous Swinging Sixties?"

"It would seem so, Mr. Deeley. I'll just confirm the date."

Leaving her bundle of clothing with Mr. Deeley, Charlie approached the counter, where Marianne was engaged in a conversation with Charlie's mum.

"You should just go along and stand in the crowd," Marianne was urging. "You never know—you might catch a glimpse of one of them."

"Some of us aren't quite as lucky as you," Charlie's mum replied. "Some of us aren't going out with dishy pop stars. Say hello to Paul McCartney for me, won't you."

"Oh, Jackie. You know I'd take you with me if I could. Giles only just managed to get two tickets. He did ask if there were more."

"I believe you," Charlie's mum said. "Thousands wouldn't." She turned to Charlie. "Hello. I like your frock. Where's it from?"

"Um," Charlie said. "A little boutique. Easy When You Know How."

"I've never heard of that one, have you?" Jackie said to Marianne.

"I haven't, but I like the name," Marianne said thoughtfully.

"You're probably going to think I'm daft," Charlie said, "but can you tell me what day it is?"

"Wednesday," Marianne answered easily. "Happens to me all the time. I woke up this morning thinking it was Monday."

"No you didn't," Jackie said. "You woke up this morning

shouting, 'Today's the day I'm going to meet the Beatles!'" She looked at Charlie. "Some people have all the luck, eh?"

"Some people," Charlie agreed. "Where's this fab meeting going to take place?"

"You really are out of it, aren't you," Marianne said. "Tonight. Just down the road at the London Pavilion."

"The premiere of their film," Jackie added. "*A Hard Day's Night.*"

"Ah…" Charlie said. "Yes. Of course. July the…er…"

"July the 6th," Marianne provided.

"1964," Jackie said humorously.

"They're expecting Princess Margaret and Lord Snowdon. Fifteen guineas a ticket."

"Yes, I know," Jackie said. "And a stuffy old champagne supper party afterwards at The Dorchester and then on to the Ad Lib Club for some late night hobnobbing with the Rolling Stones. I myself will be enjoying a blind date with a bloke Marianne's boyfriend went to school with. Not quite the same as consorting with Antony Armstrong-Jones, but I'm told he's just as good-looking."

"He is," Marianne said, confidentially, to Charlie. "I've met him. Justin Duran. Isn't that the most fab name? All terribly aristocratic and French-sounding. He isn't, of course. He's English. From Stoneford. But he's quite dishy. If I wasn't already spoken for I'd definitely go for him."

"Justin Duran," Mr. Deeley said, thoughtfully, to Charlie. "This name is very familiar."

"Oh! Do you know him too?" Marianne said.

"Indeed. I also attended school with him."

Charlie gave Mr. Deeley a look.

"Top bloke," Mr. Deeley continued. "I recall he excelled in the study of Latin, and World Geography, and had committed to memory Lacroix's *Differential and Integral Calculus*. In English, and in the original French."

"There you are," Marianne said to Jackie. "A gentleman *and* a scholar. You can't do better than that!"

• • •

Outside the boutique, Charlie burst into laughter. "That was my dad they were talking about!"

"Hence the familiarity."

"You're mad! She's going to tell him all about you, and they'll both know you're completely insane!"

"Then they will conclude that I am a rogue and a madman, who enjoys playing pranks upon unsuspecting young ladies."

"Perhaps he won't remember you."

"Why should it matter?"

"Because of the future, Mr. Deeley. Our future. You've never actually met my dad…the opportunity's never presented itself. But I've sent him photos, obviously…and I've talked about you a lot with him, and mentioned your name…I wonder if he's wondered about you…"

"I should think, Mrs. Collins, that it would be your mother who ought to remember. I *have* met her. And yet, she has no recollection of seeing me before. Unlike your grandmother, who did recall our meeting, but kept it a secret until her death. Do you not think this peculiar?"

Charlie was deep in thought. "Yes. That's very true. Mum ought to have remembered."

She looked up and considered the road, with its narrow pavement on both sides, and two lanes of cars crammed in between, and everywhere, people, young and curious, their eyes filled with adventure, their faces reflecting the optimism of the very beginning of the Swinging Sixties.

"What are we doing here, Mr. Deeley? Was it John Lennon's plectrum? Is that what brought us back to 1964?"

"Perhaps," Mr. Deeley said. They were walking north, towards Oxford Street. "Perhaps," he continued, "we are simply becoming more accustomed to the ability. I have discovered that if I wish it so, it becomes so. The plectrum was a lens for your thoughts. As was the shop, when we went inside. Did you wish to come here?"

"Not consciously," Charlie said as they passed the brown and white gables of Liberty and walked up Argyll Street.

"Palladium," said Mr. Deeley, reading the golden letters spread across the tops of a collection Corinthian columns.

"Very famous. And Grade II listed. This, Mr. Deeley, is where Beatlemania began. Sunday, the 13th of October, 1963."

"Fascinating," said Mr. Deeley, who knew about the Beatles because he'd asked Charlie one evening about a song he'd heard, *Please Please Me*, and Charlie had told him to look it up. And he had. For three days.

"Is there a purpose to it all, Mr. Deeley?"

"To Beatlemania? Most definitely. There would be no premiere of *A Hard Day's Night* this evening without it."

Charlie smiled. "You know what I mean. Is there a purpose to our time travelling? We've done this three times before...and each time, it was for a reason. We did something. We influenced something that would otherwise have been un-influenced. What's the purpose of this journey?"

"Perhaps," said Mr. Deeley, "this has something to do with the child. The half-sibling you didn't know existed. Perhaps this is when he or she came to be."

"Perhaps not a half-brother or sister at all. Perhaps a full brother or sister," Charlie said. "My mum's going to meet my dad for the first time tonight. But she didn't actually marry him until 1969. Perhaps their circumstances just didn't allow them to marry before that...and she had to give the baby up for adoption. The time we're in now, Mr. Deeley, is very different from the time we came from, when it comes to unmarried women and their babies. It would have been so difficult for her."

Charlie stopped. She stopped because Mr. Deeley had stopped, and was observing a little man on the pavement just ahead of them. He looked to be about fifty, with round, wire-framed spectacles. He wore black trousers and an old-fashioned pullover vest, underneath which was a white shirt, with rolled-up sleeves. He was playing something Celtic on a battered fiddle with exceptional skill, his violin case open on the pavement in front of him for the collection of coins.

"A busker," Charlie provided. "Usually found in Underground stations…but not all that uncommon on the surface. I expect the police will ask him to move along."

"I am acquainted with this gentleman," Mr. Deeley replied. "He is Fenwick Oldbutter."

"The time traveller?" Charlie said. "Ruby Firth gave me his business card…"

"And I consulted him, in matters to do with the interference of history." He approached the little man. "Good day, sir. Have we crossed paths by design, or by accident?"

Fenwick Oldbutter completed his tune. "The word 'accident' appears in my lexicon infrequently," he replied.

"Then by design," Mr. Deeley said. "Allow me to introduce Charlotte Duran."

Fenwick Oldbutter's eyes were bright.

"The love of your life. So pleased to meet you at last, my dear. And happy that you did not, after all, perish in the Blitz. Are you hungry?"

Charlie realized that she was, indeed, quite hungry. They had left Giles Jessop's flat just after two. It was now, unaccountably, nearly five.

"There's a hamburger restaurant round the corner," Fenwick said. "I frequent it often. Do join me. My treat."

• • •

The restaurant, near Oxford Circus, was not overly busy. The waitresses wore black frocks with white collars, and the tables were stocked with little grey pots of hot English mustard, and tomato-shaped plastic sauce holders.

"Just wait till the Yanks invade in a few years' time," Fenwick said, as their burgers arrived, on china plates with a paper napkin underneath. "I shan't bother to warn them."

"Indeed," said Mr. Deeley, applying a liberal layer of mustard to his hamburger. "It is not within your remit to warn anyone of anything, as I recall." He added mustard to Charlie's hamburger as well. "He belongs to the same circle of travellers as Mrs. Firth. And he, also, has undertaken the oath of non-interference. Although our meeting, by design, would seem to contradict his intentions."

"Did you know we were going to arrive?" Charlie asked, scraping off most of the hot mustard that Mr. Deeley had added to her hamburger and replacing it with ketchup from the squeeze bottle.

"Are you in possession of the plectrum which lately belonged to John Lennon?" Fenwick asked.

Charlie looked at him, then checked her handbag.

"Yes," she said. She paused. "Did you know Giles Jessop was going to give it to me?"

Fenwick said nothing, instead choosing to sip from his cup of tea.

"Giles Jessop is a time traveller as well?" Charlie asked.

"Let us call him a sympathetic friend. And let us also recall the knowledge I imparted to your companion, Mr. Deeley, upon another very similar occasion. The power of suggestion is your strongest ally. Your imagination was engaged. It was your own imagination which brought both of you back to this time. Nothing more, and nothing less."

"But we are here for a reason. Each journey we've undertaken has had consequences, which were brought about by our actions," Charlie pressed.

"Your interrogation of Mr. Oldbutter will, I fear, be in vain, Mrs. Collins," Mr. Deeley replied. "His infuriating adherence to the Overarching Philosophy and his steadfast loyalty to the oath prevents him from confirming anything."

"I may, however, be persuaded to discuss," Fenwick added, inscrutably. "And possibly, to suggest."

Charlie contemplated her own cup of tea.

"Have you a suggestion, then, Mr. Oldbutter?"

"I do, in fact. It would not be in anyone's best interests if Jackie Lewis were to go out with Justin Duran this evening."

"Sorry," Charlie said, "but that's my dad. They have to meet. Or I won't be born."

"The mere fact that you exist at this moment and are here, enjoying a hamburger with me and your esteemed companion, indicates to me that they did, at some point, meet," Fenwick replied humorously. "I merely suggest that it should not be tonight. When are they married?"

"1969."

"There you are then. Five years in which to discover one another. I suspect not even you know the circumstances of their first meeting."

"I've never actually asked."

"And your brother and sister?"

"I don't think they know either. It's never really come up in conversations."

"What, then, if I were to tell you, that tonight is the only opportunity your mother will have to meet Tony Quinn?"

"Who's he?"

Fenwick turned his quizzical gaze to Mr. Deeley. "A relation of yours, I believe."

"I have not heard of him."

"Perhaps, then, you simply haven't had the opportunity to explore your family tree this far into the 20th century. He is a direct descendant of your son, Thaddeus Quinn. In the year we now occupy, he plays music. On the radio. He is what you might refer to as a pirate."

"Oh!" said Charlie. "On board a pirate radio ship. I know about those."

"Unfortunately," Fenwick said, "he will die, quite tragically, aboard that same ship. Quite soon. But tonight he will be attending the premiere of *A Hard Day's Night*. He will be late…and rushing to get inside."

"Why is it so important for my mum to meet him?" Charlie asked.

She stopped, and looked at Mr. Deeley. "Oh."

"Oh, indeed," Mr. Deeley replied, and they both looked at Fenwick.

"It is true that a child will be born early next year," Fenwick said. "And that child will grow up to be someone rather important."

"Who?" Charlie asked.

"I am not at liberty to reveal that."

"And why us?"

"I cannot say."

"You might say," Mr. Deeley said, "by the means of your powers of suggestion. You might even make arrangements. Or you might procure a favour. You can say, but you merely wish not to. Another of your more infuriating habits."

"I might procure a favour from the two of you," Fenwick deferred.

"Out of everyone currently in London," Charlie replied. "Why us?"

"Out of everyone currently in London, you are the closest to Jackie Lewis...and you, Charlotte, out of everyone in London, have the most to lose if your mother fails to meet Tony Quinn this evening."

"What do I have to lose?" Charlie persisted. "This is about the birth of a child, my half-sister or brother. Not me."

"Perhaps I might show you a small story from tomorrow's *Daily Chronicle...*"

Fenwick withdrew a yellowed newspaper clipping from his trouser pocket, and handed it across the table to Charlie.

It was very short story, about a traffic accident in Central London involving a Vespa and a lorry. The two passengers aboard the little motorcycle were killed instantly. The lorry driver was unhurt, but was being treated for shock. The accident victims were identified as Jacqueline Lewis, of Stanhope Gardens, South Kensington, and Justin Duran, of Earl's Court, both aged 23.

Stunned, Charlie showed the article to Mr. Deeley, who read it with great thought, and then handed it back to Fenwick.

"And this will happen tonight?" he said.

"This will happen," Fenwick replied, "unless something else happens, which will prevent it."

"But this newspaper story is from tomorrow. It *did* happen," Charlie countered.

Fenwick remained silent as he returned the clipping to his trousers pocket.

"Perhaps," Mr. Deeley mused, "that newspaper article has its origins in another reality."

"But I'm here," Charlie objected. "So that accident couldn't have happened…could it?"

"Who is to say what reality you might return to?" Fenwick replied. "Perhaps you will be unable to return at all, if, in fact, you no longer exist. I believe this to be a paradox you ought not to risk. Consider the consequences. You might vanish." He finished his cup of tea. "And then where would that leave your poor Mr. Deeley?"

"I have encountered this situation previously," Mr. Deeley said, "and given a choice, I should prefer not to have to deal with it again. I suggest we interfere, Mrs. Collins. Lest you suddenly cease to be, and cause me untold grief for another lifetime."

• • •

"Let us hope the boutique is still open," Mr. Deeley said, as they ran back through Soho, and down Carnaby Street, "and that your mother has not yet gone home."

His hope was in vain.

The door to Marianne's Memory was locked, a "Closed" sign hanging crookedly in its window.

"No!" Charlie cried, hammering on the glass.

There was movement from within, and moments later, Marianne appeared.

"We're closed!" she mouthed, through the window, pointing at the sign.

"Please let us in!" Charlie shouted. "It's terribly important! Please!"

Marianne hesitated, then relented, unlocking the door and admitting them to the darkened shop.

"You're lucky I was just totting up the accounts in the back. What's up?"

"We are in urgent need of Justin Duran's mobile number," Mr. Deeley replied. "We must contact him."

Charlie gave him a dig in the ribs with her elbow.

"Sorry," she said, "my friend means his telephone number. He's got a peculiar way of phrasing things."

"I don't know his number," Marianne said. "He's only just moved here from Stoneford. He came for a job in the city."

"What about Giles?" Charlie asked.

Marianne telephoned her boyfriend.

"Right, ok. Thanks, love. We'll give it a try."

She hung up the phone.

"Giles only has his number at work. He hasn't got a phone at his flat. He pops out and uses the call box at the end of the road."

"Is it too late to ring him at work?" Charlie said desperately.

"I'll try," Marianne said, dialling the number. She waited. "No, no answer. It's gone half past five."

"What about Jackie?" Mr. Deeley inquired. "Will she be at home by now? Can we ring her?"

"I'm so sorry. We don't have a phone either. We've ordered one, but the Post Office takes ages to get round to installing them." She looked at Charlie and Mr. Deeley. "What is it? Is it a matter of life and death?"

"It is, actually," Charlie said. "What time is she meeting Justin?"

"Half past six." Marianne looked at her watch. "You've got time to catch them. Take the tube from Piccadilly Circus to Gloucester Road. We're in Stanhope Gardens. I'll give you the address."

• • •

As they raced through the back streets of Soho, down toward Piccadilly Circus, Mr. Deeley said: "Why did you nudge me, Mrs. Collins?"

"No mobiles, Mr. Deeley. They didn't show up properly till the 1990s. They're still tethered by landlines here. Look at all the red call boxes."

They emerged at the bottom end of Regent Street and ran towards the nearest Underground entrance. Across the road, where the fountain was, they could see crowds beginning to gather, and workers erecting metal barricades, while a huge marquee over the entrance to the London Pavilion proclaimed the presence of The Beatles in *A Hard Day's Night*.

"The fountain has moved," Mr. Deeley said, preventing Charlie from going down the stairs into the tube station.

"What?"

"The fountain topped with the Angel of Christian Charity. It is over there, in the centre of the road. I distinctly recall it being just over here in the time we have come from. Are we indeed inhabiting an alternate reality, Mrs. Collins?"

"No," Charlie said, "no...Mr. Deeley. I wish we were in an alternate reality, but they reconstructed this area in the late 1980s and moved the fountain. Everything's as it should be. Come on, we haven't got much time."

Beneath Piccadilly Circus lay the circular concourse of the Underground station.

"Tickets," Charlie said. "Money. What have you got?"

Mr. Deeley checked his pockets. "Coins," he said, offering them.

Charlie pulled her change purse out of her bag. No notes. Only more coins.

"Damn," she said.

She picked through the money in the palm of her hand.

"Five pence," she said. "Five new pence looks and weighs almost the same as an old sixpence. Excellent."

She took Mr. Deeley's coins and added her own, located a machine and bought two tickets for Gloucester Road. The machine dropped several old pennies in change into the metal tray. Charlie collected them and grabbed Mr. Deeley's hand. "This way to the Piccadilly Line," she said, pulling him towards the escalators.

• • •

"There it is."

The flat Jackie and Marianne shared was on the top floor of a five-storey stuccoed 19th century terrace, painted white, with cast iron railings and Doric columns decorating its porches and cornices over its windows.

"Another building that's Grade II listed in our time, Mr. Deeley. Very posh indeed. It doesn't look too shabby in 1964, either. I wonder how mum and Marianne can afford it. I don't think the boutique brings in enough to pay the rent on this little lot."

"Perhaps," said Mr. Deeley, "Marianne's father would rather his daughter not be domiciled in a dwelling of lesser value. Might there be money in the family?"

"I think you're right, Mr. Deeley." Charlie rang the bell for Flat 5.

They waited.

"She can't have left yet. It's not even six."

A minute later, Jackie opened the big front door, slightly out of breath.

"Oh," she said. "I was expecting Justin." She looked at Charlie, and then at Mr. Deeley. "How did you know this is where I lived?"

"Marianne gave us your address," Charlie said. "Can we come inside?"

• • •

The flat was tiny, on the very top floor of the building, and reached by way of a very long climb up five flights of narrow stairs.

"I think it's where the servants must have once lived," Jackie said. "Marianne's bedroom's a bit larger than mine. And you can see where they've put in a little kitchen and an even littler loo. Now what's this all about?"

In the tiny sitting room, Charlie and Mr. Deeley sat down on a sofa that looked as if it had originally come from a French bordello.

"You're going to think we're bonkers…" Charlie began.

"…but we are travellers in time," Mr. Deeley finished.

Charlie looked at him. And then at Jackie.

"Been smoking a bit of the weedy stuff, have you?" Jackie replied, amused. "Marianne and Giles are mad about it. It just puts me to sleep, I'm afraid."

"I do not smoke," Mr. Deeley replied.

"Anything," Charlie added. "We really are time travellers, Jackie. We're from 2014. In fact, I'm…" She paused again, and glanced at Mr. Deeley for help. Almost imperceptibly, he shook his head.

"You're what?" Jackie said. "Trippy? Or just bonkers?"

"We have come to warn you," Mr. Deeley replied. "It would be a grave error if you were to meet Mr. Duran tonight and ride away on his motorbike."

"He hasn't got a motorbike," Jackie said.

As she spoke, the bell from the front door downstairs sounded. Jackie went over to the sitting room window, which overlooked the main road and the leafy square that gave the road its name. Charlie and Mr. Deeley followed.

Down below, they could see a young man with his hair cut and combed into fringe, long in the front and long in the back, pacing nervously on the pavement. There was a gunmetal-grey Vespa with burgundy seats parked on the road behind him. The young man gave up pacing, and instead perched on the padded seat of the little motorcycle.

Charlie clung to Mr. Deeley's arm. "It's my dad," she whispered. "He's so young."

"He didn't tell me about a motorbike," Jackie said. "I'm not sure I want to ride pillion on that. It's completely impractical."

She looked down at her skirt, which was blue, and very short and narrow, and clung to her hips and legs.

"You must make an excuse," Mr. Deeley urged.

"Please," Charlie pleaded.

"Why?" Jackie asked.

"There will be an accident," Mr. Deeley said, simply. "And you will die."

Jackie stared at him. "How can you know that?" she whispered.

"We've been sent to warn you," Charlie said.

"Perhaps if you were to consider us your guardian angels," Mr. Deeley suggested gently, "it might be easier for you to understand. And accept."

Jackie looked out of the window again, then darted out of the flat and ran down the stairs. Charlie and Mr. Deeley watched as she rushed out of the front door and onto the pavement, and spent some time talking to Justin, in earnest.

They watched as the expression on his face changed from curiosity, to disappointment, then to alarm and finally concern.

They watched as he climbed aboard the Vespa and puttered away, and Jackie came back upstairs.

"I've made a date with him for next Saturday," she said, shutting the door behind her. "And to be on the safe side, we're going by bus. He borrowed the Vespa from his mate at work." She looked out of the window, thoughtfully. "He seems rather nice."

"Oh, he is!" Charlie assured her. "He won't stay working in London though. After you marry him, you'll move back to Stoneford, and he'll be quite a successful estate agent. And then you'll both retire to Portugal."

Jackie laughed. "Bloody hell," she said. "Stoneford! I don't think so. And Portugal! I'm terrible with foreign languages. Can't we just retire to Brighton or Bognor and run a little bed and breakfast place for tourists? That's more my style."

"You'll see," Charlie mused.

"Any kids, while you're predicting my future?"

"Oh yes. Three."

"Four," Mr. Deeley corrected.

"Yes," Charlie said quickly. "Four. I forgot."

"Well, now that you've managed to successfully disrupt my date with the man you're convinced I'm going to marry…what am I meant to do now?"

"Perhaps," said Mr. Deeley, "you might consider attending the premiere of that film in Piccadilly Circus."

"What, *A Hard Day's Night*? I haven't got a ticket."

"Neither do we," Charlie said.

"What, a pair of guardian angels and you can't manage a couple of tickets to the hottest film premiere in London?"

"Our employer dislikes the Beatles," Mr. Deeley replied humorously. "He prefers the classical music of Mendelssohn, the *Hebrides Overture* in particular, and the *Italian Symphony*."

Charlie looked at him. "I didn't know you knew about Mendelssohn."

"There is much you don't know about me, Mrs. Collins. Do I surprise you?"

"Yes. Constantly."

"Do you dislike it?"

"Not at all. You may continue to surprise me for as long as you wish, Mr. Deeley." Charlie turned to Jackie. "I think we should go and stand in the crowd outside the theatre and watch the celebrities arrive. We might still manage to see the Beatles."

"I think I'd rather be with Giles and Marianne. They're actually going inside and managing to *meet* the Beatles." Jackie picked up her jacket, and her handbag. "Come on then. I'm all dressed up with nowhere else to go. You owe me dinner afterwards, though. Justin was going to take me somewhere very posh and very nice. And I'm starving."

• • •

They surfaced, once more, at Piccadilly Circus, and attempted to climb the steps that led straight up from the underground concourse to the pavement in front of the Pavilion. But the exit was blocked, and through the barricade they could see a massive gathering of people, held back by a line of police.

"Come on," Jackie said. "This station's got more than one way out."

She ran around the circular concourse, past the public toilets, to the long passageway that led up into the old original Underground station building on Coventry Street. When they reached the surface, they saw a line of spectators had spilled over onto a slender paved traffic island in the middle of Coventry Street, which was surrounded by a metal fence.

"Never mind that," Jackie said. "Follow me."

She dashed across the road, dodging a bus and three cars, followed closely by Charlie and Mr. Deeley.

"Takes me back to school, this," Jackie said, impetuously, clambering over the island barricade in her mini-skirt. "Pardon my knickers."

"They are most fetching," Mr. Deeley remarked as he climbed over the railings himself, and, with practiced but unnecessary chivalry, assisted Charlie.

The line of spectators was three or four people deep on the paved island, and they all seemed to be much taller than Charlie or Jackie, although Mr. Deeley could easily see over their heads.

On the Pavilion side of the road, a striped tent had been erected from the curbside to the theatre's entrance. A line of policemen stood to the left of this, holding back another throng of spectators. Other police with huge white cuffs directed important-looking black cars to the front of the tent.

A loud cheer came from the crowd as one such car drove up and stopped, and several people climbed out.

"Who is it?" Charlie asked Mr. Deeley.

"I cannot be certain," he said. "However, I do not believe it is Mendelssohn."

Charlie turned to ask Jackie, but Jackie had disappeared.

"Can you see Jackie?" she asked Mr. Deeley.

Mr. Deeley scanned the crowd on the traffic island.

"I cannot," he said.

"Bloody hell."

Charlie dug her way through to the row of people lining the barricade facing the Pavilion. "Let me through!" she demanded, ducking under arms and cameras and bags, "I'm little! And I've lost my mum!"

She reached the front just as another car drew up, and a man climbed out, accompanied by a woman with long blonde hair.

The people around her began to shout and cheer and aim their cameras.

"John! John! Cyn! Here! Over here!"

John Lennon, Charlie thought, all worries about Jackie momentarily banished. *I've just seen John Lennon.* She remembered the plectrum in her bag, and hugged it a little bit closer to her body.

But then. Jackie. Where was she?

And she realized, too late, that she'd also lost Mr. Deeley. Hemmed in by people who were all at least six inches taller than she was, it was impossible to see where he was.

I will not panic. She hated crowds. This was such a stupid idea. *I will not panic. Where is he?*

Her attention was diverted by a commotion on the other side of the road. Behind the police barricade, beside the blocked entrance to the tube station, very near to the striped tent, a young woman, obviously unconscious, her arms dangling limply, was being handed over the heads of the onlookers. With her heart in her throat, Charlie recognized Jackie's long dark hair and her short blue miniskirt.

"Oh God—no!"

She was hemmed in on all sides. There was no way to get to Jackie except over the barricade, across the road, and over a second metal fence preventing pedestrians from doing exactly what she was now attempting.

Charlie ran around three stopped cars, two motorbikes, and four policemen. One tried to reach out and grab her. She shook him off, and clambered over the last barricade, and elbowed her way through the crowd until she found herself on other side of the road.

Jackie wasn't there.

She was, however, about twenty feet away, lying on a piece of pavement where there were no people, other than a well-dressed man who was talking to her, attempting to bring her around, and a policeman who was keeping the area clear of bystanders.

"Is she all right?" Charlie asked desperately, running to Jackie's side.

"I think so," the man replied. "She's still breathing. She's got a nice strong pulse. She's not hurt." He glanced at his watch. "We've called for an ambulance."

"Jackie," Charlie said, kneeling on the ground beside her. "Remember me?"

Jackie opened her eyes, slowly, and tried to focus on Charlie. "What's happened?"

"You fainted," said the man. "Fortunately I was nearby and caught you before you were trampled. I made sure you were carried to safety. You all right, love?"

"I fainted?"

"Yes, love. It can happen to anyone."

"Where am I?"

"Piccadilly Circus," the man said. "Outside the London Pavilion."

"Did I go to work today?"

"Yes, you did," Charlie said.

"Why am I here?"

"Premiere of *A Hard Day's Night*. Remember?"

"I don't remember," Jackie said, her face filled with confusion. "Who're you?"

"I'm Charlie. We met in your shop. I came to your flat with Mr. Deeley."

"I don't remember." Jackie said again. She looked at the man. "Who're you?"

"Tony Quinn, love. What's your name?"

"Jackie Lewis."

Why doesn't Jackie remember me? Charlie thought. "Did you hit your head when you fell?" she asked.

"She didn't," Tony replied. "I caught her before she went all the way down."

"What year is it?" Charlie asked her.

Jackie thought, but came up blank. "I don't know."

"But you do know your name?"

"Yes. Jacqueline Elizabeth Lewis."

"And when were you born?"

"January the 23rd, 1941."

She tried to sit up, but Tony Quinn made her lie back down on the pavement. "You stay like that, love, until the ambulance comes."

"What's happened?"

"You fainted, love. Outside the London Pavilion."

"I fainted?"

"Yes, love."

"Where am I?"

"Piccadilly Circus," Charlie repeated.

"Did I go to work today?"

"Yes, you did."

"Why am I here?"

Charlie looked again at the well-dressed gentleman who was kneeling on the pavement beside Jackie, holding her hand.

"It's some kind of amnesia," she said. "But it doesn't make sense...she knows her name and her birthday. She just doesn't remember anything that's happening right now."

"My sister had this," Tony Quinn said. "She was coming down with something, her body was fighting some kind of infection, and she was terribly worried about her son, who was having a bit of trouble at school...she woke up in the morning and couldn't remember a thing from Monday onward. Exactly the same as this. We'd say something to her and she wouldn't recall it two minutes later. No retention at all. She asked the same questions over and over again. We thought she'd had a stroke, but the doctor at the hospital said no. Called it something very technical. Let me think."

He paused.

"Transient global amnesia. She recovered from it completely. But she never did get her memory back from that week."

"What's happened?" Jackie asked for the third time as the ambulance finally arrived.

• • •

The ambulance had gone, speeding away with its blue lights flashing and its bell ringing. Tony Quinn had climbed into the back with Jackie, vowing to see her safely to the hospital—something he deemed far more important than attending the premiere of *A Hard Day's Night* and meeting the Beatles for the fourth or possibly the fifth time.

"Anyway," he said as the ambulance door closed, "McCartney owes me ten quid from the last blast we were at. See you again, I hope, Charlie."

And he was gone, along with Jackie.

Charlie stood alone on the pavement. The crowds had thinned considerably, and it was dark. All of the Beatles had arrived and gone inside, along with a procession of celebrity friends. Traffic was flowing normally again along Coventry Street.

"Anyway," she repeated, to herself. "Mission accomplished. Accidentally, but nonetheless accomplished. Mum has met Tony Quinn. My half-sibling will be born."

She looked for Mr. Deeley, but couldn't find him.

A terrible thought came over her…what if he had tried to go back to their present, without her, got lost somewhere along the way, and couldn't find his way home? She might never see him again. He might be lost forever, wandering in time. And what if she couldn't get back either? She'd never tried to deliberately travel by herself. She'd left all that experimentation to Mr. Deeley.

Her common sense told her she should stay put, and wait here at Piccadilly Circus until Mr. Deeley reappeared. But, for how long? It might be hours. Days.

Years.

She might end up like one of those waifs they sang about in folk songs, wandering in solitude, waiting in vain for a lover who never came back.

She was, indeed, wandering in solitude. Almost without noticing, she had wandered all the way back to Oxford Street, to the hamburger restaurant where she and Mr. Deeley had met Fenwick Oldbutter.

It was open, its warm yellow lights beckoning through large plate glass windows.

Charlie went inside, and sat down, half expecting Fenwick to reappear and congratulate her for a job well done.

Fenwick did not reappear. A waitress did, however, and Charlie ordered a hamburger and a cup of tea, realizing, as she did, that she had absolutely no way to pay for it. Her collection of coins would be as foreign to the cashier as French francs or American dimes and quarters. There was an American Express sticker on the door, but she didn't have an American Express card. And the banks hadn't yet introduced their credit cards to England.

Her burger arrived, and her tea. Charlie added a squeeze of ketchup from the tomato-shaped dispenser and waited.

Two cups of tea later, and a plate of chips, she was still waiting. With an extremely guilty conscience, she contemplated making a run for it without paying for her meal. She'd never done anything like that in her life. It was a horrible thing to consider. But she'd already cheated the Underground. And she was thinking about cheating again.

And then what? Assuming she wasn't nabbed by the police… what? Go back to Stanhope Gardens and wait for Marianne to show up? Deliver the news about Jackie…ask if she could spend the night in her bed?

She was summoning up the courage to bolt when, at last, she saw Mr. Deeley.

He was looking very jaunty in his John Stephen tie and Hardy Amies waistcoat. He glanced through the big glass window, smiled as he spotted Charlie, then opened the door and came inside.

"Where have you been?" Charlie asked him as he sat down.

"I might ask you the same thing," Mr. Deeley replied, amused. He turned to the waitress who had arrived at Charlie's table almost as quickly as he had. "I shall have the same things to eat as my friend. Many thanks."

"I can't pay for any of this," Charlie whispered, when the waitress was out of earshot. "Old money."

"Old money," Mr. Deeley replied, removing a £10 note from his trousers pocket. "Happily, I can."

"Where did you get that?"

"I shall relate what happened after you abandoned me," Mr. Deeley replied.

"I was trying to find Jackie!"

"You left me alone," Mr. Deeley said, sounding slightly miffed. "I had no choice but to negotiate my way out of the crowd. Whereupon I crossed the road, and joined another crowd—albeit with a greatly reduced number of participants—and, within some moments, I discovered myself to be inside the building."

"Which building?" Charlie asked.

"The building where the film was to be shown."

"The London Pavilion? You were inside the London Pavilion?"

"Indeed."

"How the hell did you manage that, Mr. Deeley?"

His meal arrived and he paid the waitress, who brought back his change on a china plate. Infuriatingly, he paused to drink his tea and add hot mustard and ketchup to his hamburger before continuing the tale.

"I cannot say for certain," he replied inscrutably. "In any case, I went into the cinema, and saw that there were empty seats, and so I availed myself of one, and sat down to watch the film. It was very good, by the way. Have you seen it?"

"I have," Charlie said. "Four times. And where did you get the £10?"

"After the film finished, I found I was in need of the gentlemen's toilet. And so, after asking for directions, I repaired to the facilities, whereupon I found myself standing beside a Beatle."

"You met a Beatle in the loo?"

Mr. Deeley finished his tea.

"And I engaged him in conversation about the film, and about being chased by a large number of screaming females through a railway station. I also asked him how he managed to disappear from the bath."

"John Lennon. You met John Lennon in the loo. You talked to John Lennon about *A Hard Day's Night*."

"I did, in fact. And then I explained our circumstances, that we had only recently arrived in London, and that we were, unhappily, without sufficient funds for a meal. He gave me that £10 note."

"You spare changed John Lennon in the loo for ten quid."

"And I told him we had one of his plectrums."

"What did he say?"

"He was amused. He gave me another."

Mr. Deeley removed the plectrum from the pocket of his trousers and held it out in the palm of his hand.

"He just happened to have it with him," Charlie said.

"He did. And three more. Imagine that."

Charlie smiled.

"He wished me good fortune for the future, and I wished him the same, and we parted as friends. He struck me as a very nice fellow."

"Mr. Deeley," Charlie said. "You have no idea, do you?"

"Do I not…?"

Charlie shook her head. She took out the plectrum that was in her bag, and placed it in Mr. Deeley's palm, beside its twin. She took his other hand in hers.

"Do you think we could go home now…?"

• • •

It was still a hamburger restaurant. But its wooden tables and chairs had been replaced by bright plastic, and the waitresses had been

270

replaced by a long counter, with an equally long lineup of hungry patrons queuing in front of four cash registers. There was music coming from somewhere, and the lights were glaringly bright.

"This seems a much simpler process than our previous journey," Mr. Deeley remarked. "Easy when you know how."

"Let's find a posh hotel and spend the night in London," Charlie said. "It's probably too late to get a train back to Middlehurst anyway."

"Will it have a very large and comfortable bed, with feather pillows and a bath which is big enough for two?" Mr. Deeley mused.

"I think that could certainly be arranged."

"Then do arrange it, Mrs. Collins. I am feeling particularly amorous after this day's adventures."

Charlie smiled, and kissed him. "Can't wait." She paused. "I wonder who my mum's son or daughter will turn out to be."

"If it is a descendant of mine, he or she is bound to be indescribably fascinating."

Charlie laughed, and took out her mobile. "I must look up transient global amnesia. Mum's never mentioned any of this to us."

"Perhaps," Mr. Deeley said, "it is better that she has not ever recalled this day. How will you arrange for our hotel?"

Charlie searched on her mobile and rang a number.

"We'll be there in about twenty minutes," she said.

She put her mobile back in her bag.

"Easy when you know how," she said, plucking the two plectrums out of Mr. Deeley's still open palm.

PERSISTENCE OF MEMORY

Combining the language, humor, and manners of Jane Austen's era with charming characters and colorful storytelling, *Persistence Of Memory* is a mystery, a love story, and a speculative novel about accidental time travel.

Charlie Lowe has two obsessions: saving the Stoneford Village Green from unscrupulous developers, and researching her ancestor, Louis Augustus Duran, whose mysterious origins perplex her.

When a freak lightning strike and a rogue computer virus send her back to 1825, Charlie discovers she must persuade a reluctant Sarah Foster to marry Duran, or two centuries of descendants—including herself—will cease to exist.

Unfortunately, Louis Duran turns out to be a despicable French count who spends his days impregnating a succession of unfortunate housemaids and attempting to invent the first flushing toilet in Hampshire.

A hopeless romantic, our heroine does her best to encourage the happiness of those who surround her—but will she be able to mend a matrimonial wrong, restore the Village Green to its rightful owner and, of foremost importance, conclude the tale in the company of the gentleman with whom she was always meant to be?

SKYWATCHER

Robin Harris grew up watching the 60s spy show Spy Squad, starring his dad, Evan Harris. So when the police deem the mysterious death of a Russian woman with rainbow-colored hair a suicide, Robin knows better.

Robin soon finds himself in the middle of an awesome plot that seems to be lifted directly from one of his father's old Spy Squad episodes, and, as he discovers, his father really was a spy. Now Robin and his brothers have inadvertently walked onto the scene of a real life-and-death spy drama, and as far as the free world is concerned, Robin's entrance into the family business comes not a moment too soon.

COLD PLAY

Jason Davey ran away to sea after the death of his wife, finding work as a contract entertainer aboard a cruise ship, the Star Sapphire. But when faces from his past come aboard as passengers, Jason's routine week-long trip to Alaska becomes anything but relaxing.

Jason's wife once worked for Diana Wyndham, a beautiful and eccentric actress. And hard-drinking ex-rocker Rick Redding once toured with a band Jason has strong ties to. Now Diana occupies one of the ship's luxury suites, and Rick dwells in the stateroom next door. Between them, they may know more about Jason's secret past than anyone suspects.

Jason narrates his—and the Sapphire's—story with drama, humor, and a touch of the supernatural as he tries to survive a trial by fire and ice on the journey to Juneau, Skagway, and Glacier Bay.

THE CILLA ROSE AFFAIR

A novel of espionage, intrigue, and mysterious sound waves underneath London.

Evan Harris's experiences as a spy helped make him a star playing one on TV. When Britain's best-loved breakfast show DJ dies, only Evan knows what it has to do with a pirate radio station, a long-lost diary, a suspected double agent, the London Underground, and mysterious sound waves underneath the Fitzroy Theatre.

So Evan recruits his three sons to help him unmask the traitor deep within the British spy community in a sting operation not unlike a storyline from his own cult 1960s TV show...

CPSIA information can be obtained at www.ICGtesting.com
Printed in the USA
BVOW08s1417240716

456681BV00006B/102/P